Christopher Isherwood was born in 1904 at High Lane, Cheshire, and educated at Repton School and Corpus Christi College, Cambridge.

His first novel, *All the Conspirators*, was published in 1928. In the following year he went to Berlin and remained there, supporting himself by teaching English, until Hitler came to power in 1933. While Isherwood was in Germany his second novel, *The Memorial*, was published, but it was not until 1935 that the first of the famous 'Berlin' books, *Mr Norris Changes Trains*, appeared, followed in 1937 by the novella *Sally Bowles* and in 1939 by *Goodbye to Berlin*. The late 1930s also saw the fruitful collaboration between Isherwood and the poet W. H. Auden which produced three plays (*The Dog Beneath the Skin*, *Ascent of F6* and *On the Frontier*) and a book based on their trip to China during the Japanese invasion of the country, *Journey to a War*. An autobiographical work, *Lions and Shadows*, was published in 1938. Early in 1939 Isherwood settled in the USA, where his growing interest in metaphysics and eastern philosophy led to a close association with the Vedanta Society of Los Angeles and to his cooperation on the translations of several Hindu classics, including the *Bhagavad-Gita*. He also worked as a scriptwriter in Hollywood and has taught at various Californian universities. His later work includes several more novels, a book of travel and two further volumes of autobiography.

The fascination of the subject-matter, the qualities of detached humour, irony and unerring observation of human weakness which distinguished the 'Berlin' books were largely responsible for establishing Isherwood's reputation with the general public. The highly successful play *I Am a Camera*, based on *Goodbye to Berlin*, was made into a film in 1955; the musical *Cabaret* became an Oscar-winning film in 1972, starring Liza Minnelli as Sally Bowles and Michael York as 'Herr Issyvoo'.

An American citizen since 1946, Christopher Isherwood lives in Santa Monica, California.

By the Same Author
Fiction
All the Conspirators
The Memorial
Mr Norris Changes Trains
Sally Bowles
Prater Violet
The World in the Evening
Down There on a Visit
A Single Man
A Meeting by the River

Collected Fiction
The Berlin of Sally Bowles

Plays (in collaboration with W. H. Auden)
The Dog Beneath the Skin
Ascent of F6
On the Frontier

Autobiography
Lions and Shadows
Kathleen and Frank
Christopher and His Kind

Travel
Journey to a War (in collaboration with W. H. Auden)
The Condor and the Cows

Translations
The Bhagavad-Gita (with Swami Prabhavananda)
Shankara's Jewel-Crest of Discrimination (with Swami Prabhavananda)
How to Know God; The Yoga Aphorisms of Patanjali (with Swami Prabhavananda)
Baudelaire's Intimate Journals

Miscellaneous
Exhumations
Ramakrishna and his Disciples
Vedanta for Modern Man
Vedanta for the West

CHRISTOPHER ISHERWOOD

Goodbye to Berlin

TRIAD
PANTHER

Triad/Panther Books
Granada Publishing Ltd
8 Grafton Street, London W1X 3LA

Published by Triad/Panther Books 1977
Reprinted 1978, 1979, 1981 (twice), 1983 (twice),
1985, 1986

Triad Paperbacks Ltd is an imprint of
Chatto, Bodley Head & Jonathan Cape Ltd and
Granada Publishing Ltd

First published by The Hogarth Press 1939

Copyright © Christopher Isherwood 1939

ISBN 0-586-04795-6

Printed and bound in Great Britain by
Collins, Glasgow

Set in Linotype Plantin

To
JOHN AND BEATRIX LEHMANN

CONTENTS

GOODBYE TO BERLIN

The six pieces contained in this volume form a roughly continuous narrative. They are the only existing fragments of what was originally planned as a huge episodic novel of pre-Hitler Berlin. I had intended to call it *The Lost*. My old title has been changed, however; it is too grandiose for this short loosely-connected sequence of diaries and sketches.

Readers of *Mr Norris Changes Trains* (published in the United States as *The Last of Mr Norris*) may notice that certain characters and situations in that novel overlap and contradict what I have written here – Sally Bowles, for instance, would have run into Mr Norris on Frl. Schroeder's staircase; Christopher Isherwood would certainly have come home one evening to find William Bradshaw asleep in his bed. The explanation is simple: The adventures of Mr Norris once formed part of *The Lost* itself.

Because I have given my own name to the 'I' of this narrative, readers are certainly not entitled to assume that its pages are purely autobiographical, or that its characters are libellously exact portraits of living persons. 'Christopher Isherwood' is a convenient ventriloquist's dummy, nothing more.

The first *Berlin Diary*, *The Nowaks* and *The Landauers*, have already appeared, in John Lehmann's *New Writing*. *Sally Bowles* was originally published as a separate volume by the Hogarth Press.

C. I.
September 1935

A BERLIN DIARY
(Autumn 1930)

From my window, the deep solemn massive street. Cellar-shops where the lamps burn all day, under the shadow of top-heavy balconied façades, dirty plaster frontages embossed with scrollwork and heraldic devices. The whole district is like this: street leading into street of houses like shabby monumental safes crammed with the tarnished valuables and second-hand furniture of a bankrupt middle class.

I am a camera with its shutter open, quite passive, recording, not thinking. Recording the man shaving at the window opposite and the woman in the kimono washing her hair. Some day, all this will have to be developed, carefully printed, fixed.

At eight o'clock in the evening the house-doors will be locked. The children are having supper. The shops are shut. The electric-sign is switched on over the night-bell of the little hotel on the corner, where you can hire a room by the hour. And soon the whistling will begin. Young men are calling their girls. Standing down there in the cold, they whistle up at the lighted windows of warm rooms where the beds are already turned down for the night. They want to be let in. Their signals echo down the deep hollow street, lascivious and private and sad. Because of the whistling, I do not care to stay here in the evenings. It reminds me that I am in a foreign city, alone, far from home. Sometimes I determine not to listen to it, pick up a book, try to read. But soon a call is sure to sound, so piercing, so insistent, so despairingly human, that at last I have to get up and peep through the slats of the venetian blind to make sure that it is not – as I know very well it could not possibly be – for me.

The extraordinary smell in this room when the stove is lighted and the window shut; not altogether unpleasant, a mixture of incense and stale buns. The tall tiled stove, gorgeously coloured, like an altar. The washstand like a Gothic shrine. The cupboard also is Gothic, with carved cathedral windows: Bismarck faces the King of Prussia in stained glass. My best chair would do for a bishop's throne. In the corner, three sham mediæval halberds (from a theatrical touring company?) are fastened together to form a hatstand. Frl. Schroeder unscrews the heads of the halberds and polishes them from time to time. They are heavy and sharp enough to kill.

Everything in the room is like that: unnecessarily solid, abnormally heavy and dangerously sharp. Here, at the writing-table, I am confronted by a phalanx of metal objects – a pair of candlesticks shaped like entwined serpents, an ashtray from which emerges the head of a crocodile, a paper-knife copied from a Florentine dagger, a brass dolphin holding on the end of its tail a small broken clock. What becomes of such things? How could they ever be destroyed? They will probably remain intact for thousands of years: people will treasure them in museums. Or perhaps they will merely be melted down for munitions in a war. Every morning, Frl. Schroeder arranges them very carefully in certain unvarying positions: there they stand, like an uncompromising statement of her views on Capital and Society, Religion and Sex.

All day long she goes padding about the large dingy flat. Shapeless but alert, she waddles from room to room, in carpet slippers and a flowered dressing-gown pinned ingeniously together, so that not an inch of petticoat or bodice is to be seen, flicking with her duster, peeping, spying, poking her short pointed nose into the cupboards and luggage of her lodgers. She has dark, bright, inquisitive eyes and pretty waved brown hair of which she is proud. She must be about fifty-five years old.

Long ago, before the War and the Inflation, she used to be comparatively well off. She went to the Baltic for her summer holidays and kept a maid to do the housework. For the last thirty years she has lived here and taken in lodgers. She started doing it because she liked to have company.

' "Lina," my friends used to say to me, "however can you?

How can you bear to have strange people living in your rooms and spoiling your furniture, especially when you've got the money to be independent?" And I'd always give them the same answer. "*My* lodgers aren't lodgers," I used to say. "They're my guests."

'You see, Herr Issyvoo, in those days I could afford to be very particular about the sort of people who came to live here. I could pick and choose. I only took them really well connected and well educated – proper gentlefolk (like yourself, Herr Issyvoo). I had a Freiherr once, and a Rittmeister and a Professor. They often gave me presents – a bottle of cognac or a box of chocolates or some flowers. And when one of them went away for his holidays he'd always send me a card— from London, it might be, or Paris, or Baden-Baden. Ever such pretty cards I used to get ...'

And now Frl. Schroeder has not even got a room of her own. She has to sleep in the living-room, behind a screen, on a small sofa with broken springs. As in so many of the older Berlin flats, our living-room connects the front part of the house with the back. The lodgers who live in the front have to pass through the living-room on their way to the bathroom, so that Frl. Schroeder is often disturbed during the night. 'But I drop off again at once. It doesn't worry me. I'm much too tired.' She has to do all the housework herself and it takes up most of her day. 'Twenty years ago, if anybody had told me to scrub my own floors, I'd have slapped his face for him. But you get used to it. You can get used to anything. Why, I remember the time when I'd have sooner cut off my right hand than empty this chamber ... And now,' says Frl. Schroeder, suiting the action to the word, 'My goodness! It's no more to me than pouring out a cup of tea!'

She is fond of pointing out to me the various marks and stains left by lodgers who have inhabited this room :

"Yes, Herr Issyvoo, I've got something to remember each of them by ... Look there, on the rug – I've sent it to the cleaners I don't know how often but nothing will get it out – that's where Herr Noeske was sick after his birthday party.

What in the world can he have been eating, to make a mess like that? He'd come to Berlin to study, you know. His parents lived in Brandenburg – a first-class family; oh, I assure you! They had pots of money! His Herr Papa was a surgeon, and of course he wanted his boy to follow in his footsteps ... What a charming young man! "Herr Noeske," I used to say to him, "excuse me, but you must really work harder – you with all your brains! Think of your Herr Papa and your Frau Mama; it isn't fair to them to waste their good money like that. Why, if you were to drop it in the Spree it would be better. At least it would make a splash!" I was like a mother to him. And always, when he'd got himself into some scrape – he was terribly thoughtless – he'd come straight to me: "Schroe-derschen," he used to say, "Please don't be angry with me ... We were playing cards last night and I lost the whole of this month's allowance. I daren't tell Father ..." And then he'd look at me with those great big eyes of his. I knew exactly what he was after, the scamp! But I hadn't the heart to refuse. So I'd sit down and write a letter to his Frau Mama and beg her to forgive him just that once and send some more money. And she always would ... Of course, as a woman, I knew how to appeal to a mother's feelings, although I've never had any children of my own ... What are you smiling at, Herr Issyvoo? Well, well! Mistakes will happen, you know!"

'And that's where the Herr Rittmeister always upset his coffee over the wall-paper. He used to sit there on the couch with his fiancée. "Herr Rittmeister," I used to say to him, "do please drink your coffee at the table. If you'll excuse my saying so, there's plenty of time for the other thing after-wards ..." But no, he always would sit on the couch. And then, sure enough, when he began to get a bit excited in his feelings, over went the coffee-cups ... Such a handsome gentleman! His Frau Mama and his sister came to visit us sometimes. They liked coming up to Berlin. "Fräulein Schroe-der," they used to tell me, "you don't know how lucky you are to be living here, right in the middle of things. We're only country cousins – we envy you! And now tell us all the latest Court scandals!" Of course, they were only joking. They had the sweetest little house, not far from Halberstadt, in the Harz. They used to show me pictures of it. A perfect dream!'

'You see those ink-stains on the carpet? That's where Herr Professor Koch used to shake his fountain-pen. I told him of it a hundred times. In the end, I even laid sheets of blotting-paper on the floor around his chair. He was so absent-minded ... Such a dear old gentleman! And so simple. I was very fond of him. If I mended a shirt for him or darned his socks, he'd thank me with the tears in his eyes. He liked a bit of fun, too. Sometimes, when he heard me coming, he'd turn out the light and hide behind the door; and then he'd roar like a lion to frighten me. Just like a child ...'

Frl. Schroeder can go on like this, without repeating herself, by the hour. When I have been listening to her for some time, I find myself relapsing into a curious trance-like state of depression. I begin to feel profoundly unhappy. Where are all those lodgers now? Where, in another ten years, shall I be, myself? Certainly not here. How many seas and frontiers shall I have to travel, on foot, on horseback, by car, push-bike, aeroplane, steamer, train, lift, moving-staircase and tram? How much money shall I need for that enormous journey? How much food must I gradually, wearily consume on my way? How many pairs of shoes shall I wear out? How many thousands of cigarettes shall I smoke? How many cups of tea shall I drink and how many glasses of beer? What an awful tasteless prospect! And yet to have to die .. A sudden vague pang of apprehension grips my bowels and I have to excuse myself in order to go to the lavatory.

Hearing that I was once a medical student, she confides to me that she is very unhappy because of the size of her bosom. She suffers from palpitations and is sure that these must be caused by the strain on her heart. She wonders if she should have an operation. Some of her acquaintances advise her to, others are against it:

'Oh dear, it's such a weight to have to carry about with you! And just think – Herr Issyvoo: I used to be as slim as you are!'

'I suppose you had a great many admirers, Frl. Schroeder?'

Yes, she has had dozens. But only one Friend. He was married man, living apart from his wife, who would not divorce him.

'We were together eleven years. Then he died of pneumonia. Sometimes I wake up in the night when it's cold and wish he was there. You never seem to get really warm, sleeping alone.'

There are four other lodgers in this flat. Next door to me, in the big front-room, is Frl. Kost. In the room opposite, overlooking the courtyard, is Frl. Mayr. At the back, beyond the living-room, is Bobby. And behind Bobby's room, over the bathroom, at the top of a ladder, is a tiny attic which Frl. Schroeder refers to, for some occult reason, as 'The Swedish Pavilion.' This she lets, at twenty marks a month, to a commercial traveller who is out all day and most of the night. I occasionally come upon him on Sunday mornings, in the kitchen, shuffling about in his vest and trousers, apologetically hunting for a box of matches.

Bobby is a mixer at a west-end bar called the Troika. I don't know his real name. He has adopted this one because English Christian names are fashionable just now in the Berlin demi-monde. He is a pale worried-looking smartly dressed young man with thin sleek black hair. During the early afternoon, just after he has got out of bed, he walks about the flat in shirt-sleeves, wearing a hairnet.

Frl. Schroeder and Bobby are on intimate terms. He tickles her and slaps her bottom; she hits him over the head with a frying-pan or a mop. The first time I surprised them scuffling like this, they were both rather embarrassed. Now they take my presence as a matter of course.

Frl. Kost is a blonde florid girl with large silly blue eyes. When we meet, coming to and from the bathroom in our dressing-gowns, she modestly avoids my glance. She is plump but has a good figure.

One day I asked Frl. Schroeder straight out: What was Frl. Kost's profession?

'Profession? Ha, ha, that's good! That's just the word for it!

Oh, yes, she's got a fine profession. Like this—'

And with the air of doing something extremely comic, she began waddling across the kitchen like a duck, mincingly holding a duster between her finger and thumb. Just by the door, she twirled triumphantly round, flourishing the duster as though it were a silk handkerchief, and kissed her hand to me mockingly:

'Ja, ja, Herr Issyvoo! That's how they do it.'

'I don't quite understand, Frl. Schroeder. Do you mean that she's a tight-rope walker?'

'He, he, he! Very good indeed, Herr Issyvoo! Yes, that's right! That's it! She walks along the line for her living. That just describes her!'

One evening, soon after this, I met Frl. Kost on the stairs, with a Japanese. Frl. Schroeder explained to me later that he is one of Frl. Kost's best customers. She asked Frl. Kost how they spent the time together when not actually in bed, for the Japanese can speak hardly any German.

'Oh, well,' said Frl. Kost, 'we play the gramophone together, you know, and eat chocolates, and then we laugh a lot. He's very fond of laughing ...'

Frl. Schroeder really quite likes Frl. Kost and certainly hasn't any moral objections to her trade: nevertheless, when she is angry because Frl. Kost has broken the spout of the teapot or omitted to make crosses for her telephone-calls on the slate in the living-room, then invariably she exclaims:

'But after all, what else can you expect from a woman of that sort, a common prostitute! Why, Herr Issyvoo, do you know what she used to be? A servant girl! And then she got to be on intimate terms with her employer and one fine day, of course, she found herself in certain circumstances ... And when that little difficulty was removed, she had to go trot-trot ...'

Frl. Mayr is a music-hall *jodlerin* – one of the best, so Frl. Schroeder reverently assures me, in the whole of Germany. Frl. Schroeder doesn't altogether like Frl. Mayr, but she stands in great awe of her; as well she may. Frl. Mayr has a bull-dog jaw, enormous arms and coarse string-coloured hair.

She speaks a Bavarian dialect with peculiarly aggressive emphasis. When at home, she sits up like a war-horse at the living-room table, helping Frl. Schroeder to lay cards. They are both adept fortune-tellers and neither would dream of beginning the day without consulting the omens. The chief thing they both want to know at present is: when will Frl. Mayr get another engagement? This question interests Frl. Schroeder quite as much as Frl. Mayr, because Frl. Mayr is behind-hand with the rent.

At the corner of the Motzstrasse, when the weather is fine, there stands a shabby pop-eyed man beside a portable canvas booth. On the sides of the booth are pinned astrological diagrams and autographed letters of recommendation from satisfied clients. Frl. Schroeder goes to consult him whenever she can afford the mark for his fee. In fact, he plays a most important part in her life. Her behaviour towards him is a mixture of cajolery and threats. If the good things he promises her come true she will kiss him, she says, invite him to dinner, buy him a gold watch: if they don't, she will throttle him, box his ears, report him to the police. Among other prophecies, the astrologer has told her that she will win some money in the Prussian State Lottery. So far, she has had no luck. But she is always discussing what she will do with her winnings. We are all to have presents, of course. I am to get a hat, because Frl. Schroeder thinks it very improper that a gentleman of my education should go about without one.

When not engaged in laying cards, Frl. Mayr drinks tea and lectures Frl. Schroeder on her past theatrical triumphs:

'And the Manager said to me: "Fritzi, Heaven must have sent you here! My leading lady's fallen ill. You're to leave for Copenhagen to-night." And what's more, he wouldn't take no for an answer. "Fritzi," he said (he always called me that), "Fritzi, you aren't going to let an old friend down?" And so I went ...' Frl. Mayr sips her tea reminiscently: 'A charming man. And so well-bred.' She smiles: 'Familiar ... but he always knew how to behave himself.'

Frl. Schroeder nods eagerly, drinking in every word, revelling in it:

'I suppose some of those managers must be cheeky devils? (Have some more sausage, Frl. Mayr?)'

'(Thank you, Frl. Schroeder; just a little morsel.) Yes, some of them ... you wouldn't believe! But I could always take care of myself. Even when I was quite a slip of a girl ...'

The muscles of Frl. Mayr's nude fleshy arms ripple unappetisingly. She sticks out her chin:

'I'm a Bavarian, and a Bavarian never forgets an injury.'

Coming into the living-room yesterday evening, I found Frl. Schroeder and Frl. Mayr lying flat on their stomachs with ears pressed to the carpet. At intervals, they exchanged grins of delight or joyfully pinched each other, with simultaneous exclamations of *Ssh!*

'Hark!' whispered Frl. Schroeder, 'He's smashing all the furniture!'

'He's beating her black and blue!' exclaimed Frl. Mayr, in raptures.

'Bang! Just listen to that!'

'Ssh! Ssh!'

'Ssh!'

Frl. Schroeder was quite beside herself. When I asked what was the matter, she clambered to her feet, waddled forward and, taking me round the waist, danced a little waltz with me: 'Herr Issyvoo! Herr Issyvoo! Herr Issyvoo!" until she was breathless.

'But whatever has happened?' I asked.

'Ssh!' commanded Frl. Mayr from the floor. 'Ssh! They've started again!'

In the flat directly beneath ours lives a certain Frau Glanterneck. She is a Galician Jewess, in itself a reason why Frl. Mayr should be her enemy: for Frl. Mayr, needless to say, is an ardent Nazi. And quite apart from this, it seems that Frau Glanterneck and Frl. Mayr once had words on the stairs about Frl. Mayr's yodelling. Frau Glanterneck, perhaps because she is a non-Aryan, said that she preferred the noises made by cats. Thereby, she insulted not merely Frl. Mayr, but all Bavarian, all German women: and it was Frl. Mayr's pleasant duty to avenge them.

About a fortnight ago, it became known among the neighbours that Frau Glanterneck, who is sixty years old and as ugly as a witch, had been advertising in the newspaper for a husband. What was more, an applicant had already appeared: a widowed butcher from Halle. He had seen Frau Glanterneck and was nevertheless prepared to marry her. Here was Frl. Mayr's chance. By roundabout inquiries, she discovered the butcher's name and address and wrote him an anonymous letter. Was he aware that Frau Glanterneck had (*a*) bugs in her flat, (*b*) been arrested for fraud and released on the ground that she was insane, (*c*) leased out her own bedroom for immoral purposes, and (*d*) slept in the bed afterwards without changing the sheets? And now the butcher had arrived to confront Frau Glanterneck with the letter. One could hear both of them quite distinctly: the growling of the enraged Prussian and the shrill screaming of the Jewess. Now and then came the thud of a fist against wood and, occasionally, the crash of glass. The row lasted over an hour.

This morning we hear that the neighbours have complained to the portress of the disturbance and that Frau Glanterneck is to be seen with a black eye. The marriage is off.

The inhabitants of this street know me by sight already. At the grocer's, people no longer turn their heads on hearing my English accent as I order a pound of butter. At the street corner, after dark, the three whores no longer whisper throatily: 'Komm, Süsser!' as I pass.

The three whores are all plainly over fifty years old. They do not attempt to conceal their age. They are not noticeably rouged or powdered. They wear baggy old fur coats and longish skirts and matronly hats. I happened to mention them to Bobby and he explained to me that there is a recognized demand for the comfortable type of woman. Many middle-aged men prefer them to girls. They even attract boys in their 'teens. A boy, explained Bobby, feels shy with a girl of his own age but not with a woman old enough to be his mother. Like most barmen, Bobby is a great expert on sexual questions.

The other evening, I went to call on him during business hours.

It was still very early, about nine o'clock, when I arrived at the Troika. The place was much larger and grander than I had expected. A commissionaire braided like an archduke regarded my hatless head with suspicion until I spoke to him in English. A smart cloak-room girl insisted on taking my overcoat, which hides the worst stains on my baggy flannel trousers. A page-boy, seated on the counter, didn't rise to open the inner door. Bobby, to my relief, was at his place behind a blue and silver bar. I made towards him as towards an old friend. He greeted me most amiably:

'Good evening, Mr Isherwood. Very glad to see you here.'

I ordered a beer and settled myself on a stool in the corner. With my back to the wall, I could survey the whole room.

'How's business?' I asked.

Bobby's care-worn, powdered, night-dweller's face became grave. He inclined his head towards me, over the bar, with confidential flattering seriousness:

'Not much good, Mr Isherwood. The kind of public we have nowadays ... you wouldn't believe it! Why, a year ago, we'd have turned them away at the door. They order a beer and think they've got the right to sit here the whole evening.'

Bobby spoke with extreme bitterness. I began to feel uncomfortable:

'What'll you drink?' I asked, guiltily gulping down my beer: and added, lest there should be any misunderstanding: 'I'd like a whisky and soda.'

Bobby said he'd have one too.

The room was nearly empty. I looked the few guests over, trying to see them through Bobby's disillusioned eyes. There were three attractive, well-dressed girls sitting at the bar: the one nearest to me was particularly elegant, she had quite a cosmopolitan air. But during a lull in the conversation, I caught fragments of her talk with the other barman. She spoke broad Berlin dialect. She was tired and bored; her mouth dropped. A young man approached her and joined in the discussion; a handsome broad-shouldered boy in a well-cut dinner-jacket, who might well have been an English public-school prefect on holiday.

'Nee, nee,' I heard him say. 'Bei mir nicht!' He grinned and made a curt, brutal gesture of the streets.

Over in the corner sat a page-boy, talking to the little old lavatory attendant in his white jacket. The boy said something, laughed and broke off suddenly into a huge yawn. The three musicians on their platform were chatting, evidently unwilling to begin until they had an audience worth playing to. At one of the tables, I thought I saw a genuine guest, a stout man with a moustache. After a moment, however, I caught his eye, he made me a little bow and I knew that he must be the manager.

The door opened. Two men and two women came in. The women were elderly, had thick legs, cropped hair and costly evening-gowns. The men were lethargic, pale, probably Dutch. Here, unmistakably, was Money. In an instant, the Troika was transformed. The manager, the cigarette boy and the lavatory attendant rose simultaneously to their feet. The lavatory attendant disappeared. The manager said something in a furious undertone to the cigarette-boy, who also disappeared. He then advanced, bowing and smiling, to the guests' table and shook hands with the two men. The cigarette-boy reappeared with his tray, followed by a waiter who hurried foward with the wine-list. Meanwhile, the three-man orchestra struck up briskly. The girls at the bar turned on their stools, smiling a not-too-direct invitation. The gigolos advanced to them as if to complete strangers, bowed formally and asked, in cultured tones, for the pleasure of a dance. The page-boy, spruce, discreetly grinning, swaying from the waist like a flower, crossed the room with his tray of cigarettes: 'Zigarren! Zigaretten!' His voice was mocking, clear-pitched like an actor's. And in the same tone, yet more loudly, mockingly, joyfully, so that we could all hear, the waiter ordered from Bobby: 'Heidsick Monopol!'

With absurd, solicitous gravity, the dancers performed their intricate evolutions, showing in their every movement a consciousness of the part they were playing. And the saxophonist, letting his instrument swing loose from the ribbon around his neck, advanced to the edge of the platform with his little megaphone:

> Sie werden lachen,
> Ich lieb'
> Meine eigene Frau ...

He sang with a knowing leer, including us all in the conspiracy, charging his voice with innuendo, rolling his eyes in an epileptic pantomime of extreme joy. Bobby, suave, sleek, five years younger, handled the bottle. And meanwhile the two flaccid gentlemen chatted to each other, probably about business, without a glance at the night-life they had called into being; while their women sat silent, looking neglected, puzzled, uncomfortable and very bored.

Frl. Hippi Bernstein, my first pupil, lives in the Grünewald, in a house built almost entirely of glass. Most of the richest Berlin families inhabit the Grünewald. It is difficult to understand why. Their villas, in all known styles of expensive ugliness, ranging from the eccentric-rococo folly to the cubist flat-roofed steel-and-glass box, are crowded together in this dank, dreary pinewood. Few of them can afford large gardens, for the ground is fabulously dear: their only view is of their neighbour's backyard, each one protected by a wire fence and a savage dog. Terror of burglary and revolution has reduced these miserable people to a state of siege. They have neither privacy nor sunshine. The district is really a millionaire's slum.

When I rang the bell at the garden gate, a young footman came out with a key from the house, followed by a large growling Alsatian.

'He won't bite you while I'm here,' the footman reassured me, grinning.

The hall of the Bernstein's house has metal-studded doors and a steamer clock fasted to the wall with bolt-heads. There are modernist lamps, designed to look like pressure-gauges, thermometers and switchboard dials. But the furniture doesn't match the house and its fittings. The place is like a power-station which the engineers have tried to make comfortable with chairs and tables from an old-fashioned, highly respectable boarding-house. On the austere metal walls, hang highly varnished nineteenth-century landscapes in massive gold frames. Herr Bernstein probably ordered the villa from a popular *avant-garde* architect in a moment of recklessness; was horrified at the result and tried to cover it up as much as possible with the family belongings.

Frl. Hippi is a fat pretty girl, about nineteen years old, with glossy chestnut hair, good teeth and big cow-eyes. She has a lazy, jolly, self-indulgent laugh and a well-formed bust. She speaks schoolgirl English with a slight American accent, quite nicely, to her own complete satisfaction. She has clearly no intention of doing any work. When I tried weakly to suggest a plan for our lessons, she kept interrupting to offer me chocolates, coffee, cigarettes: 'Excuse me a minute, there isn't some fruit,' she smiled, picking up the receiver of the house-telephone: 'Anna, please bring some oranges.'

When the maid arrived with the oranges, I was forced, despite my protests, to make a regular meal, with a plate, knife and fork. This destroyed the last pretence of the teacher-pupil relationship. I felt like a policeman being given a meal in the kitchen by an attractive cook. Frl. Hippi sat watching me eat, with her good-natured, lazy smile:

'Tell me, please, why you come to Germany?'

She is inquisitive about me, but only like a cow idly poking with its head between the bars of a gate. She doesn't particularly want the gate to open. I said that I found Germany very interesting:

'The political and economic situation,' I improvised authoritatively, in my schoolmaster voice, 'is more interesting in Germany than in any other European country.'

'Except Russia, of course,' I added experimentally.

But Frl. Hippi didn't react. She just blandly smiled:

'I think it shall be dull for you here? You do not have many friends in Berlin, no?'

'No. Not many.'

This seemed to please and amuse her:

'You don't know some nice girls?'

Here the buzzer of the house-telephone sounded. Lazily smiling, she picked up the receiver, but appeared not to listen to the tinny voice which issued from it. I could hear quite distinctly the real voice of Frau Bernstein, Hippi's mother, speaking from the next room.

'Have you left your *red* book in here?' repeated Frl. Hippi mockingly and smiling at me as though this were a joke which I must share: 'No, I don't see it. It must be in the study. Ring up Daddy. Yes, he's working there.' In dumb show, she offered me another orange. I shook my head politely. We both smiled: 'Mummy, what have we got for lunch to-day? Yes? Really? Splendid!'

'Do you not know no nice girls?'

She hung up the receiver and returned to her cross-examination:

'*Any* nice girls ...' I corrected evasively. But Frl. Hippi merely smiled, waiting for the answer to her question.

'Yes. One,' I had at length to add, thinking of Frl. Kost.

'Only one?' She raised her eyebrows in comic surprise. 'And tell me, please, do you find German girls different than English girls?'

I blushed. 'Do you find German girls ...' I began to correct her and stopped, realizing just in time that I wasn't absolutely sure whether one says *different from* or *different to*.

'Do you find German girls different than English girls?' she repeated, with smiling persistence.

I blushed deeper than ever. 'Yes. Very different,' I said boldly.

'How are they different?'

Mercifully the telephone buzzed again. This was somebody from the kitchen, to say that lunch would be an hour earlier than usual. Herr Bernstein was going to the city that afternoon.

'I am so sorry,' said Frl. Hippi, rising, 'but for to-day we

must finish. And we shall see us again on Friday? Then good-
bye, Mr Isherwood. And I thank you very much.'

She fished in her bag and handed me an envelope which
I stuck awkwardly into my pocket and tore open only when I
was out of sight of the Bernsteins' house. It contained a five-
mark piece. I threw it into the air, missed it, found it after
five minutes' hunt, buried in sand, and ran all the way to the
tram-stop, singing and kicking stones about the road. I felt
extraordinarily guilty and elated, as though I'd successfully
committed a small theft.

It is a mere waste of time even pretending to teach Frl.
Hippi anything. If she doesn't know a word, she says it in
German. If I correct her, she repeats it in German. I am glad,
of course, that she's so lazy and only afraid that Frau Bernstein may discover how little progress her daughter is making.
But this is very unlikely. Most rich people, once they have
decided to trust you at all, can be imposed upon to almost
any extent. The only real problem for the private tutor is to
get inside the front door.

As for Hippi, she seems to enjoy my visits. From something she said the other day, I gather she boasts to her school
friends that she has got a genuine English teacher. We understand each other very well. I am bribed with fruit not to be
tiresome about the English language: she, for her part, tells
her parents that I am the best teacher she ever had. We gossip
in German about the things which interest her. And every
three or four minutes, we are interrupted while she plays her
part in the family game of exchanging entirely unimportant
messages over the house-telephone.

Hippi never worries about the future. Like everyone else
in Berlin, she refers continually to the political situation, but
only briefly, with a conventional melancholy, as when one
speaks of religion. It is quite unreal to her. She means to go
to the university, travel about, have a jolly good time and
eventually, of course, marry. She already has a great many
boy friends. We spend a lot of time talking about them. One
has a wonderful car. Another has an aeroplane. Another has

fought seven duels. Another has discovered a knack of putting out street-lamps by giving them a smart kick in a certain spot. One night, on the way back from a dance, Hippi and he put out all the street-lamps in the neighbourhood.

To-day, lunch was early at the Bernsteins'; so I was invited to it, instead of giving my 'lesson.' The whole family was present: Frau Bernstein, stout and placid; Herr Bernstein, small and shaky and sly. There was also a younger sister, a schoolgirl of twelve, very fat. She ate and ate, quite unmoved by Hippi's jokes and warnings that she'd burst. They all seem very fond of each other, in their cosy, stuffy way. There was a little domestic argument, because Herr Bernstein didn't want his wife to go shopping in the car that afternoon. During the last few days, there has been a lot of Nazi rioting in the city.

'You can go in the tram,' said Herr Bernstein. 'I will not have them throwing stones at my beautiful car.'

'And suppose they throw stones at me?' asked Frau Bernstein good-humouredly.

'Ach, what does that matter? If they throw stones at you, I will buy you a sticking-plaster for your head. It will cost me only five groschen. But if they throw stones at my car, it will cost me perhaps five hundred marks.'

And so the matter was settled. Herr Bernstein then turned his attention to me:

'You can't complain that we treat you badly here, young man, eh? Not only do we give you a nice dinner, but we pay for you eating it!'

I saw from Hippi's expression that this was going a bit far, even for the Bernstein sense of humour; so I laughed and said:

'Will you pay me a mark extra for every helping I eat?'

This amused Herr Bernstein very much; but he was careful to show that he knew I hadn't meant it seriously.

During the last week, our household has been plunged into a terrific row.

It began when Frl. Kost came to Frl. Schroeder and announced that fifty marks had been stolen from her room. She was very much upset; especially, she explained, as this was the money she'd put aside towards the rent and the telephone bill. The fifty-mark note had been lying in the drawer of the cupboard, just inside the door of Frl. Kost's room.

Frl. Schroeder's immediate suggestion was, not unnaturally, that the money had been stolen by one of Frl. Kost's customers. Frl. Kost said that this was quite impossible, as none of them had visited her during the last three days. Moreover, she added, *her* friends were all absolutely above suspicion. They were well-to-do gentlemen, to whom a miserable fifty-mark note was a mere bagatelle. This annoyed Frl. Schroeder very much indeed:

'I suppose she's trying to make out that one of *us* did it! Of all the cheek! Why, Herr Issyvoo, will you believe me, I could have chopped her into little pieces!'

'Yes, Frl. Schroeder. I'm sure you could.'

Frl. Schroeder then developed the theory that the money hadn't been stolen at all and that this was a trick of Frl. Kost's to avoid paying the rent. She hinted so much to Frl. Kost, who was furious. Frl. Kost said that, in any case, she'd raise the money in a few days: which she already has. She also gave notice to leave her room at the end of the month.

Meanwhile, I have discovered, quite by accident, that Frl. Kost has been having an affair with Bobby. As I came in, one evening, I happened to notice that there was no light in Frl. Kost's room. You can always see this, because there is a frosted glass pane in her door to light the hall of the flat. Later, as I lay in bed reading, I heard Frl. Kost's door open and Bobby's voice, laughing and whispering. After much creaking of boards and muffled laughter, Bobby tiptoed out of the flat, shutting the door as quietly as possible behind him. A moment later, he re-entered with a great deal of noise and went straight through into the living-room, where I heard him wishing Frl. Schroeder good-night.

If Frl. Schroeder doesn't actually know of this, she at least suspects it. This explains her fury against Frl. Kost: for the truth is, she is terribly jealous. The most grotesque and embarrassing incidents have been taking place. One morning, when I wanted to visit the bathroom, Frl. Kost was using it already. Frl. Schroeder rushed to the door before I could stop her and ordered Frl. Kost to come out at once: and when Frl. Kost naturally didn't obey, Frl. Schroeder began, despite my protests, hammering on the door with her fists. 'Come out of my bathroom!' she screamed. 'Come out this minute, or I'll call the police to fetch you out!'

After this she burst into tears. The crying brought on palpitations. Bobby had to carry her to the sofa, gasping and sobbing. While we were all standing round, rather helpless, Frl. Mayr appeared in the doorway with a face like a hangman and said, in a terrible voice, to Frl. Kost: 'Think yourself lucky, my girl, if you haven't murdered her!' She then took complete charge of the situation, ordered us all out of the room and sent me down to the grocer's for a bottle of Baldrian Drops. When I returned, she was seated beside the sofa, stroking Frl. Schroeder's hand and murmuring, in her most tragic tones: 'Lina, my poor little child ... what have they done to you?'

One afternoon, early in October, I was invited to black coffee at Fritz Wendel's flat. Fritz always invited you to 'Black coffee,' with emphasis on the black. He was very proud of his coffee. People used to say that it was the strongest in Berlin.

Fritz himself was dressed in his usual coffee-party costume – a very thick white yachting sweater and very light blue flannel trousers. He greeted me with his full-lipped, luscious smile:

' 'lo, Chris!'

'Hullo, Fritz. How are you?'

'Fine.' He bent over the coffee-machine, his sleek black hair unplastering itself from his scalp and falling in richly scented locks over his eyes. 'This darn thing doesn't go,' he added.

'How's business?' I asked.

'Lousy and terrible.' Fritz grinned richly. 'Or I pull off a new deal in the next month or I go as a gigolo.'

'*Either* ... or ...,' I corrected, from force of professional habit.

'I'm speaking a lousy English just now,' drawled Fritz, with great self-satisfaction. 'Sally says maybe she'll give me a few lessons.'

'Who's Sally?'

'Why, I forgot. You don't know Sally. Too bad of me. Eventually she's coming around here this afternoon.'

'Is she nice?'

Fritz rolled his naughty black eyes, handing me a rum-moistened cigarette from his patent tin:

'*Mar*-vellous!' he drawled. 'Eventually I believe I'm getting crazy about her.'

'And who is she? What does she do?'

'She's an English girl, an actress: sings at the Lady Windermere – hot stuff, believe me!'

'That doesn't sound much like an English girl, I must say.'

'Eventually she's got a bit of French in her. Her mother was French.'

A few minutes later, Sally herself arrived.

'Am I terribly late, Fritz darling?'

'Only half of an hour, I suppose,' Fritz drawled, beaming with proprietary pleasure. 'May I introduce Mr Isherwood – Miss Bowles? Mr Isherwood is commonly known as Chris.'

'I'm not,' I said. 'Fritz is about the only person who's ever called me Chris in my life.'

Sally laughed. She was dressed in black silk, with a small cape over her shoulders and a little cap like a page-boy's stuck jauntily on one side of her head:

'Do you mind if I use your telephone, sweet?'

'Sure. Go right ahead.' Fritz caught my eye. 'Come into the other room, Chris. I want to show you something.' He was evidently longing to hear my first impressions of Sally, his new acquisition.

'For heaven's sake, don't leave me alone with this man!' she exclaimed. 'Or he'll seduce me down the telephone. He's most terribly passionate.'

As she dialled the number, I noticed that her finger-nails were painted emerald green, a colour unfortunately chosen, for it called attention to her hands, which were much stained by cigarette-smoking and as dirty as a little girl's. She was dark enough to be Fritz's sister. Her face was long and thin, powdered dead white. She had very large brown eyes which should have been darker, to match her hair and the pencil she used for her eyebrows.

'Hilloo,' she cooed, pursing her brilliant cherry lips as though she were going to kiss the mouthpiece: 'Ist das Du, mein Liebling?' Her mouth opened in a fatuously sweet smile. Fritz and I sat watching her, like a performance at the theatre. 'Was wollen wir machen, Morgen Abend? Oh, wie wunderbar ... Nein, nein, ich werde bleiben Heute Abend zu Hause. Ja, ja, ich werde wirklich bleiben zu Hause ...

Auf Wiedersehen, mein Liebling ...'

She hung up the receiver and turned to us triumphantly.

'That's the man I slept with last night,' she announced. 'He makes love marvellously. He's an absolute genius at business and he's terribly rich—' She came and sat down on the sofa beside Fritz, sinking back into the cushions with a sigh: 'Give me some coffee, will you, darling? I'm simply dying of thirst.'

And soon we were on to Fritz's favourite topic: he pronounced it Larv.

'On the average,' he told us. 'I'm having a big affair every two years.'

'And how long is it since you had your last?' Sally asked.

'Exactly one year and eleven months!' Fritz gave her his naughtiest glance.

'How marvellous!' Sally puckered up her nose and laughed a silvery little stage-laugh: 'Doo tell me – what was the last one like?'

This, of course, started Fritz off on a complete autobiography. We had the story of his seduction in Paris, details of a holiday flirtation at Las Palmas, the four chief New York romances, a disappointment in Chicago and a conquest in Boston; then back to Paris for a little recreation, a very beautiful episode in Vienna, to London to be consoled and, finally, Berlin.

'You know, Fritz darling,' said Sally, puckering up her nose at me, 'I believe the trouble with you is that you've never really found the right woman.'

'Maybe that's true—' Fritz took this idea very seriously. His black eyes became liquid and sentimental: 'Maybe I'm still looking for my ideal ...'

'But you'll find her one day, I'm absolutely certain you will.' Sally included me, with a glance, in the game of laughing at Fritz.

'You think so?' Fritz grinned lusciously, sparkling at her.

'Don't you think so?' Sally appealed to me.

'I'm sure I don't know,' I said. 'Because I've never been able to discover what Fritz's ideal is.'

For some reason, this seemed to please Fritz. He took it as a kind of testimonial: 'And Chris knows me pretty well,' he chimed in, 'If Chris doesn't know, well, I guess no one does.'

Then it was time for Sally to go.

'I'm supposed to meet a man at the Adlon at five,' she explained. 'And it's six already! Never mind, it'll do the old swine good to wait. He wants me to be his mistress, but I've told him I'm damned if I will till he's paid all my debts. Why are men always such beasts?' Opening her bag, she rapidly retouched her lips and eyebrows: 'Oh, by the way, Fritz darling, could you be a perfect angel and lend me ten marks? I haven't got a bean for a taxi.'

'Why sure!' Fritz put his hand into his pocket and paid up without hesitation, like a hero.

Sally turned to me: 'I say, will you come and have tea with me sometime? Give me your telephone number. I'll ring you up.'

I suppose, I thought, she imagines I've got cash. Well, this will be a lesson to her, once for all. I wrote my number in her tiny leather book. Fritz saw her out.

'Well!' he came bounding back into the room and gleefully shut the door: 'What do you think of her Chris? Didn't I tell you she was a good-looker?'

'You did indeed!'

'I'm getting crazier about her each time I see her!' With a sigh of pleasure, he helped himself to a cigarette: 'More coffee, Chris?'

'No, thank you very much.'

'You know, Chris, I think she took a fancy to you, too!'

'Oh, rot!'

'Honestly, I do!' Fritz seemed pleased. 'Eventually I guess we'll be seeing a lot of her from now on!'

When I got back to Frl. Schroeder's, I felt so giddy that I had to lie down for half an hour on my bed. Fritz's black coffee was as poisonous as ever.

A few days later, he took me to hear Sally sing. The Lady Windermere (which now, I hear, no longer exists) was an arty 'informal' bar, just off the Tauentzien-strasse, which the proprietor had evidently tried to make look as much as possible like Montparnasse. The walls were covered with sketches on menu-cards, caricatures and signed theatrical photographs – ('To the one and only Lady Winder-mere.' 'To Johnny, with all my heart.') The Fan itself, four times life size, was displayed above the bar. There was a big piano on a platform in the middle of the room.

I was curious to see how Sally would behave. I had imagined her, for some reason, rather nervous, but she wasn't, in the least. She had a surprisingly deep husky voice. She sang badly, without any expression, her hands hanging down at her sides – yet her performance was, in its own way, effec-tive because of her startling appearance and her air of not caring a curse what people thought of her. Her arms hanging carelessly limp, and a take-it-or-leave-it grin on her face, she sang:

> Now I know why Mother
> Told me to be true;
> She meant me for Someone
> Exactly like you.

There was quite a lot of applause. The pianist, a handsome young man with blond wavy hair, stood up and solemnly kissed Sally's hand. Then she sang two more songs, one in French and the other in German. These weren't so well received.

After the singing, there was a good deal more hand-kissing and a general movement towards the bar.

Sally seemed to know everybody in the place. She called them all Thou and Darling. For a would-be demi-mondaine, she seemed to have surprisingly little business sense or tact. She wasted a lot of time making advances to an elderly gentleman who would obviously have preferred a chat with the barman. Later, we all got rather drunk. Then Sally had to go off to an appointment, and the manager came and sat at our table. He and Fritz talked English Peerage. Fritz was in his element.

I decided, as so often before, never to visit a place of this sort again.

Then Sally rang up, as she had promised, to invite me to tea.

She lived a long way down the Kurfürstendamm on the last dreary stretch which rises to Halensee. I was shown into a big gloomy half-furnished room by a fat untidy landlady with a pouchy sagging jowl like a toad. There was a broken-down sofa in one corner and a faded picture of an eighteenth-century battle, with the wounded reclining on their elbows in graceful attitudes, admiring the prancings of Frederick the Great's horse.

'Oh, hullo, Chris darling!' cried Sally from the doorway. 'How sweet of you to come! I was feeling most terribly lonely. I've been crying on Frau Karpf's chest. Nicht wahr, Frau Karpf?' She appealed to the toad landlady, 'ich habe geweint aur Dein Brust.' Frau Karpf shook her bosom in a toad-like chuckle.

'Would you rather have coffee, Chris, or tea?' Sally continued. 'You can have either. Only I don't recommend the tea much. I don't know what Frau Karpf does to it; I think she empties all the kitchen slops together into a jug and boils them up with tea-leaves.'

'I'll have coffee, then.'

'Frau Karpf, Leibling, willst Du sein ein Engel und bring zwei Tassen von Kaffee?' Sally's German was not merely incorrect; it was all her own. She pronounced every word in a mincing, specially 'foreign' manner. You could tell that she was speaking a foreign language from her expression alone. 'Chris darling, will you be an angel and draw the curtains?'

I did so, although it was still quite light outside. Sally, meanwhile, had switched on the table-lamp. As I turned from the window, she curled herself up delicately on the sofa like a cat, and, opening her bag, felt for a cigarette. But hardly was the pose complete before she'd jumped to her feet again:

'Would you like a Prairie Oyster?' She produced glasses, eggs and a bottle of Worcester sauce from the boot-cupboard

under the dismantled washstand: 'I practically live on them.'
Dexterously, she broke the eggs into the glasses, added the
sauce and stirred up the mixture with the end of a fountain-
pen: 'They're about all I can afford.' She was back on the
sofa again, daintily curled up.

She was wearing the same black dress to-day, but without
the cape. Instead, she had a little white collar and white cuffs.
They produced a kind of theatrically chaste effect, like a nun
in grand opera. 'What are you laughing at, Chris?' she asked.

'I don't know,' I said. But still I couldn't stop grinning.
There was, at that moment, something so extraordinarily
comic in Sally's appearance. She was really beautiful, with her
little dark head, big eyes and finely arched nose – and so
absurdly conscious of all these features. There she lay, as
complacently feminine as a turtle-dove, with her poised self-
conscious head and daintily arranged hands.

'Chris, you swine, do tell me why you're laughing?'

'I really haven't the faintest idea.'

At this, she began to laugh, too: 'You are mad, you know!'

'Have you been here long?' I asked, looking round the
large gloomy room.

'Ever since I arrived in Berlin. Let's see – that was about
two months ago.'

I asked what had made her decide to come out to Germany
at all. Had she come alone? No, she'd come with a girl
friend. An actress. Older than Sally. The girl had been to
Berlin before. She'd told Sally that they'd certainly be able
to get work with the Ufa. So Sally borrowed ten pounds from
a nice old gentleman and joined her.

She hadn't told her parents anything about it until the two
of them had actually arrived in Germany: 'I wish you'd met
Diana. She was the most marvellous gold-digger you can
imagine. She'd get hold of men anywhere – it didn't matter
whether she could speak their language or not. She made me
nearly die of laughing. I absolutely adored her.'

But when they'd been together in Berlin three weeks and
no job had appeared, Diana had got hold of a banker,
who'd taken her off with him to Paris.

'And left you here alone? I must say I think that was pretty rotten of her.'

'Oh, I don't know ... Everyone's got to look after themselves. I expect, in her place, I'd have done the same.'

'I bet you wouldn't!'

'Anyhow, I'm all right. I can always get along alone.'

'How old are you, Sally?'

'Nineteen.'

'Good God! And I thought you were about twenty-five!'

'I know. Everyone does.'

Frau Karpf came shuffling in with two cups of coffee on a tarnished metal tray.

'Oh, Frau Karpf, Leibling, wie wunderbar von Dich!'

'Whatever makes you stay in this house?' I asked, when the landlady had gone out: 'I'm sure you could get a much nicer room than this.'

'Yes, I know I could.'

'Well then, why don't you?'

'Oh, I don't know. I'm lazy, I suppose.'

'What do you have to pay here?'

'Eighty marks a month.'

'With breakfast included?'

'No – I don't think so.'

'You don't *think* so?' I exclaimed severely. 'But surely you must know for certain?'

Sally took this meekly: 'Yes, it's stupid of me, I suppose. But, you see, I just give the old girl money when I've got some. So it's rather difficult to reckon it all up exactly.'

'But, good heavens, Sally – I only pay fifty a month for my room, with breakfast, and it's ever so much nicer than this one!'

Sally nodded, but continued apologetically: 'And another thing is, you see, Christopher darling, I don't quite know what Frau Karpf would do if I were to leave her. I'm sure she'd never get another lodger. Nobody else would be able to stand her face and her smell and everything. As it is, she owes three months' rent. They'd turn her out at once if they knew she hadn't any lodgers: and if they do that, she says she'll commit suicide.'

'All the same, I don't see why you should sacrifice yourself for her.'

'I'm not sacrificing myself, really. I quite like being here, you know. Frau Karpf and I understand each other. She's more or less what I'll be in thirty years' time. A respectable sort of landlady would probably turn me out after a week.'

'My landlady wouldn't turn you out.'

Sally smiled vaguely, screwing up her nose: 'How do you like the coffee, Chris darling?'

'I prefer it to Fritz's,' I said evasively.

Sally laughed: 'Isn't Fritz marvellous? I adore him. I adore the way he says, "I give a damn." '

' "Hell, I give a damn." ' I tried to imitate Fritz. We both laughed. Sally lit another cigarette: she smoked the whole time. I noticed how old her hands looked in the lamplight. They were nervous, veined and very thin – the hands of a middle-aged woman. The green finger-nails seemed not to belong to them at all; to have settled on them by chance – like hard, bright, ugly little beetles. 'It's a funny thing,' she added meditatively. 'Fritz and I have never slept together, you know.' She paused, asked with interest: 'Did you think we had?'

'Well, yes – I suppose I did.'

'We haven't. Not once ...' she yawned. 'And now I don't suppose we ever shall.'

We smoked for some minutes in silence. Then Sally began to tell me about her family. She was the daughter of a Lancashire mill-owner. Her mother was a Miss Bowles, an heiress with an estate, and so, when she and Mr Jackson were married, they joined their names together: 'Daddy's a terrible snob, although he pretends not to be. My real name's Jackson-Bowles; but, of course, I can't possibly call myself that on the stage. People would think I was crazy.'

'I thought Fritz told me your mother was French?'

'No, of course not! ' Sally seemed quite annoyed. 'Fritz is an idiot. He's always inventing things.'

Sally had one sister, named Betty. 'She's an absolute angel. I adore her. She's seventeen, but she's still most terribly innocent. Mummy's bringing her up to be very county. Betty would nearly die if she knew what an old whore I am. She knows absolutely nothing whatever about men.'

'But why aren't you county, too, Sally?'

'I don't know. I suppose that's Daddy's side of the family coming out. You'd love Daddy. He doesn't care a damn for anyone. He's the most marvellous business man. And about once a month he gets absolutely dead tight and horrifies all Mummy's smart friends. It was he who said I could go to London and learn acting.'

'You must have left school very young?'

'Yes. I couldn't bear school. I got myself expelled.'

'However did you do that?'

'I told the headmistress I was going to have a baby.'

'Oh rot, Sally, you didn't!'

'I did, honestly! There was the most terrible commotion. They got a doctor to examine me, and sent for my parents. When they found out there was nothing the matter, they were most frightfully disappointed. The headmistress said that a girl who could even think of anything so disgusting couldn't possibly be allowed to stay on and corrupt the other girls. So I got my own way. And then I pestered Daddy till he said I might go to London.

Sally had settled down in London, at a hostel, with other girl students. There, in spite of supervision, she had managed to spend large portions of the night at young men's flats: 'The first man who seduced me had no idea I was a virgin until I told him afterwards. He was marvellous. I adored him. He was an absolute genius at comedy parts. He's sure to be terribly famous, one day.'

After a time, Sally had got crowd-work in films and finally a small part in a touring company. Then she had met Diana.

'And how much longer shall you stay in Berlin?' I asked.

'Heaven knows. This job at the Lady Windermere only lasts another week. I got it through a man I met at the Eden Bar. But he's gone off to Vienna now. I must ring up the Ufa people again, I suppose. And then there's an awful old Jew who takes me out sometimes. He's always promising to get me a contract but he only wants to sleep with me, the old swine. I think the men in this country are awful. They've none of them got any money, and they expect you to let them seduce you if they give you a box of chocolates.'

'How on earth are you going to manage when this job comes to an end?'

'Oh well, I get a small allowance from home, you know. Not that that'll last much longer. Mummy's already threatened to stop it if I don't come back to England soon ... Of course, they think I'm here with a girl friend. If Mummy knew I was on my own, she'd simply pass right out. Anyhow, I'll get enough to support myself somehow, soon. I loathe taking money from them. Daddy's business is in a frightfully bad way now, from the slump.'

'I say, Sally – if you ever really get into a mess I wish you'd let me know.'

Sally laughed: 'That's terribly sweet of you, Chris. But I don't sponge on my friends.'

'Isn't Fritz your friend?' It had jumped out of my mouth. But Sally didn't seem to mind a bit.

'Oh yes, I'm awfully fond of Fritz, of course. But he's got pots of cash. Somehow, when people have cash, you feel differently about them—I don't know why.'

'And how do you know I haven't got pots of cash, too?'

'You?' Sally burst out laughing. 'Why, I knew you were hard-up the first moment I set eyes on you!'

The afternoon Sally came to tea with me, Frl. Schroeder was beside herself with excitement. She put on her best dress for the occasion and waved her hair. When the door-bell rang, she threw open the door with a flourish: 'Herr Issyvoo,' she announced, winking knowingly at me and speaking very loud, 'there's a lady to see you!'

I then formally introduced Sally and Frl. Schroeder to each other. Frl. Schroeder was overflowing with politeness: she addressed Sally repeatedly as 'Gnädiges Fräulein.' Sally, with her page-boy cap stuck over one ear, laughed her silvery laugh and sat down elegantly on the sofa. Frl. Schroeder hovered about her in unfeigned admiration and amazement. She had evidently never seen anyone like Sally before. When she brought in the tea there were, in place of the usual little chunks of pale unappetizing pastry, a plateful of jam tarts arranged in the shape of a star. I noticed also that Frl. Schroeder had provided us with two tiny paper serviettes, perforated at the edges to resemble lace. (When, later I complimented her on these preparations, she told me that she had always used the serviettes when the Herr Rittmeister had had his fiancée to tea. 'Oh, yes, Herr Issyvoo. You can depend on me! I know what pleases a young lady!')

'Do you mind if I lie down on your sofa, darling?' Sally asked, as soon as we were alone.

'No, of course not.'

Sally pulled off her cap, swung her little velvet shoes up on to the sofa, opened her bag and began powdering: 'I'm most terribly tired. I didn't sleep a wink last night. I've got a marvellous new lover.'

I began to put out the tea. Sally gave me a sidelong glance:

'Do I shock you when I talk like that, Christopher darling?'

'Not in the least.'

'But you don't like it?'

'It's no business of mine.' I handed her the tea-glass.

'Oh, for God's sake,' cried Sally, 'don't start being English! Of course it's your business what you think!'

'Well then, if you want to know, it rather bores me.'

This annoyed her even more than I had intended. Her tone changed: she said coldly: 'I thought you'd understand.' She sighed: 'But I forgot – you're a man.'

'I'm sorry, Sally, I can't help being a man, of course ... But please don't be angry with me. I only meant that when you talk like that it's really just nervousness. You're naturally rather shy with strangers, I think: so you've got into this trick of trying to bounce them into approving or disapproving of you, violently. I know, because I try it myself, sometimes ... Only I wish you wouldn't try it on me, because it just doesn't work and it only makes me feel embarrassed. If you go to bed with every single man in Berlin and come and tell me about it each time, you still won't convince me that you're *La Dame aux Camélias* – because, really and truly, you know, you aren't.'

'No ... I suppose I'm not—' Sally's voice was carefully impersonal. She was beginning to enjoy this conversation. I had succeeded in flattering her in some new way: 'Then what *am* I, exactly, Christopher darling?'

'You're the daughter of Mr and Mrs Jackson-Bowles.'

Sally sipped her tea: 'Yes ... I think I see what you mean ... Perhaps you're right ... Then you think I ought to give up having lovers altogether?'

'Certainly I don't. As long as you're sure you're really enjoying yourself.'

'Of course,' said Sally gravely, after a pause, 'I'd never let love interfere with my work. Work comes before everything ... But I don't believe that a woman can be a great actress who hasn't had any love-affairs—' she broke off suddenly: 'What are you laughing at, Chris?'

'I'm not laughing.'

'You're always laughing at me. Do you think I'm the most ghastly idiot?'

'No, Sally. I don't think you're an idiot at all. It's quite true, I *was* laughing. People I like often make me want to laugh at them. I don't know why.'

'Then you do like me, Christopher darling?'

'Yes, of course I like you Sally. What did you think?'

'But you're not in love with me, are you?'

'No. I'm not in love with you.'

'I'm awfully glad. I've wanted you to like me ever since we first met. But I'm glad you're not in love with me, because, somehow, I couldn't possibly be in love with you – so, if you had been, everything would have been spoilt.'

'Well then, that's very lucky, isn't it?'

'Yes, very ...' Sally hesitated. 'There's something I want to confess to you, Chris darling . . . I'm not sure if you'll understand or not.'

'Remember, I'm only a man, Sally.'

Sally laughed: 'It's the most idiotic little thing. But somehow, I'd hate it if you found out without my telling you ... You know, the other day, you said Fritz had told you my mother was French?'

'Yes, I remember.'

'And I said he must have invented it? Well, he hadn't ... You see, I'd told him she was.'

'But why on earth did you do that?'

We both began to laugh. 'Goodness knows,' said Sally. 'I suppose I wanted to impress him.'

'But what is there impressive in having a French mother?'

'I'm a bit mad like that sometimes, Chris. You must be patient with me.'

'All right, Sally, I'll be patient.'

'And you'll swear on your honour not to tell Fritz?'

'I swear.'

'If you do, you swine,' exclaimed Sally, laughing and picking up the paper-knife dagger from my writing-table, 'I'll cut your throat!'

Afterwards, I asked Frl. Schroeder what she'd thought of Sally. She was in raptures: 'Like a picture, Herr Issyvoo! And so elegant: such beautiful hands and feet! One can see that she belongs to the very best society ... You know, Herr Issyvoo, I should never have expected you to have a lady friend like that! You always seem so quiet ...'

'Ah, well, Frl. Schroeder, it's often the quiet ones—'

She went off into her little scream of laughter, swaying backwards and forwards on her short legs:

'Quite right, Herr Issyvoo! Quite right!'

On New Year's Eve, Sally came to live at Frl. Schroeder's. It had all been arranged at the last moment. Sally, her suspicions sharpened by my repeated warnings, had caught out Frau Karpf in a particularly gross and clumsy piece of swindling. So she had hardened her heart and given notice. She was to have Frl. Kost's old room. Frl. Schroeder was, of course, enchanted.

We all had our Sylvester Abend dinner at home: Frl.
Schroeder, Frl. Mayr, Sally, Bobby, a mixer colleague from
the Troika and myself. It was a great success. Bobby, already
restored to favour, flirted daringly with Frl. Schroeder. Frl.
Mayr and Sally, talking as one great artiste to another, discussed the possibilities of music-hall work in England. Sally
told some really startling lies, which she obviously for the
moment half-believed, about how she'd appeared at the
Palladium and the London Coliseum. Frl. Mayr capped them
with a story of how she'd been drawn through the streets of
Munich in a carriage by excited students. From this point it
did not take Sally long to persuade Frl. Mayr to sing *Sennerin
Abschied von der Alm*, which, after claret cup and a bottle
of very inexpensive cognac, so exactly suited my mood that
I shed a few tears. We all joined in the repeats and the final,
ear-splitting *Juch-he!* Then Sally sang 'I've got those Little
Boy Blues' with so much expression that Bobby's mixer colleague, taking it personally, seized her round the waist and
had to be restrained by Bobby, who reminded him firmly that
it was time to be getting along to business.

Sally and I went with them to the Troika, where we met
Fritz. With him was Klaus Linke, the young pianist who used
to accompany Sally when she sang at the Lady Windermere.
Later, Fritz and I went off alone. Fritz seemed rather depressed: he wouldn't tell me why. Some girls did classical
figure-tableaux behind gauze. And then there was a big danc-
ing-hall with telephones on the tables. We had the usual kind
of conversations: 'Pardon me, Madame, I feel sure from your
voice that you're a fascinating little blonde with long black
eyelashes – just my type. How did I know? Aha, that's my
secret! Yes – quite right: I'm tall, dark, broad-shouldered,
military appearance, and the tiniest little moustache ... You
don't believe me? Then come and see for yourself!' The
couples were dancing with hands on each other's hips, yelling
in each other's faces, streaming with sweat. An orchestra in
Bavarian costume whooped and drank and perspired beer.
The place stank like a zoo. After this, I think I strayed off
alone and wandered for hours and hours through a jungle of

paper streamers. Next morning, when I woke, the bed was full of them.

I had been up and dressed for some time when Sally returned home. She came straight into my room, looking tired but very pleased with herself.

'Hullo, darling! What time is it?'

'Nearly lunch-time.'

'I say, is it really? How marvellous! I'm practically starving. I've had nothing for breakfast but a cup of coffee ...' She paused expectantly, waiting for my next question.

'Where have you been?' I asked.

'But, darling,' Sally opened her eyes very wide in affected surprise: 'I thought you knew!'

'I haven't the least idea.'

'Nonsense!'

'Really I haven't, Sally.'

'Oh, Christopher darling, how can you be such a liar! Why, it was obvious that you'd planned the whole thing! The way you got rid of Fritz – he looked so cross! Klaus and I nearly died of laughing.'

All the same, she wasn't quite at her ease. For the first time, I saw her blush.

'Have you got a cigarette, Chris?'

I gave her one and lit the match. She blew out a long cloud of smoke and walked slowly to the window:

'I'm most terribly in love with him.'

She turned, frowning slightly; crossed to the sofa and curled herself up carefully, arranging her hands and feet: 'At least, I think I am,' she added.

I allowed a respectful pause to elapse before asking: 'And is Klaus in love with you?'

'He absolutely adores me.' Sally was very serious indeed. She smoked for several minutes: 'He says he fell in love with me the first time we met, at the Lady Windermere. But as long as we were working together, he didn't dare to say anything. He was afraid it might put me off my singing ... He says that, before he met me, he'd no idea what a marvellously beautiful thing a woman's body is. He's only had about three women before, in his life ...'

I lit a cigarette.

'Of course, Chris, I don't suppose you really understand ... It's awfully hard to explain ...'

'I'm sure it is.'

'I'm seeing him again at four o'clock.' Sally's tone was slightly defiant.

'In that case, you'd better get some sleep. I'll ask Frl. Schroeder to scramble you some eggs; or I'll do them myself if she's still too drunk. You get into bed. You can eat them there.'

'Thanks, Chris darling. You are an angel.' Sally yawned. 'What on earth I should do without you, I don't know.'

After this, Sally and Klaus saw each other every day. They generally met at our house; and, once, Klaus stayed the whole night. Frl. Schroeder didn't say much to me about it, but I could see that she was rather shocked. Not that she disapproved of Klaus: she thought him very attractive. But she regarded Sally as my property, and it shocked her to see me standing so tamely to one side. I am sure, however, that if I hadn't known about the affair, and if Sally had really been deceiving me, Frl. Schroeder would have assisted at the conspiracy with the greatest relish.

Meanwhile, Klaus and I were a little shy of each other. When we happened to meet on the stairs, we bowed coldly, like enemies.

About the middle of January, Klaus left suddenly, for England. Quite unexpectedly he had got the offer of a very good job, synchronizing music for the films. The afternoon he came to say good-bye there was a positively surgical atmosphere in the flat, as though Sally were undergoing a dangerous operation. Frl. Schroeder and Frl. Mayr sat in the living-room and laid cards. The results, Frl. Schroeder later assured me, couldn't have been better. The eight of clubs had appeared three times in a favourable conjunction.

* * *

Sally spent the whole of the next day curled up on the sofa in her room, with pencil and paper on her lap. She was writing poems. She wouldn't let me see them. She smoked cigarette after cigarette, and mixed Prairie Oysters, but refused to eat more than a few mouthfuls of Frl. Schroeder's omelette.

'Can't I bring you something in, Sally?'

'No thanks, Chris darling. I just don't want to eat anything at all. I feel all marvellous and ethereal, as if I was a kind of most wonderful saint, or something. You've no idea how glorious it feels ... Have a chocolate, darling? Klaus gave me three boxes. If I eat any more, I shall be sick.'

'Thank you.'

'I don't suppose I shall ever marry him. It would ruin our careers. You see, Christopher, he adores me so terribly that it wouldn't be good for him to always have me hanging about.'

'You might marry after you're both famous.'

Sally considered this:

'No ... That would spoil everything. We should be trying all the time to live up to our old selves, if you know what I mean. And we should both be different ... He was so marvellously primitive: just like a faun. He made me feel like a most marvellous nymph, or something, miles away from anywhere, in the middle of the forest.'

The first letter from Klaus duly arrived. We had all been anxiously awaiting it; and Frl. Schroeder woke me up specially early to tell me that it had come. Perhaps she was afraid that she would never get a chance of reading it herself and relied on me to tell her the contents. If so, her fears were groundless. Sally not only showed the letter to Frl. Schroeder, Frl. Mayr, Bobby and myself, she even read selections from it aloud in the presence of the porter's wife, who had come up to collect the rent.

From the first, the letter left a nasty taste in my mouth. Its whole tone was egotistical and a bit patronizing. Klaus didn't like London, he said. He felt lonely there. The food disagreed with him. And the people at the studio treated him with lack of consideration. He wished Sally were with him: she could have helped him in many ways. However, now that he was in England, he would try to make the best of it. He would work hard and earn money; and Sally was to work hard too. Work would cheer her up and keep her from getting depressed. At the end of the latter came various endearments, rather too slickly applied. Reading them, one felt: he's written this kind of thing several times before.

Sally was delighted, however. Klaus' exhortation made such an impression upon her that she at once rang up several film companies, a theatrical agency and half a dozen of her 'business' acquaintances. Nothing definite came of all this, it is true; but she remained very optimistic throughout the next twenty-four hours – even her dreams, she told me, had been full of contracts and four-figure cheques: 'It's the most marvellous feeling, Chris. I know I'm going right ahead now and going to become the most wonderful actress in the world.'

One morning, about a week after this, I went into Sally's room and found her holding a letter in her hand. I recognized Klaus' handwriting at once.

'Good morning, Chris darling.'

'Good morning, Sally.'

'How did you sleep?' Her tone was unnaturally bright and chatty.

'All right, thanks. How did you?'

'Fairly all right ... Filthy weather, isn't it?'

'Yes.' I walked over to the window to look. It was.

Sally smiled conversationally: 'Do you know what this swine's gone and done?'

'What swine?' I wasn't going to be caught out.

'Oh Chris! For God's sake, don't be so dense!'

'I'm very sorry. I'm afraid I'm a bit slow in the uptake this morning.'

'I can't be bothered to explain, darling.' Sally held out the letter. 'Here, read this, will you? Of all the blasted impudence! Read it aloud. I want to hear how it sounds.'

'Mein liebes, armes Kind,' the letter began. Klaus called Sally his poor dear child because, as he explained, he was afraid that what he had to tell her would make her terribly unhappy. Nevertheless, he must say it: he must tell her that he had come to a decision. She mustn't imagine that this had been easy for him: it had been very difficult and painful. All the same, he knew he was right. In a word, they must part.

'I see now,' wrote Klaus, 'that I behaved very selfishly. I thought only of my own pleasure. But now I realize that I must have had a bad influence on you. My dear little girl, you have adored me too much. If we should continue to be together, you would soon have no will and no mind of your own.' Klaus went on to advise Sally to live for her work. 'Work is the only thing which matters, as I myself have found.' He was very much concerned that Sally shouldn't upset herself unduly: 'You must be brave, Sally, my poor darling child.'

Right at the end of the letter, it all came out:

'I was invited a few nights ago to a party at the house of Lady Klein, a leader of the English aristocracy. I met there a very beautiful and intelligent young English girl named Miss Gore-Eckersley. She is related to an English lord whose name I couldn't quite hear – you will probably know which one I mean. We have met twice since then and had wonderful conversations about many things. I do not think I have ever met a girl who could understand my mind so well as she does—'

'That's a new one on me,' broke in Sally bitterly, with a short laugh: 'I never suspected the boy of having a mind at all.'

At this moment we were interrupted by Frl. Schroeder who had come, sniffing secrets, to ask if Sally would like a bath. I left them together to make the most of the occasion.

'I can't be angry with the fool,' said Sally, later in the day, pacing up and down the room and furiously smoking: 'I just feel sorry for him in a motherly sort of way. But what on earth'll happen to *his* work, if he chucks himself at these women's heads, I can't imagine.'

She made another turn of the room:

'I think if he'd been having a proper affair with another

woman, and had only told me about it after it'd been going on for a long time, I'd have minded more. But this girl! Why, I don't suppose she's even his mistress.'

'Obviously not,' I agreed. 'I say, shall we have a Prairie Oyster?'

'How marvellous you are, Chris! You always think of just the right thing. I wish I could fall in love with you. Klaus isn't worth your little finger.'

'I know he isn't.'

'The blasted cheek,' exclaimed Sally gulping the Worcester sauce and licking her upper lip, 'of his saying I adored him! ... The worst of it is, I did!'

That evening I went into her room and found her with pen and paper before her:

'I've written about a million letters to him and torn them all up.'

'It's no good, Sally. Let's go to the cinema.'

'Right you are, Chris darling.' Sally wiped her eyes with the corner of her tiny handkerchief: 'It's no use bothering, is it?'

'Not a bit of use.'

'And now I jolly well *will* be a great actress – just to show him!'

'That's the spirit!'

We went to a little cinema in the Bülowstrasse, where they were showing a film about a girl who sacrificed her stage career for the sake of a Great Love, Home and Children. We laughed so much that we had to leave before the end.

'I feel ever so much better now,' said Sally, as we were coming away.

'I'm glad'.

'Perhaps, after all, I can't have been properly in love with him ... What do you think?'

'It's rather difficult for me to say.'

'I've often thought I was in love with a man, and then I found I wasn't. But this time,' Sally's voice was regretful, 'I really did feel *sure* of it ... And now, somehow, everything seems to have got a bit confused ...'

'Perhaps you're suffering from shock,' I suggested.

Sally was very pleased with this idea: 'Do you know, I expect I am! ... You know, Chris, you do understand women most marvellously: better than any man I've ever met ... I'm sure that some day you'll write the most marvellous novel which'll sell simply millions of copies.'

'Thank you for believing in me, Sally!'

'Do you believe in me, too, Chris?'

'Of course I do.'

'No, but honestly?'

'Well ... I'm quite certain you'll make a terrific success at something – only I'm not sure what it'll be ... I mean, there's so many things you could do if you tried, aren't there?'

'I suppose there are.' Sally became thoughtful. 'At least, sometimes I feel like that ... And sometimes I feel I'm no damn' use at anything ... Why, I can't even keep a man faithful to me for the inside of a month.'

'Oh, Sally, don't let's start all that again!'

'All right, Chris – we won't start all that. Let's go and have a drink.'

During the weeks that followed, Sally and I were together most of the day. Curled up on the sofa in the big dingy room, she smoked, drank Prairie Oysters, talked endlessly of the future. When the weather was fine, and I hadn't any lessons to give, we strolled as far as the Wittenbergplatz and sat on a bench in the sunshine, discussing the people who went past. Everybody stared at Sally, in her canary yellow beret and shabby fur coat, like the skin of a mangy old dog.

'I wonder,' she was fond of remarking, 'what they'd say if they knew that we two old tramps were to be the most marvellous novelist and the greatest actress in the world.'

'They'd probably be very much surprised.'

'I expect we shall look back on this time when we're driving about in our Mercedes, and think: After all, it wasn't such bad fun!'

'It wouldn't be such bad fun if we had that Mercedes now.'

We talked continually about wealth, fame, huge contracts for Sally, record-breaking sales for the novels I should one day write. 'I think,' said Sally, 'it must be marvellous to be a novelist. You're frightfully dreamy and unpractical and un-businesslike, and people imagine they can fairly swindle you as much as they want – and then you sit down and write a book about them which fairly shows them what swine they all are, and it's the most terrific success and you make pots of money.'

'I expect the trouble with me is that I'm not quite dreamy enough ...'

'... If only I could get a really rich man as my lover. Let's see ... I shouldn't want more than three thousand a year, and a flat and a decent car. I'd do anything, just now, to get rich. If you're rich you can afford to stand out for a really good contract; you don't have to snap up the first offer you get ... Of course, I'd be absolutely faithful to the man who kept me—'

Sally said things like this very seriously and evidently believed she meant them. She was in a curious state of mind, restless and nervy. Often she flew into a temper for no special reason. She talked incessantly about getting work, but made no effort to do so. Her allowance hadn't been stopped, so far, however, and we were living very cheaply, since Sally no longer cared to go out in the evenings or to see other people at all. Once, Fritz came to tea. I left them alone together afterwards to go and write a letter. When I came back Fritz had gone and Sally was in tears:

'That man *bores* me so!' she sobbed. 'I hate him! I should like to kill him!'

But in a few minutes she was quite calm again. I started to mix the inevitable Prairie Oyster. Sally, curled up on the sofa, was thoughtfully smoking:

'I wonder,' she said suddenly, 'if I'm going to have a baby.'

'Good God!' I nearly dropped the glass: 'Do you really think you are?'

'I don't know. With me it's so difficult to tell: I'm so

irregular ... I've felt sick sometimes. It's probably something I've eaten ...'

'But hadn't you better see a doctor?'

'Oh, I suppose so.' Sally yawned listlessly. 'There's no
hurry.'

'Of course there's a hurry! You'll go and see a doctor
to-morrow!'

'Look here, Chris, who the hell do you think you're ordering about? I wish now I hadn't said anything about it at all!'
Sally was on the point of bursting into tears again.

'Oh, all right! All right!' I hastily tried to calm her. 'Do
just what you like. It's no business of mine.'

'Sorry, darling. I didn't mean to be snappy. I'll see how
I feel in the morning. Perhaps I will go and see that doctor,
after all.'

But of course, she didn't. Next day, indeed, she seemed
much brighter: 'Let's go out this evening, Chris. I'm getting
sick of this room. Let's go and see some life!'

'Right you are, Sally. Where would you like to go?'

'Let's go to the Troika and talk to that old idiot Bobby.
Perhaps he'll stand us a drink – you never know!'

Bobby didn't stand us any drinks; but Sally's suggestion
proved to have been a good one, nevertheless. For it was
while sitting at the bar of the Troika that we first got into
conversation with Clive.

From that moment onwards we were with him almost
continuously; either separately or together. I never once saw
him sober. Clive told us that he drank half a bottle of whisky
before breakfast, and I had no reason to disbelieve him. He
often began to explain to us why he drank so much – it was
because he was very unhappy. But why he was so unhappy
I never found out, because Sally always interrupted to say
that it was time to be going out or moving on to the next place
or smoking a cigarette or having another glass of whisky. She
was drinking nearly as much whisky as Clive himself. It never
seemed to make her really drunk, but sometimes her eyes
looked awful, as though they had been boiled. Every day the

layer of make-up on her face seemed to get thicker.

Clive was a very big man, good-looking in a heavy Roman way, and just beginning to get fat. He had about him that sad, American air of vagueness which is always attractive; doubly attractive in one who possessed so much money. He was vague, wistful, a bit lost: dimly anxious to have a good time and uncertain how to set about getting it. He seemed never to be quite sure whether he was really enjoying himself, whether what we were doing was *really* fun. He had constantly to be reassured. *Was* this the genuine article? *Was* this the real guaranteed height of a Good Time? It was? Yes, yes, of course – it was marvellous! It was great! Ha, ha, ha! His big school-boyish laugh rolled out, re-echoed, became rather forced and died away abruptly on that puzzled note of enquiry. He couldn't venture a step without our support. Yet, even as he appealed to us, I thought I could sometimes detect odd sly flashes of sarcasm. What did he really think of us?

Every morning, Clive sent round a hired car to fetch us to the hotel where he was staying. The chaffeur always brought with him a wonderful bouquet of flowers, ordered from the most expensive flower-shop in the Linden. One morning I had a lesson to give and arranged with Sally to join them later. On arriving at the hotel, I found that Clive and Sally had left early to fly to Dresden. There was a note from Clive apologizing profusely and inviting me to lunch at the hotel restaurant, by myself, as his guest. But I didn't. I was afraid of that look in the head waiter's eye. In the evening, when Clive and Sally returned, Clive had brought me a present: it was a parcel of six silk shirts. 'He wanted to get you a gold cigarette case,' Sally whispered in my ear, 'but I told him shirts would be better. Yours are in such a state ... Besides, we've got to go slow at present. We don't want him to think we're gold-diggers ...'

I accepted them gratefully. What else could I do? Clive had corrupted us utterly. It was understood that he was going to put up the money to launch Sally upon a stage career. He often spoke of this, in a thoroughly nice way, as though it were a very trivial matter, to be settled, without fuss, between friends. But no sooner had he touched on the subject than his attention seemed to wander off again – his thoughts were as easily distracted as those of a child. Sometimes Sally was very hard put to it, I could see, to hide her impatience. 'Just leave us alone for a bit now, darling,' she would whisper to me, 'Clive and I are going to talk business.' But however tactfully Sally tried to bring him to the point, she never quite succeeded. When I rejoined them, half an hour later, I would find Clive smiling and sipping his whisky; and Sally also smiling, to conceal her extreme irritation.

'I adore him,' Sally told me, repeatedly and very solemnly, whenever we were alone together. She was intensely earnest in believing this. It was like a dogma in a newly adopted religious creed: Sally adores Clive. It is a very solemn undertaking to adore a millionaire. Sally's features began to assume, with increasing frequency, the rapt expression of the theatrical nun. And indeed, when Clive, with his charming vagueness, gave a particularly flagrant professional beggar a twenty-mark note, we would exchange glances of genuine awe. The waste of so much good money affected us both like something inspired, a kind of miracle.

There came an afternoon when Clive seemed more nearly sober than usual. He began to make plans. In a few days we were all three of us to leave Berlin, for good. The Orient Express would take us to Athens. Thence, we should fly to Egypt. From Egypt to Marseilles. From Marseilles, by boat to South America. Then Tahiti. Singapore. Japan. Clive pronounced the names as though they had been stations on the Wannsee railway, quite as a matter of course: he had been there already. He knew it all. His matter-of-fact boredom gradually infused reality into the preposterous conversation. After all, he could do it. I began seriously to believe that he meant to do it. With a mere gesture of his wealth, he could alter the whole course of our lives.

What would become of us? Once started, we should never go back. We could never leave him. Sally, of course, he would

marry. I should occupy an ill-defined position: a kind of
private secretary without duties. With a flash of vision, I
saw myself ten years hence, in flannels and black and white
shoes, gone heavier round the jowl, and a bit glassy, pouring
out a drink in the lounge of a Californian hotel.

'Come and cast an eye at the funeral,' Clive was saying.

'What funeral, darling?' Sally asked, patiently. This was a
new kind of interruption.

'Why, say, haven't you noticed it?' Clive laughed. 'It's a
most elegant funeral. It's been going past for the last hour.'

We all three went out on to the balcony of Clive's room.
Sure enough, the street below was full of people. They were
burying Hermann Müller. Ranks of pale steadfast clerks,
government officials, trade union secretaries – the whole drab
weary pageant of Prussian Social Democracy – trudged past
under their banners towards the silhouetted arches of the
Brandenburger Tor, from which the long black streamers
stirred slowly in an evening breeze.

'Say, who was this guy, anyway?' asked Clive, looking
down. 'I guess he must have been a big swell?'

'God knows,' Sally answered, yawning. 'Look, Clive darling, isn't it a marvellous sunset?'

She was quite right. We had nothing to do with those
Germans down there, marching, or with the dead man in the
coffin, or with the words on the banners. In a few days, I
thought, we shall have forfeited all kinship with ninety-nine
per cent of the population of the world, with the men and
women who earn their living, who insure their lives, who are
anxious about the future of their children. Perhaps in the
Middle Ages people felt like this, when they believed themselves to have sold their souls to the Devil. It was a curious,
exhilarating, not unpleasant sensation: but, at the same time,
I felt slightly scared. Yes, I said to myself, I've done it, now.
I am lost.

Next morning, we arrived at the hotel at the usual time.
The porter eyed us, I thought, rather queerly.

'Whom did you wish to see, Madam?'

The question seemed so extraordinary that we both laughed.

'Why, number 365, of course,' Sally answered. 'Who did you think? Don't you know us by this time?'

'I'm afraid you can't do that, Madam. The gentleman in 365 left early this morning.'

'Left? You mean he's gone out for the day? That's funny! What time will he be back?'

'He didn't say anything about coming back, Madam. He was travelling to Budapest.'

As we stood there goggling at him, a waiter hurried up with a note.

'Dear Sally and Chris,' it said, 'I can't stick this darned town any longer, so am off. Hoping to see you sometime, Clive.

'(These are in case I forgot anything.)'

In the envelope were three hundred-mark notes. These, the fading flowers, Sally's four pairs of shoes and two hats (bought in Dresden) and my six shirts were our total assets from Clive's visit. At first, Sally was very angry. Then we both began to laugh:

'Well, Chris, I'm afraid we're not much use as gold-diggers, are we, darling?'

We spent most of the day discussing whether Clive's departure was a premeditated trick. I was inclined to think it wasn't. I imagined him leaving every new town and every new set of acquaintances in much the same sort of way. I sympathized with him, a good deal.

Then came the question of what was to be done with the money. Sally decided to put by two hundred and fifty marks for some new clothes: fifty marks we would blow that evening.

But blowing the fifty marks wasn't as much fun as we'd imagined it would be. Sally felt ill and couldn't eat the wonderful dinner we'd ordered. We were both depressed.

'You know, Chris, I'm beginning to think that men are always going to leave me. The more I think about it, the more men I remember who have. It's ghastly, really.'

'I'll never leave you, Sally.'

'Won't you, darling? ... But seriously, I believe I'm a sort of Ideal Woman, if you know what I mean. I'm the sort of woman who can take men away from their wives, but I could never keep anybody for long. And that's because I'm the type which every man imagines he wants, until he gets me; and then he finds he doesn't really, after all.'

'Well, you'd rather be that than the Ugly Duckling with the Heart of Gold, wouldn't you?'

'... I could kick myself, the way I behaved to Clive. I ought never to have bothered him about money, the way I did. I expect he thought I was just a common little whore, like all the others. And I really did adore him – in a way ... If I'd married him, I'd have made a man out of him. I'd have got him to give up drinking.'

'You set him such a good example.'

We both laughed.

'The old swine might at least have left me with a decent cheque.'

'Never mind, darling. There's more where he came from.'

'I don't care,' said Sally. 'I'm sick of being a whore. I'll never look at a man with money again.'

Next morning, Sally felt very ill. We both put it down to the drink. She stayed in bed the whole morning and when she got up she fainted. I wanted her to see a doctor straight away, but she wouldn't. About tea-time, she fainted again and looked so bad afterwards that Frl. Schroeder and I sent for a doctor without consulting her at all.

The doctor, when he arrived, stayed a long time. Frl. Schroeder and I sat waiting in the living-room to hear his diagnosis. But, very much to our surprise, he left the flat suddenly, in a great hurry, without even looking in to wish us good afternoon. I went at once to Sally's room. Sally was sitting up in bed, with a rather fixed grin on her face:

'Well, Christopher darling, I've been made an April Fool of.'

'What do you mean?'

Sally tried to laugh:

'He says I'm going to have a baby.'

'Oh my God!'

'Don't looked so scared, darling! I've been more or less expecting it, you know.'

'It's Klaus's, I suppose?'

'Yes.'

'And what are you going to do about it?'

'Not have it, of course.' Sally reached for a cigarette. I sat stupidly staring at my shoes.

'Will the doctor ...'

'No, he won't. I asked him straight out. He was terribly shocked. I said: "My dear man, what do you imagine would happen to the unfortunate child if it was born? Do I look as if I'd make a good mother?"'

'And what did he say to that?'

'He seemed to think it was quite beside the point. The only thing which matters to him is his professional reputation.'

'Well then, we've got to find someone without a professional reputation, that's all.'

'I should think,' said Sally, 'we'd better ask Frl. Schroeder.'

So Frl. Schroeder was consulted. She took it very well: she was alarmed but extremely practical. Yes, she knew of somebody. A friend of a friend's friend had once had difficulties. And the doctor was a fully qualified man, very clever indeed. The only trouble was, he might be rather expensive.

'Thank goodness,' Sally interjected, 'we haven't spent all that swine Clive's money!'

'I must say, I think Klaus ought—'

'Look here, Chris. Let me tell you this once for all: if I catch you writing to Klaus about this business, I'll never forgive you and I'll never speak to you again!'

'Oh, very well ... Of course I won't. It was just a suggestion, that's all.'

I didn't like the doctor. He kept stroking and pinching Sally's arm and pawing her hand. However, he seemed the right man for the job. Sally was to go into his private nursing-home as soon as there was a vacancy for her. Everything was perfectly official and above-board. In a few polished sentences, the dapper little doctor dispelled the least whiff of sinister illegality. Sally's state of health, he explained, made it quite impossible for her to undergo the risks of childbirth: there would be a certificate to that effect. Needless to say, the certificate would cost a lot of money. So would the nursing-home and so would the operation itself. The doctor wanted two hundred and fifty marks down before he would make any arrangements at all. In the end, we beat him down to two hundred. Sally wanted the extra fifty, she explained to me later, to get some new nightdresses.

At last, it was spring. The cafés were putting up wooden platforms on the pavement and the ice-cream shops were opening, with their rainbow-wheels. We drove to the nursing-home in an open taxi. Because of the lovely weather, Sally was in better spirits than I had seen her in for weeks. But Frl. Schroeder, though she bravely tried to smile, was on the verge of tears. 'The doctor isn't a Jew, I hope?' Frl. Mayr asked me sternly. 'Don't you let one of those filthy Jews touch her. They always try to get a job of that kind, the beasts!'

Sally had a nice room, clean and cheerful, with a balcony. I called there again in the evening. Lying there in bed without her make-up, she looked years younger, like a little girl:

'Hullo, darling . . . They haven't killed me yet, you see. But they've been doing their best to . . . Isn't this a funny place? . . . I wish that pig Klaus could see me . . . This is what comes of not understanding his *mind* . . .'

She was a bit feverish and laughed a great deal. One of the nurses came in for a moment, as if looking for something, and went out again almost immediately.

'She was dying to get a peep at you,' Sally explained. 'You see, I told her you were the father. You don't mind, do you darling . . .'

'Not at all. It's a compliment.'

'It makes everything so much simpler. Otherwise, if there's no one, they think it so odd. And I don't care for being sort of looked down on and pitied as the poor betrayed girl who gets abandoned by her lover. It isn't particularly flattering for me, is it? So I told her we were most terribly in love but fearfully hard up, so that we couldn't afford to marry, and how we dreamed of the time when we'd both be rich and famous and then we'd have a family of ten, just to make up for this one. The nurse was awfully touched, poor girl. In fact, she wept. To-night, when she's on duty, she's going to show me pictures of *her* young man. Isn't it sweet?'

Next day, Frl. Schroeder and I went round to the nursing-home together. We found Sally lying flat, with the bedclothes up to her chin:

'Oh, hullo, you two! Won't you sit down? What time is it?' She turned uneasily in bed and rubbed her eyes: 'Where did all these flowers come from?'

'We brought them.'

'How marvellous of you!' Sally smiled vacantly. 'Sorry to be such a fool to-day ... It's this bloody chloroform ... My head's full of it.'

We only stayed a few minutes. On the way home, Frl. Schroeder was terribly upset: 'Will you believe it, Herr Issy-voo, I couldn't take it more to heart if it was my own daughter? Why, when I see the poor child suffering like that, I'd rather it was myself lying there in her place – I would indeed!'

Next day Sally was much better. We all went to visit her: Frl. Schroeder, Frl. Mayr, Bobby and Fritz. Fritz, of course, hadn't the faintest idea what had really happened. Sally, he had been told, was being operated upon for a small internal ulcer. As always is the way with people when they aren't in the know, he made all kinds of unintentional and startlingly apt references to storks, gooseberry-bushes, perambulators and babies generally; and even recounted a special new item of scandal about a well-known Berlin society lady who was said to have undergone a recent illegal operation. Sally and I avoided each other's eyes.

On the evening of the next day, I visited her at the nursing-home for the last time. She was to leave in the morning. She was alone and we sat together on the balcony. She seemed

More or less all right now and could walk about the room.

'I told the Sister I didn't want to see anybody to-day except you.' Sally yawned languidly. 'People make me feel so tired.'

'Would you rather I went away too?'

'Oh, no,' said Sally, without much enthusiasm, 'if you go, one of the nurses will only come in and begin to chatter; and if I'm not lively and bright with her, they'll say I have to stay in this hellish place a couple of extra days, and I couldn't stand that.'

She stared out moodily over the quiet street:

'You know, Chris, in some ways I wish I'd had that kid ... It would have been rather marvellous to have had it. The last day or two, I've been sort of feeling what it would be like to be a mother. Do you know, last night, I sat here for a long time by myself and held this cushion in my arms and imagined it was my baby? And I felt a most marvellous sort of shut-off feeling from all the rest of the world. I imagined how it'd grow up and how I'd work for it, and how, after I'd put it to bed at nights, I'd go out and make love to filthy old men to get money to pay for its food and clothes ... It's all very well for you to grin like that, Chris ... I did really!'

'Well, why don't you marry and have one?'

'I don't know ... I feel as if I'd lost faith in men. I just haven't any use for them at all ... Even you, Christopher, if you were to go out into the street now and be run over by a taxi ... I should be sorry in a way, of course, but I shouldn't really *care* a damn.'

'Thank you, Sally.'

We both laughed.

'I didn't mean that, of course, darling – at least, not personally. You mustn't mind what I say while I'm like this. I get all sorts of crazy ideas into my head. Having babies makes you feel awfully primitive, like a sort of wild animal or something, defending its young. Only the trouble is, I haven't any young to defend ... I expect that's what makes me so frightfully bad-tempered to everybody just now.'

* * *

It was partly as the result of this conversation that I suddenly decided, that evening, to cancel all my lessons, leave Berlin as soon as possible, go to some place on the Baltic and try to start working. Since Christmas, I had hardly written a word.

Sally, when I told her my idea, was rather relieved, I think. We both needed a change. We talked vaguely of her joining me later; but, even then, I felt that she wouldn't. Her plans were very uncertain. Later, she might go to Paris, or to the Alps, or to the South of France, she said – if she could get the cash. 'But probably,' she added, 'I shall just stay on here. I should be quite happy. I seem to have got sort of used to this place.'

I returned to Berlin towards the middle of July.

All this time I had heard nothing of Sally, beyond half a dozen postcards, exchanged during the first month of my absence. I wasn't much surprised to find she'd left her room in our flat:

'Of course, I quite understand her going. I couldn't make her as comfortable as she'd the right to expect; especially as we haven't any running water in the bedrooms.' Poor Frl. Schroeder's eyes had filled with tears. 'But it was a terrible disappointment to me, all the same ... Frl. Bowles behaved very handsomely, I can't complain about that. She insisted on paying for her room until the end of July. I was entitled to the money, of course, because she didn't give notice until the twenty-first – but I'd never have mentioned it ... She was such a charming young lady—'

'Have you got her address?'

'Oh yes, and the telephone number. You'll be ringing her up, of course. She'll be delighted to see you ... The other gentlemen came and went, but you were her real friend, Herr Issyvoo. You know, I always used to hope that you two would get married. You'd have made an ideal couple. You always had such a good steady influence on her, and she used to brighten you up a bit when you got too deep in your books

and studies ... Oh yes, Herr Issyvoo, you may laugh – but
you never can tell! Perhaps it isn't too late yet!'

Next morning, Frl. Schroeder woke me in great excitement:

'Herr Issyvoo, what do you think! They've shut the Darmstädter und National! There'll be thousands ruined, I
shouldn't wonder! The milkman says we'll have civil war in
a fortnight! Whatever do you say to that!'

As soon as I'd got dressed, I went down into the street.
Sure enough, there was a crowd outside the branch bank on
the Nollendorfplatz corner, a lot of men with leather satchels
and women with stringbags – women like Frl. Schroeder herself. The iron lattices were drawn down over the bank windows. Most of the people were staring intently and rather
stupidly at the locked door. In the middle of the door was
fixed a small notice, beautifully printed in Gothic type, like
a page from a classic author. The notice said the Reichs-
president had guaranteed the deposits. Everything was quite
all right. Only the bank wasn't going to open.

A little boy was playing with a hoop amongst the crowd.
The hoop ran against a woman's legs. She flew out at him at
once: 'Du, sei bloss nicht so frech! Cheeky little brat! What
do you want here!' Another woman joined in, attacking the
scared boy: 'Get out! You can't understand it, can you?' And
another asked, in furious sarcasm: 'Have you got your money
in the bank too, perhaps?' The boy fled before their pent-up,
exploding rage.

In the afternoon it was very hot. The details of the new
emergency decrees were in the early evening papers – terse,
governmentally inspired. One alarmist headline stood out
boldly, barred with blood-red ink: 'Everything Collapses!'
A Nazi journalist reminded his readers that to-morrow, the
fourteenth of July, was a day of national rejoicing in France;
and doubtless, he added, the French would rejoice with
especial fervour this year, at the prospect of Germany's down-
fall. Going into an outfitter's, I bought myself a pair of
ready-made flannel trousers for twelve marks fifty – a gesture

of confidence by England. Then I got into the Underground to go and visit Sally.

She was living in a block of three-room flats, designed as an Artists' Colony, not far from the Breitenbachplatz. When I rang the bell, she opened the door to me herself:

'Hillooo, Chris, you old swine!'

'Hullo, Sally darling!'

'How are you? ... Be careful, darling, you'll make me untidy. I've got to go out in a few minutes.'

I had never seen her all in white before. It suited her. But her face looked thinner and older. Her hair was cut in a new way and beautifully waved.

'You're very smart,' I said.

'Am I?' Sally smiled her pleased, dreamy, selfconscious smile. I followed her into the sitting-room of the flat. One wall was entirely window. There was some cherry-coloured wooden furniture and a very low divan with gaudy fringed cushions. A fluffy white miniature dog jumped to its feet and yapped. Sally picked it up and went through the gestures of kissing it, just not touching it with her lips:

'Freddi, mein Liebling, Du bist *soo* süss!'

'Yours?' I asked, noticing the improvement in her German accent.

'No. He belongs to Gerda, the girl I share this flat with.'

'Have you known her long?'

'Only a week or two.'

'What's she like?'

'Not bad. As stingy as hell. I have to pay for practically everything.'

'It's nice here.'

'Do you think so? Yes, I suppose it's all right. Better than that hole in the Nollendorfstrasse, anyhow.'

'What made you leave? Did you and Frl. Schroeder have a row?'

'No, not exactly. Only I got so sick of hearing her talk. She nearly talked my head off. She's an awful old bore, really.'

'She's very fond of you.'

Sally shrugged her shoulders with a slight impatient listless movement. Throughout this conversation. I noticed that she avoided my eyes. There was a long pause. I felt puzzled and vaguely embarrassed. I began to wonder how soon I could make an excuse to go.

Then the telephone bell rang. Sally yawned, pulled the instrument across on to her lap:

'Hilloo, who's there? Yes, it's me . . . No . . . No . . . I've really no idea . . . *Really* I haven't! I'm to guess?' Her nose wrinkled: 'Is it Erwin? No? Paul? No? Wait a minute . . . Let me see . . .'

'And now, darling, I must fly!' cried Sally, when, at last, the conversation was over: 'I'm about two hours late already!'

'Got a new boy friend?'

But Sally ignored my grin. She lit a cigarette with a faint expression of distaste.

'I've got to see a man on business,' she said briefly.

'And when shall we meet again?'

'I'll have to see, darling . . . I've got such a lot on, just at present . . . I shall be out in the country all day to-morrow, and probably the day after . . . I'll let you know . . . I may be going to Frankfurt quite soon.'

'Have you got a job there?'

'No. Not exactly.' Sally's voice was brief, dismissing this subject. 'I've decided not to try for any film work until the autumn, anyhow. I shall take a thorough rest.'

'You seem to have made a lot of new friends.'

Again, Sally's manner became vague, carefully casual:

'Yes, I suppose I have . . . It's probably a reaction from all those months at Frl. Shroeder's, when I never saw a soul.'

'Well,' I couldn't resist a malicious grin. 'I hope for your sake that none of your new friends have got their money in the Darmstädter und National.'

'Why?' She was interested at once. 'What's the matter with it?'

'Do you really mean to say you haven't heard?'

'Of course not. I never read the papers, and I haven't been out to-day, yet.'

I told her the news of the crisis. At the end of it, she was looking quite scared.

'But why on earth,' she exclaimed impatiently, 'didn't you tell me all this before? It may be serious.'

'I'm sorry, Sally. I took it for granted that you'd know already ... especially as you seem to be moving in financial circles, nowadays—'

But she ignored this little dig. She was frowning, deep in her own thoughts:

'If it was *very* serious, Leo would have rung up and told me ...' she murmured at length. And this reflection appeared to ease her mind considerably.

We walked out together to the corner of the street, where Sally picked up a taxi.

'It's an awful nuisance living so far off,' she said. 'I'm probably going to get a car soon.'

'By the way,' she added just as we were parting, 'what was it like on Ruegen?'

'I bathed a lot.'

'Well, good-bye, darling. I'll see you sometime.'

'Good-bye, Sally. Enjoy yourself.'

About a week after this, Sally rang me up:

'Can you come round at once, Chris? It's very important. I want you to do me a favour.'

This time, also, I found Sally alone in the flat.

'Do you want to earn some money, darling?' she greeted me.

'Of course.'

'Splendid! You see, it's like this ...' She was in a fluffy pink dressing-wrap and inclined to be breathless: 'There's a man I know who's starting a magazine. It's going to be most terribly highbrow and artistic, with lots of marvellous modern photographs, ink-pots and girls' heads upside down – you know the sort of thing ... The point is each number is going to take a special country and kind of review it, with articles about the manners and customs, and all that ... Well, the first country they're going to do is England and they want me to write an article on the English Girl . . . Of course, I haven't the foggiest idea what to say, so what I thought was: you could write the article in my name and get the money – I only want not to disoblige this man who's editing the paper, because he may be terribly useful to me in other ways, later on ...'

'All right, I'll try.'

'Oh, marvellous!'

'How soon do you want it done?'

'You see, darling, that's the whole point. I must have it at once ... Otherwise it's no earthly use, because I promised it four days ago and I simply must give it him this evening ... It needn't be very long. About five hundred words.'

'Well, I'll do my best ...'

'Good. That's wonderful ... Sit down wherever you like. Here's some paper. You've got a pen? Oh, and here's a dictionary, in case there's a word you can't spell ... I'll just be having my bath.'

When, three-quarters of an hour later, Sally came in dressed for the day, I had finished. Frankly, I was rather pleased with my effort.

She read it through carefully, a slow frown gathering between her beautifully pencilled eyebrows. When she had finished, she laid down the manuscript with a sigh:

'I'm sorry, Chris. It won't do at all.'

'Won't do?' I was genuinely taken aback.

'Of course, I dare say it's very good from a literary point of view, and all that ...'

'Well then, what's wrong with it?'

'It's not nearly snappy enough.' Sally was quite final. 'It's not the kind of thing this man wants, at all.'

I shrugged my shoulders: 'I'm sorry, Sally. I did my best. But journalism isn't really in my line, you know.'

There was a resentful pause. My vanity was piqued.

'My goodness, I know who'll do it for me if I ask him!' cried Sally, suddenly jumping up. 'Why on earth didn't I think of him before?' She grabbed the telephone and dialled a number: 'Oh, hilloo, Kurt darling ...'

In three minutes, she had explained all about the article. Replacing the receiver on its stand, she announced triumphantly: 'That's marvellous! He's going to do it at once ...' She paused impressively and added: 'That was Kurt Rosenthal.'

'Who's he?'

'You've never heard of him?' This annoyed Sally; she pretended to be immensely surprised: 'I thought you took an interest in the cinema? He's miles the best young scenario writer. He earns pots of money. He's only doing this as a favour to me, of course ... He says he'll dictate it to his secretary while he's shaving and then send it straight round to the editor's flat ... He's marvellous!'

'Are you sure it'll be what the editor wants, this time?'

'Of course it will! Kurt's an absolute genius. He can do anything. Just now, he's writing a novel in his spare time. He's so fearfully busy, he can only dictate it while he's having breakfast. He showed me the first few chapters, the other day. Honestly, I think it's easily the best novel I've ever read.'

'Indeed?'

'That's the sort of writer I admire,' Sally continued. She was careful to avoid my eye. 'He's terribly ambitious and he works the whole time; and he can write anything – anything you like: scenarios, novels, plays, poetry, advertisements ... He's not a bit stuck-up about it either. Not like these young men who, because they've written one book, start talking about Art and imagining they're the most wonderful authors in the world ... They make me sick ...'

Irritated as I was with her, I couldn't help laughing:

'Since when have you disapproved of me so violently, Sally?'

'I don't disapprove of you' – but she couldn't look me in the face – 'not exactly.'

'I merely make you sick?'

'I don't know what it is ... You seem to have changed, somehow ...'

'How have I changed?'

'It's difficult to explain ... You don't seem to have any energy or want to get anywhere. You're so dilettante. It annoys me.'

'I'm sorry.' But my would-be facetious tone sounded rather forced. Sally frowned down at her tiny black shoes.

'You must remember I'm a woman, Christopher. All women like men to be strong and decided and following out their careers. A woman wants to be motherly to a man and protect his weak side, but he must have a strong side too, which she can respect ... If you ever care for a woman. I don't advise you to let her see that you've got no ambition. Otherwise she'll get to despise you. '

'Yes, I see ... And that's the principle on which you choose your friends – your *new* friends?'

She flared up at this:

'It's very easy for you to sneer at my friends for having good business heads. If they've got money, it's because they've worked for it ... I suppose you consider yourself better than they are?'

'Yes, Sally, since you ask me – if they're at all as I imagine them – I do.'

'There you go, Christopher! That's typical of you. That's what annoys me about you: you're conceited and lazy. If you say things like that, you ought to be able to prove them.'

'How does one prove that one's better than somebody else? Besides, that's not what I said. I said I considered myself better – it's simply a matter of taste.'

Sally made no reply. She lit a cigarette, slightly frowning.

'You say I seem to have changed,' I continued. 'To be quite frank, I've been thinking the same about *you*.'

Sally didn't seem surprised: 'Have you, Christopher? Perhaps you're right. I don't know ... Or perhaps we've neither of us changed. Perhaps we're just seeing each other as we really are. We're awfully different in lots of ways, you know.'

'Yes, I've noticed that.'

'I think,' said Sally, smoking meditatively, her eyes on her shoes, 'that we may have sort of outgrown each other, a bit.'

'Perhaps we have ...' I smiled: Sally's real meaning was so obvious: 'At any rate, we needn't quarrel about it, need we?'

'Of course not, darling.'

There was a pause. Then I said that I must be going. We were both rather embarrassed, now, and extra polite.

'Are you certain you won't have a cup of coffee?'

'No, thanks awfully.'

'Have some tea? It's specially good. I got it as a present.'

'No, thanks very much indeed, Sally. I really must be getting along.'

'Must you?' She sounded, after all, rather relieved. 'Be sure and ring me up some time soon, won't you?'

'Yes, rather.'

It wasn't until I had actually left the house and was walking quickly away up the street that I realized how angry and ashamed I felt. What an utter little bitch she is, I thought. After all, I told myself, it's only what I've always known she was like – right from the start. No, that wasn't true: I hadn't known it. I'd flattered myself – why not be frank about it? – that she was fond of me. Well, I'd been wrong, it seemed; but could I blame her for that? Yet I did blame her, I was furious with her; nothing would have pleased me more, at that moment, than to see her soundly whipped. Indeed, I was so absurdly upset that I began to wonder whether I hadn't, all this time, in my own peculiar way, been in love with Sally myself.

But no, it wasn't love either – it was worse. It was the cheapest, most childish kind of wounded vanity. Not that I cared a curse what she thought of my article – well, just a little, perhaps, but only a very little; my literary self-conceit was proof against anything *she* could say – it was her criticism of myself. The awful sexual flair women have for taking the stuffing out of a man! It was no use telling myself that Sally had the vocabulary and mentality of a twelve-year-old schoolgirl, that she was altogether comic and preposterous; it was no use – I only knew that I'd been somehow made to feel a sham. Wasn't I a bit of a sham anyway – though not for her ridiculous reasons – with my arty talk to lady pupils and my newly-acquired parlour-socialism? Yes, I was. But she knew nothing about that. I could quite easily have impressed her. That was the most humiliating part of the whole business; I had mis-managed our interview from the very beginning. I had blushed and squabbled, instead of being wonderful, convincing, superior, fatherly, mature. I had tried to compete with her beastly little Kurt on his own ground; just the very thing, of course, which Sally wanted and expected me to do! After all these months, I had made the one really fatal mistake – I had let her see that I was not only incompetent but jealous. Yes, vulgarly jealous. I could have kicked myself. The mere thought made me prickly with shame from head to foot.

Well, the mischief was done, now. There was only one thing for it, and that was to forget the whole affair. And of course it would be impossible for me ever to see Sally again.

It must have been about ten days after this that I was visited, one morning, by a small pale dark-haired young man who spoke American fluently with a slight foreign accent. His name, he told me, was George P Sandars. He had seen my English-teaching advertisement in the BZ am Mittag.

'When would you like to begin?' I asked him.

But the young man shook his head hastily. Oh no, he hadn't come to take lessons, at all. Rather disappointed, I waited politely for him to explain the reason of his visit. He seemed in no hurry to do this. Instead, he accepted a cigarette, sat down and began to talk chattily about the States. Had I ever been to Chicago? No? Well, had I heard of James L Schraube? I hadn't? The young man uttered a faint sigh. He had the air of being very patient with me, and with the world in general. He had evidently been over the same ground with a good many other people already. James L Schraube, he explained, was a very big man in Chicago: he owned a whole chain of restaurants and several cinemas. He had two large country houses and a yacht on Lake Michigan. And he possessed no less than four cars. By this time, I was beginning to drum with my fingers on the table. A pained expression passed over the young man's face. He excused himself for taking up my valuable time; he had only told me about Mr Schraube, he said, because he thought I might be interested – his tone implied a gentle rebuke – and because Mr Schraube, had I known him, would certainly have vouched for his friend Sandars' respectability. However . . . it couldn't be helped . . . well, would I lend him two hundred marks? He needed the money in order to start a business; it was a unique opportunity, which he would miss altogether if he didn't find the money before to-morrow morning. He would pay me back within three days. If I gave him the money now he would return that same evening with papers to prove that the whole thing was perfectly genuine.

No? Ah well . . . He didn't seem unduly surprised. He rose to go at once, like a business man who has wasted a valuable twenty minutes on a prospective customer: the loss, he contrived politely to imply, was mine, not his. Already at the door, he paused for a moment: Did I happen, by any chance, to know some film actresses? He was travelling, as a sideline, in a new kind of face-cream specially invented to keep the skin from getting dried up by the studio lights. It was being used by all the Hollywood stars already, but in Europe it was still quite unknown. If he could find half a dozen actresses to use and recommend it, they should have free sample jars and permanent supplies at half-price.

After a moment's hesitation, I gave him Sally's address. I don't know quite why I did it. Partly, of course, to get rid of the young man, who showed signs of wishing to sit down again and continue our conversation. Partly, perhaps, out of malice. It would do Sally no harm to have to put up with his chatter for an hour or two: she had told me that she liked men with ambition. Perhaps she would even get a jar of the face-cream – if it existed at all. And if he touched her for the two hundred marks – well, that wouldn't matter so very much, either. He couldn't deceive a baby.

'But whatever you do,' I warned him, 'don't say that I sent you.'

He agreed to this at once, with a slight smile. He must have had his own explanation of my request, for he didn't appear to find it in the least strange. He raised his hat politely as he went downstairs. By the next morning, I had forgotten about his visit altogether.

A few days later, Sally herself rang me up. I had been called away in the middle of a lesson to answer the telephone and was very ungracious.

'Oh, is that you, Christopher darling?'

'Yes. It's me.'

'I say, can you come round and see me at once?'

'No.'

'Oh ...' My refusal evidently gave Sally a shock. There was a little pause, then she continued, in a tone of unwonted humility: 'I suppose you're most terribly busy?'

'Yes. I am.'

'Well ... would you mind frightfully if I came round to see you?'

'What about?'

'Darling' – Sally sounded positively desperate – 'I can't possibly explain to you over the telephone ... It's something really serious.'

'Oh, I see' – I tried to make this as nasty as possible – 'another magazine article, I suppose?'

Nevertheless, as soon as I'd said that, we both had to laugh.

'Chris, you are a brute!' Sally tinkled gaily along the wire: then checked herself abruptly: 'No, darling – this time I promise you: it's most terribly serious, really and truly it is.' She paused; then impressively added: 'And you're the only person who can possibly help.'

'Oh, all right ...' I was more than half melted already. 'Come in an hour.'

*   *   *

'Well, darling, I'll begin at the very beginning, shall I? ...
Yesterday morning, a man rang me up and asked if he could
come round and see me. He said it was on very important
business; and as he seemed to know my name and everything
of course I said: Yes, certainly, come at once ... So he came.
He told me his name was Rakowski – Paul Rakowski – and
that he was a European agent of Metro-Goldwyn-Mayer and
that he'd come to make me an offer. He said they were
looking out for an English actress who spoke German to act
in a comedy film they were going to shoot on the Italian
Riviera. He was most frightfully convincing about it all; he
told me who the director was and the camera-man and the
art-director and who'd written the script. Naturally, I hadn't
heard of any of them before. But that didn't seem so surprising: in fact, it really made it sound much more real, because
most people would have chosen one of the names you see in
the newspapers ... Anyhow, he said that, now he'd seen me,
he was sure I'd be just the person for the part, and he could
practically promise it to me, as long as the test was all right ...
so of course I was simply thrilled and I asked when the test
would be and he said not for a day or two, as he had to make
arrangements with the Ufa people ... So then we began to
talk about Hollywood and he told me all kinds of stories – I
suppose they *could* have been things he'd read in fan maga-
zines, but somehow I'm pretty sure they weren't – and then
he told me how they make sound-effects and how they do the
trick work; he was really most awfully interesting and he
certainly must have been inside a great many studios ...
Anyhow, when we'd finished talking about Hollywood, he
started to tell me about the rest of America and the people
he knew, and about the gangsters and about New York. He
said he'd only just arrived from there and all his luggage was
still in the customs at Hamburg. As a matter of fact, I *had*
been thinking to myself that it seemed rather queer he was
so shabbily dressed; but after he said that, of course, I thought
it was quite natural ... Well – now you must promise not to
laugh at this part of the story, Chris, or I simply shan't be able
to tell you – presently he started making the most passionate

love to me. At first I was rather angry with him, for sort of mixing business with pleasure; but then, after a bit, I didn't mind so much: he was quite attractive, in a Russian kind of way ... And the end of it was, he invited me to have dinner with him; so we went to Horcher's and had one of the most marvellous dinners I've ever had in my life (that's one consolation); only, when the bill came, he said "Oh, by the way, darling, could you lend me three hundred marks until tomorrow? I've only got dollar bills on me, and I'll have to get them changed at the Bank." So, of course, I gave them to him: as bad luck would have it, I had quite a lot of money on me, that evening ... And then he said: 'Let's have a bottle of champagne to celebrate your film contract.' So I agreed, and I suppose by that time I must have been pretty tight because when he asked me to spend the night with him, I said Yes. We went to one of those little hotels in the Augsburgerstrasse – I forget its name, but I can find it again, easily ... It was the most ghastly hole ... Anyhow, I don't remember much more about what happened that evening. It was early this morning that I started to think about things properly, while he was still asleep; and I began to wonder if everything was really quite all right ... I hadn't noticed his underclothes before: they gave me a bit of a shock. You'd expect an important film man to wear silk next his skin, wouldn't you? Well, his were the most extraordinary kind of stuff like camelhair or something; they looked as if they might have belonged to John the Baptist. And then he had a regular Woolworth's tin clip for his tie. It wasn't so much that his things were shabby; but you could see they'd never been any good, even when they were new ... I was just making up my mind to get out of bed and take a look inside his pockets, when he woke up and it was too late. So we ordered breakfast ... I don't know if he thought I was madly in love with him by this time and wouldn't notice, or whether he just couldn't be bothered to go on pretending, but this morning he was like a completely different person – just a common little guttersnipe. He ate his jam off the blade of his knife, and of course most of it went on the sheets. And he sucked the insides out of the eggs with a most terrific squelching noise. I couldn't help laughing at him, and that made him quite cross ... Then he said: "I must have beer!" Well, I said, all right; ring down to the office and ask for some. To tell you the truth, I was beginning to be a bit frightened of him. He'd started to scowl in the most cavemannish way; I felt sure he must be mad. So I thought I'd humour him as much as I could ... Anyhow, he seemed to think I'd made quite a good suggestion, and he picked up the telephone and had a long conversation and got awfully angry, because he said they refused to send beer up to the rooms. I realize now that he must have been holding the hook all the time and just acting; but he did it most awfully well, and anyhow I was much too scared to notice things much. I thought he'd probably start murdering me because he couldn't get his beer ... However, he took it quite quietly. He said he must get dressed and go downstairs and fetch it himself. All right, I said ... Well, I waited and waited and he didn't come back. So at last I rang the bell and asked the maid if she'd seen him go out. And she said: "Oh yes, the gentleman paid the bill and went away about an hour ago ... He said you weren't to be disturbed." I was so surprised, I just said: "Oh, right, thanks ..." The funny thing was, I'd so absolutely made up my mind by this time that he was a looney that I'd stopped suspecting him of being a swindler. Perhaps that was what he wanted ... Anyhow, he wasn't such a looney, after all, because, when I looked in my bag, I found he'd helped himself to all the rest of my money, as well as the change from the three hundred marks I'd lent him the night before ... What really annoys me about the whole business is that I bet he thinks I'll be ashamed to go to the police. Well, I'll just show him he's wrong—'

'I say, Sally, what exactly did this young man look like?'

'He was about your height. Pale. Dark. You could tell he wasn't a born American; he spoke with a foreign accent—'

'Can you remember if he mentioned a man named Schraube, who lives in Chicago?'

'Let's see ... Yes, of course he did! He talked about him a lot ... But, Chris, how on earth did you know?'

'Well, it's like this ... Look here, Sally, I've got a most awful confession to make to you ... I don't know if you'll ever forgive me ...'

We went to the Alexanderplatz that same afternoon.

The interview was even more embarrassing than I had expected. For myself at any rate. Sally, if she felt uncomfortable, did not show it by so much as the movement of an eyelid. She detailed the facts of the case to the two bespectacled police officials with such brisk bright matter-of-factness that one might have supposed she had come to complain about a strayed lapdog or an umbrella lost in a bus. The two officials – both obviously fathers of families – were at first inclined to be shocked. They dipped their pens excessively in the violet ink, made nervous inhibited circular movements with their elbows before beginning to write, and were very curt and gruff.

'Now about this hotel,' said the elder of them sternly: 'I suppose you knew, before going there, that it was an hotel of a certain kind?'

'Well, you didn't expect us to go to the Bristol, did you?' Sally's tone was very mild and reasonable: 'They wouldn't have let us in there without luggage, anyway.'

'Ah, so you had no luggage?' The younger one pounced upon this fact triumphantly, as of supreme importance. His violet copperplate policehand began to travel steadily across a ruled sheet of foolscap paper. Deeply inspired by his theme, he paid not the slightest attention to Sally's retort:

'I don't usually pack a suitcase when a man asks me out to dinner.'

The elder one caught the point, however, at once:

'So it wasn't till you were at the restaurant that this young man invited you to – er – accompany him to the hotel?'

'It wasn't till after dinner.'

'My dear young lady,' the elder one sat back in his chair,

very much the sarcastic father, 'may I enquire whether it is your usual custom to accept invitations of this kind from perfect strangers?'

Sally smiled sweetly. She was innocence and candour itself:

'But, you see, Herr Kommissar, he wasn't a perfect stranger. He was my fiancé.'

That made both of them sit up with a jerk. The younger one even made a small blot in the middle of his virgin page – the only blot, perhaps to be found in all the spotless dossiers of the Polizeipräsidium.

'You mean to tell me, Frl. Bowles' – but in spite of his gruffness, there was already a gleam in the elder one's eye – 'You mean to tell me that you became engaged to this man when you'd only known him a single afternoon?'

'Certainly.'

'Isn't that, well – rather unusual?'

'I suppose it is,' Sally seriously agreed. 'But nowadays, you know, a girl can't afford to keep a man waiting. If he asks her once and she refuses him, he may try somebody else. It's all these surplus women—'

At this, the elder official frankly exploded. Pushing back his chair, he laughed himself quite purple in the face. It was nearly a minute before he could speak at all. The young one was much more decorous; he produced a large handkerchief and pretended to blow his nose. But the nose-blowing developed into a kind of sneeze which became a guffaw; and soon he too had abandoned all attempt to take Sally seriously. The rest of the interview was conducted with comic-opera informality, accompanied by ponderous essays in gallantry. The elder official, particularly, became quite daring; I think they were both sorry that I was present. They wanted her to themselves.

'Now don't you worry, Frl. Bowles,' they told her, patting her hand at parting, 'we'll find him for you, if we have to turn Berlin inside out to do it!'

'Well!' I exclaimed admiringly, as soon as we were out

of earshot, 'you do know how to handle them, I must say!'

Sally smiled dreamily: she was feeling very pleased with herself: 'How do you mean, exactly, darling?'

'You know as well as I do – getting them to laugh like that: telling them he was your fiancé! It was really inspired!'

But Sally didn't laugh. Instead, she coloured a little, looking down at her feet. A comically guilty, childish expression came over her face:

'You see, Chris, it happened to be quite true—'

'True!'

'Yes, darling.' Now, for the first time, Sally was really embarrassed: she began speaking very fast: 'I simply couldn't tell you this morning: after everything that's happened, it would have sounded too idiotic for words ... He asked me to marry him while we were at the restaurant, and I said Yes ... You see, I thought that, being in films, he was probably quite used to quick engagements, like that: after all, in Hollywood, it's quite the usual thing ... And, as he was an American, I thought we could get divorced again easily, any time we wanted to ... And it would have been a good thing for my career – I mean, if he'd been genuine – wouldn't it? ... We were to have got married to-day, if it could have been managed ... It seems funny to think of, now—'

'But Sally!' I stood still. I gaped at her. I had to laugh: 'Well really ... You know, you're the most extraordinary creature I ever met in my life!'

Sally giggled a little, like a naughty child which has unintentionally succeeded in amusing the grown-ups:

'I always told you I was a bit mad, didn't I? Now perhaps you'll believe it—'

It was more than a week before the police could give us any news. Then, one morning, two detectives called to see me. A young man answering to our description had been traced and was under observation. The police knew his address, but wanted me to identify him before making the arrest. Would I come round with them at once to a snack-bar in the Kleiststrasse? He was to be seen there, about this time, almost

every day. I should be able to point him out to them in the
crowd and leave again at once, without any fuss or unpleasant-
ness.

I didn't like the idea much, but there was no getting out of
it now. The snack-bar, when we arrived, was crowded, for
this was the lunch-hour. I caught sight of the young man
almost immediately: he was standing at the counter, by the
tea-urn, cup in hand. Seen thus, alone and off his guard, he
seemed rather pathetic: he looked shabbier and far younger
– a mere boy. I very nearly said: 'He isn't here.' But what
would have been the use? They'd have got him, anyway. 'Yes,
that's him.' I told the detectives. 'Over there.' They nodded.
I turned and hurried away down the street, feeling guilty and
telling myself: I'll never help the police again.

A few days later, Sally came round to tell me the rest of
the story: 'I had to see him, of course . . . I felt an awful brute;
he looked so wretched. All he said was: "I thought you were
my friend." I'd have told him he could keep the money, but
he'd spent it all, anyway . . . The police said he really had been
to the States, but he isn't American; he's a Pole . . . He won't
be prosecuted, that's one comfort. The doctor's seen him and
he's going to be sent to a home. I hope they treat him decently
there . . .'

'So he was a looney, after all?'

'I suppose so. A sort of mild one . . .' Sally smiled. 'Not
very flattering to me, is it? Oh, and Chris, do you know how
old he was? You'd never guess!'

'Round about twenty, I should think.'

'Sixteen!'

'Oh, rot!'

'Yes, honestly . . . The case would have to have been tried
in the Children's Court!'

We both laughed. 'You know, Sally,' I said, 'what I really
like about you is that you're so awfully easy to take in. People
who never get taken in are so dreary.'

'So you still like me, Chris darling?'

'Yes, Sally. I still like you.'

'I was afraid you'd be angry with me – about the other day.'

'I was. Very.'

'But you're not, now?'

'No ... I don't think so.'

'It's no good my trying to apologize, or explain, or anything ... I get like that, sometimes ... I expect you understand, don't you, Chris?'

'Yes,' I said. 'I expect I do.'

I have never seen her since. About a fortnight later, just when I was thinking I ought really to ring her up, I got a post-card from Paris: 'Arrived here last night. Will write properly to-morrow. Heaps of love.' No letter followed. A month after this, another post-card arrived from Rome, giving no address: 'Am writing in a day or two,' it said. That was six years ago.

So now I am writing to her.

When you read this, Sally – if you ever do – please accept it as a tribute, the sincerest I can pay, to yourself and to our friendship.

And send me another post-card.

ON RUEGEN ISLAND
(Summer 1931)

I wake early and go out to sit on the verandah in my pyjamas. The wood casts long shadows over the fields. Birds call with sudden uncanny violence, like alarm-clocks going off. The birch-trees hang down laden over the rutted, sandy earth of the country road. A soft bar of cloud is moving up from the line of trees along the lake. A man with a bicycle is watching his horse graze on a patch of grass by the path; he wants to disentangle the horse's hoof from its tether-rope. He pushes the horse with both hands, but it won't budge. And now an old woman in a shawl comes walking with a little boy. The boy wears a dark sailor suit; he is very pale and his neck is bandaged. They soon turn back. A man passes on a bicycle and shouts something to the man with the horse. His voice rings out, quite clear yet unintelligible, in the morning stillness. A cock crows. The creak of the bicycle, going past. The dew on the white table and chairs in the garden arbour, and dripping from the heavy lilac. Another cock crows, much louder and nearer. And I think I can hear the sea, or very distant bells.

The village is hidden in the woods, away up to the left. It consists almost entirely of boarding-houses, in various styles of seaside architecture – sham Moorish, old Bavarian, Taj Mahal, and the rococo doll's house, with white fretwork balconies. Behind the woods is the sea. You can reach it without going through the village, by a zig-zag path, which brings you out abruptly to the edge of some sandy cliffs, with the beach below you, and the tepid shallow Baltic lying almost at your feet. This end of the bay is quite deserted; the official bathing-beach is round the corner of the headland. The white onion-domes of the Strand Restaurant at Baabe wobble in the distance, behind fluid waves of heat, a kilometre away.

In the wood are rabbits and adders and deer. Yesterday morning I saw a roe being chased by a Borzoi dog, right across the fields and in amongst the trees. The dog couldn't catch the roe, although it seemed to be going much the faster of the two, moving in long graceful bounds, while the roe went bucketing over the earth with wild rigid jerks, like a grand piano bewitched.

There are two people staying in this house, besides myself. One of them is an Englishman, named Peter Wilkinson, about my own age. The other is a German working-class boy from Berlin, named Otto Nowak. He is sixteen or seventeen years old.

Peter – as I already call him; we got rather tight the first evening, and quickly made friends – is thin and dark and nervous. He wears horn-rimmed glasses. When he gets excited, he digs his hands down between his knees and clenches them together. Thick veins stand out at the sides of his temples. He trembles all over with suppressed, nervous laughter, until Otto, rather irritated, exclaims: *'Mensch, reg' Dich bloss nicht so auf!'*

Otto has a face like a very ripe peach. His hair is fair and thick, growing low on his forehead. He has small sparkling eyes, full of naughtiness, and a wide, disarming grin, which is much too innocent to be true. When he grins, two large dimples appear in his peach-bloom cheeks. At present, he makes up to me assiduously, flattering me, laughing at my jokes, never missing an opportunity of giving me a crafty, understanding wink. I think he looks upon me as a potential ally in his dealings with Peter.

This morning we all bathed together. Peter and Otto are busy building a large sand fort. I lay and watched Peter as he worked furiously, enjoying the glare, digging away savagely with his child's spade, like a chain-gang convict under the eyes of an armed warder. Throughout the long, hot morning, he never sat still for a moment. He and Otto swam, dug, wrestled, ran races or played with a rubber football, up and down the sands. Peter is skinny but wiry. In his games with Otto, he holds his own, it seems, only by an immense, furious effort of will. It is Peter's will against Otto's body. Otto is his whole body; Peter is only his head. Otto moves fluidly, effortlessly;

his gestures have the savage, unconscious grace of a cruel, elegant animal. Peter drives himself about, lashing his stiff, ungraceful body with the whip of his merciless will.

Otto is outrageously conceited. Peter has bought him a chest-expander, and, with this, he exercises solemnly at all hours of the day. Coming into their bedroom, after lunch, to look for Peter, I found Otto wrestling with the expander like Laocoön, in front of the looking-glass, all alone: 'Look, Christoph!' he gasped. 'You see, I can do it! All five strands!' Otto certainly has a superb pair of shoulders and chest for a boy of his age – but his body is nevertheless somehow slightly ridiculous. The beautiful ripe lines of the torso taper away too suddenly to his rather absurd little buttocks and spindly, immature legs. And these struggles with the chest-expander are daily making him more and more top-heavy.

This evening Otto had a touch of sunstroke, and went to bed early, with a headache. Peter and I walked up to the village, alone. In the Bavarian café, where the band makes a noise like Hell unchained, Peter bawled into my ear the story of his life.

Peter is the youngest of a family of four. He has two sisters, both married. One of the sisters lives in the country and hunts. The other is what the newspapers call ' a popular society hostess.' Peter's elder brother is a scientist and explorer. He has been on expeditions to the Congo, the New Hebrides and the Great Barrier Reef. He plays chess, speaks with the voice of a man of sixty, and has never, to the best of Peter's belief, performed the sexual act. The only member of the family with whom Peter is at present on speaking terms is his hunting sister, but they seldom meet, because Peter hates his brother-in-law.

Peter was delicate, as a boy. He did not go to a preparatory school but, when he was thirteen, his father sent him to a public school. His father and mother had a row about this which lasted until Peter, with his mother's encouragement, developed heart trouble and had to be removed at the end of his second term. Once escaped, Peter began to hate his mother for having petted and coddled him into a funk. She saw that he could not forgive her and so, as Peter was the only one of her children whom she cared for, she got ill herself and soon afterwards died.

It was too late to send Peter back to school again, so Mr Wilkinson engaged a tutor. The tutor was a very high-church young man who intended to become a priest. He took cold baths in winter and had crimpy hair and a Grecian jaw. Mr Wilkinson disliked him from the first, and the elder brother made satirical remarks, so Peter threw himself passionately on to the tutor's side. The two of them went for walking-tours in the Lake District and discussed the meaning of the Sacrament amidst austere moorland scenery. This kind of talk got them, inevitably, into a complicated emotional tangle which was abruptly unravelled, one evening, during a fearful row in a barn. Next morning, the tutor left, leaving a ten-page letter behind him. Peter meditated suicide. He heard later indirectly that the tutor had grown a moustache and gone out to Australia. So Peter got another tutor, and finally went up to Oxford.

Hating his father's business and his brother's science, he made music and literature into a religious cult. For the first year, he liked Oxford very much indeed. He went out to tea parties and ventured to talk. To his pleasure and surprise, people appeared to be listening to what he said. It wasn't until he had done this often that he began to notice their air of slight embarrassment. 'Somehow or other,' said Peter, 'I always struck the wrong note.'

Meanwhile, at home, in the big Mayfair house, with its four bath-rooms and garage for three cars, where there was always too much to eat, the Wilkinson family was slowly falling to pieces, like something gone rotten. Mr Wilkinson with his diseased kidneys, his whisky, and his knowledge of 'handling men,' was angry and confused and a bit pathetic. He snapped and growled at his children when they passed near him, like a surly old dog. At meals nobody ever spoke. They avoided each other's eyes, and hurried upstairs afterwards to write letters, full of hatred and satire, to their intimate friends. Only Peter had no friend to write to. He shut himself up in his tasteless, expensive bedroom and read and read.

And now it was the same at Oxford. Peter no longer went

to tea-parties. He worked all day, and, just before the exam-
inations, he had a nervous breakdown. The doctor advised a
complete change of scene, other interests. Peter's father let
him play at farming for six months in Devonshire, then he began to talk of the business. Mr Wilkinson had been unable to
persuade any of his other children to take even a polite interest
in the source of their incomes. They were all unassailable in
their different worlds. One of his daughters was about to marry
into the peerage, the other frequently hunted with the Prince
of Wales. His elder son read papers to the Royal Geographical
Society. Only Peter hadn't any justification for his existence.
The other children behaved selfishly, but knew what they
wanted. Peter also behaved selfishly, and didn't know.

However, at the critical moment, Peter's uncle, his mother's
brother, died. This uncle lived in Canada. He had seen Peter
once as a child and had taken a fancy to him, so he left him
all his money, not very much but enough to live on, comfort-
ably.

Peter went to Paris and began studying music. His teacher
told him that he would never be more than a good second-rate
amateur, but he only worked all the harder. He worked merely
to avoid thinking, and had another nervous breakdown, less
serious than the first. At this time, he was convinced that he
would soon go mad. He paid a visit to London and found only
his father at home. They had a furious quarrel on the first
evening; thereafter, they hardly exchanged a word. After a
week of silence and huge meals, Peter had a mild attack of
homicidal mania. All through breakfast, he couldn't take his
eyes off a pimple on his father's throat. He was fingering the
bread-knife. Suddenly the left side of his face began to twitch.
It twitched and twitched, so that he had to cover his cheek with
his hand. He felt certain that his father had noticed this, and
was intentionally refusing to remark on it – was, in fact, deliberately torturing him. At last, Peter could stand it no longer.
He jumped up and rushed out of the room, out of the house,
into the garden, where he flung himself face downwards on the
wet lawn. There he lay, too frightened to move. After a quarter
of an hour, the twitching stopped.

That evening Peter walked along Regent Street and picked up a whore. They went back together to the girl's room, and talked for hours. He told her the whole story of his life at home, gave her ten pounds and left her without even kissing her. Next morning a mysterious rash appeared on his left thigh. The doctor seemed at a loss to explain its origin, but prescribed some ointment. The rash became fainter, but did not altogether disappear until last month. Soon after the Regent Street episode, Peter also began to have trouble with his left eye.

For some time already, he had played with the idea of consulting a psychoanalyst. His final choice was an orthodox Freudian with a sleepy, ill-tempered voice and very large feet. Peter took an immediate dislike to him, and told him so. The Freudian made notes on a piece of paper, but did not seem offended. Peter later discovered that he was quite uninterested in anything except Chinese art. They met three times a week, and each visit cost two guineas.

After six months Peter abandoned the Freudian, and started going to a new analyst, a Finnish lady with white hair and a bright conversational manner. Peter found her easy to talk to. He told her, to the best of his ability, everything he had ever done, ever said, ever thought, or ever dreamed. Sometimes, in moments of discouragement, he told her stories which were absolutely untrue, or anecdotes collected from case-books. Afterwards, he would confess to these lies, and they would discuss his motives for telling them, and agree that they were very interesting. On red-letter nights Peter would have a dream, and this gave them a topic of conversation for the next few weeks. The analysis lasted nearly two years, and was never completed.

This year Peter got bored with the Finnish lady. He heard of a good man in Berlin. Well, why not? At any rate, it would be a change. It was also an economy. The Berlin man only cost fifteen marks a visit.

'And you're still going to him?' I asked.

'No . . .' Peter smiled. 'I can't afford to, you see.'

Last month, a day or two after his arrival, Peter went out to Wannsee, to bathe. The water was still chilly, and there were

not many people about. Peter had noticed a boy who was turning somersaults by himself, on the sand. Later the boy came
up and asked him for a match. They got into conversation. It
was Otto Nowak.

'Otto was quite horrified when I told him about the analyst.
"What!" he said, "you give that man fifteen marks a day just
for letting you talk to him! You give me ten marks and I'll
talk to you all day, and all night as well!" ' Peter began to shake
all over with laughter, flushing scarlet and wringing his hands.

Curiously enough, Otto wasn't being altogether preposterous
when he offered to take the analyst's place. Like many very
animal people, he has considerable instinctive powers of heal-
ing – when he chooses to use them. At such times, his treat-
ment of Peter is unerringly correct. Peter will be sitting at the
table, hunched up, his downward-curving mouth lined with
childhood fears: a perfect case-picture of his twisted, expensive
upbringing. Then in comes Otto, grins, dimples, knocks over
a chair, slaps Peter on the back, rubs his hands and exclaims
fatuously: '*Ja, ja . . . so ist die Sache!*' And, in a moment, Peter
is transformed. He relaxes, begins to hold himself naturally;
the tightness disappears from his mouth, his eyes lose their
hunted look. As long as the spell lasts, he is just like an ordinary person.

Peter tells me that, before he met Otto, he was so terrified
of infection that he would wash his hands with carbolic after
picking up a cat. Nowadays, he often drinks out of the same
glass as Otto, uses his sponge, and will share the same plate.

Dancing has begun at the Kurhaus and the café on the lake.
We saw the announcements of the first dance two days ago,
while we were taking our evening walk up the main street of
the village. I noticed that Otto glanced at the poster wistfully,
and that Peter had seen him do this. Neither of them, however,
made any comment.

Yesterday was chilly and wet. Otto suggested that we should
hire a boat and go fishing on the lake: Peter was pleased with
this plan, and agreed at once. But when we had waited three
quarters of an hour in the drizzle for a catch, he began to get

irritable. On the way back to the shore, Otto kept splashing with his oars – at first because he couldn't row properly, later merely to annoy Peter. Peter got very angry indeed, and swore at Otto, who sulked.

After supper, Otto announced that he was going to dance at the Kurhaus. Peter took this without a word, in ominous silence, the corners of his mouth beginning to drop; and Otto, either genuinely unconscious of his disapproval or deliberately overlooking it, assumed that the matter was settled.

After he had gone out, Peter and I sat upstairs in my cold room, listening to the pattering of the rain on the window:

'I though it couldn't last,' said Peter gloomily. 'This is the beginning. You'll see.'

'Nonsense, Peter. The beginning of what? It's quite natural that Otto should want to dance sometimes. You mustn't be so possessive.'

'Oh, I know, I know. As usual, I'm being utterly unreasonable ... All the same, this is the beginning ...'

Rather to my own surprise the event proved me right. Otto arrived back from the Kurhaus before ten o'clock. He had been disappointed. There had been very few people there, and the band was poor:

'I'll never go again,' he added, with a languishing smile at me. 'From now on I'll stay every evening with you and Chistoph. It's much more fun when we're all three together, isn't it?'

Yesterday morning, while we were lying in our fort on the beach, a little fair-haired man with ferrety blue eyes and a small moustache came up to us and asked us to join in a game with him. Otto, always over-enthusiastic about strangers, accepted at once, so that Peter and I had either to be rude or follow his example.

The little man, after introducing himself as a surgeon from a Berlin hospital, at once took command, assigning to us the places where we were to stand. He was very firm about this – instantly ordering me back when I attempted to edge a little nearer, so as not to have such a long distance to throw. Then it appeared that Peter was throwing in quite the wrong way: the little doctor stopped the game in order to demonstrate this. Peter was amused at first, and then rather annoyed. He retorted with considerable rudeness, but the doctor's skin wasn't pierced. 'You hold yourself so stiff,' he explained, smiling. 'That is an error. You should relax completely – like this – you understand? Now try again, and I will keep my hand on your shoulder-blade to see whether you really relax ... No, Again you do not!'

He seemed delighted, as if this failure of Peter's were a special triumph for his own methods of teaching. His eye met Otto's. Otto grinned understandingly.

Our meeting with the doctor put Peter in a bad temper for the rest of the day. In order to tease him, Otto pretended to like the doctor very much: 'That's the sort of chap I'd like to have for a friend,' he said with a spiteful smile. 'A real sportsman! You ought to take up sport, Peter! Then you'd have a figure like he has!'

Had Peter been in another mood, this remark would probably have made him smile. As it was, he got very angry: 'You'd better go off with your doctor now, if you like him so much!'

Otto grinned teasingly. 'He hasn't asked me to – yet!'

Yesterday evening, Otto went out to dance at the Kurhaus and didn't return till late.

There are now a good many summer visitors to the village. The bathing-beach by the pier, with its array of banners, begins to look like a mediæval camp. Each family has its own enormous hooded wicker beach-chair, and each chair flies a little flag. There are the German city-flags – Hamburg, Hanover, Dresden, Rostock and Berlin, as well as the National, Republican and Nazi colours. Each chair is encircled by a low sand bulwark upon which the occupants have set inscriptions in fircones: *Waldesruh. Familie Walter. Stahlhelm. Heil Hitler!* Many of the forts are also decorated with the Nazi swastika. The other morning I saw a child of about five years old, stark naked, marching along all by himself with a swastika flag over his shoulder and singing *'Deutschland über alles.'*

The little doctor fairly revels in this atmosphere. Nearly every morning he arrives, on a missionary visit, to our fort. 'You really ought to come round to the other beach,' he tells us. 'It's much more amusing there. I'd introduce you to some nice girls. The young people here are a magnificent lot! I, as a doctor, know how to appreciate them. The other day I was over at Hiddensee. Nothing but Jews! It's a pleasure to get back here and see real Nordic types!'

'Let's go to the other beach,' urged Otto. 'It's so dull here. There's hardly anyone about.'

'You can go if you like,' Peter retorted with angry sarcasm: 'I'm afraid I should be rather out of place. I had a grandmother who was partly Spanish.'

But the little doctor won't let us alone. Our opposition and more or less openly expressed dislike seem actually to fascinate him. Otto is always betraying us into his hands. One day, when the doctor was speaking enthusiastically about Hitler, Otto said, 'It's no good your talking like that to Christoph, Herr Doktor. He's a communist!'

This seemed positively to delight the doctor. His ferrety blue eyes gleamed with triumph. He laid his hand affectionately on my shoulder.

'But you *can't* be a communist! You *can't*!'

'Why can't I?' I asked coldly, moving away. I hate him to touch me.

'Because there isn't any such thing as communism. It's just an hallucination. A mental disease. People only imagine that they're communists. They aren't really.'

'What are they, then?'

But he wasn't listening. He fixed me with his triumphant, ferrety smile.

'Five years ago I used to think as you do. But my work at the clinic has convinced me that communism is a mere hallucination. What people need is discipline, self-control. I can tell you this as a doctor. I know it from my own experience.'

This morning we were all together in my room, ready to start out to bathe. The atmosphere was electric, because Peter and Otto were still carrying on an obscure quarrel which they had begun before breakfast, in their own bedroom. I was turning over the pages of a book, not paying much attention to them. Suddenly Peter slapped Otto hard on both cheeks. They closed immediately and staggered grappling about the room, knocking over the chairs. I looked on, getting out of their way as well as I could. It was funny, and, at the same time, unpleasant, because rage made their faces strange and ugly. Presently Otto got Peter down on the ground and began twisting his arm: 'Have you had enough?' he kept asking. He grinned: at that moment he was really hideous, positively deformed with malice. I knew that Otto was glad to have me there, because my presence was an extra humiliation for Peter. So I laughed, as though the whole thing were a joke, and went out of the room. I walked through the woods to Baabe, and bathed from the beach beyond. I felt I didn't want to see either of them again for several hours.

If Otto wishes to humiliate Peter, Peter in his different way, also wishes to humiliate Otto. He wants to force Otto into making a certain kind of submission to his will, and this submission Otto refuses instinctively to make. Otto is naturally and healthily selfish, like an animal. If there are two chairs in a room, he will take the more comfortable one without hesitation, because it never even occurs to him to consider Peter's comfort. Peter's selfishness is much less honest, more civilized, more perverse. Appealed to in the right way, he will make and sacrifice, however unreasonable and unnecessary. But when Otto takes the better chair as if by right, then Peter immediately sees a challenge which he dare not refuse to accept. I suppose that – given their two natures – there is no possible escape from this situation. Peter is bound to go on fighting to win Otto's submission. When, at last, he ceases to do so, it will merely mean that he has lost interest in Otto altogether.

The really destructive feature of their relationship is its inherent quality of boredom. It is quite natural for Peter often to feel bored with Otto – they have scarcely a single interest in common – but Peter, for sentimental reasons, will never admit that this is so. When Otto, who has no such motives for pretending, says. 'It's so dull here!' I invariably see Peter wince and look pained. Yet Otto is actually far less often bored than Peter himself; he finds Peter's company genuinely amusing, and is quite glad to be with him most of the day. Often, when Otto has been chattering rubbish for an hour without stopping, I can see that Peter really longs for him to be quiet and go away. But to admit this would be, in Peter's eyes, a total defeat, so he only laughs and rubs his hands, tacitly appealing to me to support him in his pretence of finding Otto inexhaustibly delightful and funny.

On our way back through the woods, after my bathe, I saw the ferrety little blond doctor advancing to meet me. It was too late to turn back. I said 'Good Morning' as politely and coldly as possible. The doctor was dressed in running-shorts and a sweater; he explained that he had been taking a 'Waldlauf.' 'But I think I shall turn back now,' he added. 'Wouldn't you like to run with me a little?'

'I'm afraid I can't,' I said rashly, 'you see, I twisted my ankle a bit yesterday.'

I could have bitten my tongue out as I saw the gleam of triumph in his eyes. 'Ah, you've sprained your ankle? Please let me look at it!' Squirming with dislike, I had to submit to his prodding fingers. 'But it is nothing, I assure you. You have no cause for alarm.'

As we walked the doctor began to question me about Peter and Otto, twisting his head to look up at me, as he delivered each sharp, inquisitive little thrust. He was fairly consumed with curiosity.

'My work in the clinic has taught me that it is no use trying to help this type of boy. Your friend is very generous and very well meaning, but he makes a great mistake. This type of boy always reverts. From a scientific point of view, I find him exceedingly interesting.'

As though he were about to say something specially momentous, the doctor suddenly stood still in the middle of the path, paused a moment to engage my attention, and smilingly announced:

'He has a criminal head!'

'And you think that people with criminal heads should be left to become criminals?'

'Certainly not. I believe in discipline. These boys ought to be put into labour-camps.'

'And what are you going to do with them when you've got them there? You say that they can't be altered, anyhow, so I suppose you'd keep them locked up for the rest of their lives?'

The doctor laughed delightedly, as though this were a joke against himself which he could, nevertheless, appreciate. He laid a caressing hand on my arm:

'You are an idealist! Do not imagine that I don't understand your point of view. But it is unscientific, quite unscientific. You and your friend do not understand such boys as Otto. I understand them. Every week, one or two such boys come to my clinic, and I must operate on them for adenoids, or mastoid, or poisoned tonsils. So, you see, I know them through and through!'

'I should have thought it would be more accurate to say you knew their throats and ears.'

Perhaps my German wasn't quite equal to rendering the sense of this last remark. At all events, the doctor ignored it completely. 'I know this type of boy very well,' he repeated, 'It is a bad degenerate type. You cannot make anything out of these boys. Their tonsils are almost invariably diseased.'

There are perpetual little rows going on between Peter and Otto, yet I cannot say that I find living with them actually unpleasant. Just now, I am very much taken up with my new novel. Thinking about it, I often go out for long walks, alone. Indeed, I find myself making more and more frequent excuses to leave them to themselves; and this is selfish, because, when I am with them, I can often choke off the beginnings of a quarrel by changing the subject or making a joke. Peter, I know, resents my desertions. 'You're quite an ascetic,' he said maliciously the other day, 'always withdrawing for your contemplations.' Once, when I was sitting in a café near the pier, listening to the band, Peter and Otto came past. 'So this is where you've been hiding!' Peter exclaimed. I saw that, for the moment, he really disliked me.

One evening, we were all walking up the main street, which was crowded with summer visitors. Otto said to Peter, with his most spiteful grin: 'Why must you always look in the same direction as I do?' This was surprisingly acute, for, whenever Otto turned his head to stare at a girl, Peter's eyes mechanically followed his glance with instinctive jealousy. We passed the photographer's window, in which, every day, the latest groups snapped by the beach camera-men are displayed. Otto paused to examine one of the new pictures with great attention, as though its subject were particularly attractive. I saw Peter's lips contract. He was struggling with himself, but he couldn't resist his own jealous curiosity – he stopped too. The photograph was of a fat old man with a long beard, waving a Berlin flag. Otto, seeing that his trap had been successful, laughed maliciously.

Invariably, after supper, Otto goes dancing at the Kurhaus or the café by the lake. He no longer bothers to ask Peter's permission to do this; he has established the right to have his evenings to himself. Peter and I generally go out too, into the village. We lean over the rail of the pier for a long time without speaking, staring down at the cheap jewellery of the Kurhaus lights reflected in the black water, each busy with his own thoughts. Sometimes we go into the Bavarian café and Peter gets steadily drunk – his stern, Puritan mouth contracting slightly with distaste as he raises the glass to his lips. I say nothing. There is too much to say. Peter, I know, wants me to make some provocative remark about Otto which will give him the exquisite relief of losing his temper. I don't, and we drink – keeping up a desultory conversation about books and concerts and plays. Later, when we are returning home, Peter's footsteps will gradually quicken until, as we enter the house, he leaves me and runs upstairs to his bedroom. Often we don't get back till half-past twelve or a quarter to one, but it is very seldom that we find Otto already there.

*   *   *

Down by the railway station, there is a holiday home for children from the Hamburg slums. Otto has got to know one of the teachers from this home, and they go out dancing together nearly every evening. Sometimes the girl, with her little troop of children, comes marching past the house. The children glance up at the windows and, if Otto happens to be looking out, indulge in precocious jokes. They nudge and pluck at their young teacher's arm to persuade her to look up, too.

On these occasions, the girl smiles coyly and shoots one glance at Otto from under her eyelashes, while Peter, watching behind the curtains, mutters through clenched teeth: 'Bitch ... bitch ... bitch ...' This persecution annoys him more than the actual friendship itself. We always seem to be running across the children when we are out walking in the woods. The children sing as they march – patriotic songs about the Homeland – in voices as shrill as birds. From far off, we hear them approaching, and have to turn hastily in the opposite direction. It is, as Peter says, like Captain Hook and the Crocodile.'

Peter has made a scene, and Otto has told his friend that she mustn't bring her troop past the house any more. But now they have begun bathing on our beach, not very far from the fort. The first morning this happened, Otto's glance kept turning in their direction. Peter was aware of this, of course, and remained plunged in gloomy silence.

'What's the matter with you to-day, Peter?' said Otto. 'Why are you so horrid to me?'

'Horrid to you?' Peter laughed savagely.

'Oh, very well then,' Otto jumped up. 'I see you don't want me here.' And, bounding over the rampart of our fort, he began to run along the beach towards the teacher and her children, very gracefully, displaying his figure to the best possible advantage.

Yesterday evening, there was a gala dance at the Kurhaus. In a mood of unusual generosity, Otto had promised Peter not to be later than a quarter to one, so Peter sat up with a book to wait for him. I didn't feel tired, and wanted to finish a chapter, so suggested that he should come into my room and wait there.

I worked. Peter read. The hours went slowly by. Suddenly I looked at my watch and saw that it was a quarter past two. Peter had dozed off in his chair. Just as I was wondering whether I should wake him, I heard Otto coming up the stairs. His footsteps sounded drunk. Finding no one in his room, he banged open my door. Peter sat up with a start.

Otto lolled grinning against the doorpost. He made me a half-tipsy salute. 'Have you been reading all this time?' he asked Peter.

'Yes,' said Peter, very self-controlled.

'Why?' Otto smiled fatuously.

'Because I couldn't sleep.'

'Why couldn't you sleep?'

'You know quite well,' said Peter between his teeth.

Otto yawned in his most offensive manner. 'I don't know and I don't care ... Don't make such a fuss.'

Peter rose to his feet. 'God, you little swine!' he said, smacking Otto's face hard with the flat of his hand. Otto didn't attempt to defend himself. He gave Peter an extraordinarily vindictive look out of his bright little eyes, 'Good!' He spoke rather thickly. 'To-morrow I shall go back to Berlin.' He turned unsteadily on his heel.

'Otto, come here,' said Peter. I saw that, in another moment, he would burst into tears of rage. He followed Otto out on to the landing. 'Come here,' he said again, in a sharp tone of command.

'Oh, leave me alone,' said Otto, 'I'm sick of you. I want to sleep now. To-morrow I'm going back to Berlin.'

This morning, however, peace has been restored – at a price. Otto's repentance has taken the form of a sentimental outburst over his family: 'Here I've been enjoying myself and never thinking of them ... Poor mother has to work like a dog, and her lungs are so bad ... Let's send her some money, shall we, Peter? Let's send her fifty marks ...' Otto's generosity reminded him of his own needs. In addition to the money for Frau Nowak, Peter has been talked into ordering Otto a new suit, which will cost a hundred and eighty, as well as a pair of shoes, a dressing-gown, and a hat.

In return for this outlay, Otto has volunteered to break off his relations with the teacher. (We now discover that, in any case, she is leaving the island to-morrow.) After supper, she appeared, walking up and down outside the house.

'Just let her wait till she's tired,' said Otto. 'I'm not going down to her.'

Presently the girl, made bold by impatience, began to whistle. This sent Otto into a frenzy of glee. Throwing open the window, he danced up and down, waving his arms and making hideous faces at the teacher who, for her part, seemed struck dumb with amazement at this extraordinary exhibition.

'Get away from here!' Otto yelled. 'Get out!'

The girl turned, and walked slowly away, a rather pathetic figure, into the gathering darkness.

'I think you might have said good-bye to her,' said Peter, who could afford to be magnanimous, now that he saw his enemy routed.

But Otto wouldn't hear of it.

'What's the use of all those rotten girls, anyhow? Every night they came pestering me to dance with them ... And you know how I am, Peter – I'm so easily persuaded ... Of course, it was horrid of me to leave you alone, but what could I do? It was all their fault, really ...'

Our life has now entered upon a new phase. Otto's resolutions were short-lived. Peter and I are alone together most of the day. The teacher has left, and with her, Otto's last inducement to bathe with us from the fort. He now goes off, every morning, to the bathing-beach by the pier, to flirt and play ball with his dancing-partners of the evening. The little doctor has also disappeared, and Peter and I are free to bathe and loll in the sun as unathletically as we wish.

After supper, the ritual of Otto's preparations for the dance begins. Sitting in my bedroom, I hear Peter's footsteps cross the landing, light and springy with relief – for now comes the only time of day when Peter feels himself altogether excused from taking any interest in Otto's activities. When he taps on my door, I shut my book at once. I have been out already to the village to buy half-a-pound of peppermint creams. Peter says good-bye to Otto, with a vain lingering hope that, perhaps to-night, he will, after all, be punctual: 'Till half-past twelve, then ...'

'Till one,' Otto bargains.

'All right,' Peter concedes. 'Till one. But don't be late.'

'No, Peter, I won't be late.'

As we open the garden gate and cross the road into the wood, Otto waves to us from the balcony. I have to be careful to hide the peppermint creams under my coat, in case he should see them. Laughing guiltily, munching the peppermints, we take the woodland path to Baabe. We always spend our evenings in Baabe, nowadays. We like it better than our own village. Its single sandy street of low-roofed houses among the pine-trees has a romantic, colonial air; it is like a ramshackle, lost settlement somewhere in the backwoods, where people come to look for a non-existent gold mine and remain, stranded, for the rest of their lives.

In the little restaurant, we eat strawberries and cream, and talk to the young waiter. The waiter hates Germany and longs to go to America. '*Hier ist nichts los.*' During the season, he is allowed no free time at all, and in the winter he earns nothing. Most of the Baabe boys are Nazis. Two of them come into the restaurant sometimes and engage us in good-humoured political arguments. They tell us about their field-exercises and military games.

'You're preparing for war,' says Peter indignantly. On these occasions – although he has really not the slightest interest in politics – he gets quite heated.

'Excuse me,' one of the boys contradicts, 'that's quite wrong. The Führer does not want war. Our programme stands for peace, with honour. All the same ...' he adds wistfully, his face lighting up, 'war can be fine, you know! Think of the ancient Greeks!'

'The ancient Greeks,' I object, 'didn't use poison gas.'

The boys are rather scornful at this quibble. One of them answers loftily. 'That's a purely technical question.'

At half-past ten we go down, with most of the other inhabitants, to the railway station, to watch the arrival of the last train. It is generally empty. It goes clanging away through the dark woods, sounding its harsh bell. At last it is late enough to start home; this time, we take the road. Across the meadows, you can see the illuminated entrance of the café by the lake, where Otto goes to dance.

'The lights of Hell are shining brightly this evening,' Peter is fond of remarking.

Peter's jealousy has turned into insomnia. He has begun taking sleeping tablets, but admits that they seldom have any effect. They merely made him feel drowsy next morning, after breakfast. He often goes to sleep for an hour or two in our fort, on the shore.

This morning the weather was cool and dull, the sea oyster-grey. Peter and I hired a boat, rowed out beyond the pier, then let ourselves drift, gently, away from the land. Peter lit a cigarette. He said abruptly:

'I wonder how much longer this will go on ...'

'As long as you let it, I suppose.'

'Yes ... We seem to have got into a pretty static condition, don't we? I suppose there's no particular reason why Otto and I should ever stop behaving to each other as we do at present ...' He paused, added: 'Unless, of course I stop giving him money.'

'What do you think would happen, then?'

Peter paddled idly in the water with his fingers. 'He'd leave me.'

The boat drifted on for several minutes. I asked: 'You don't think he cares for you, at all?'

'At the beginning he did, perhaps ... Not now. There's nothing between us now but my cash.'

'Do you still care for him?'

'No ... I don't know. Perhaps ... I still hate him, sometimes – if that's a sign of caring.'

'It might be.'

There was a long pause. Peter dried his fingers on his handkerchief. His mouth twitched nervously.

'Well,' he said at last, 'what do you advise me to do?'

'What do you want to do?'

Peter's mouth gave another twitch.

'I suppose, really, I want to leave him.'

'Then you'd better leave him.'

'At once?'

'The sooner the better. Give him a nice present and send him back to Berlin this afternoon.'

Peter shook his head, smiled sadly:

'I can't.'

There was another long pause. Then Peter said: 'I'm sorry Christopher ... You're absolutely right, I know. If I were in your place, I'd say the same thing ... But I can't. Things have got to go on as they are – until something happens. They can't last much longer, anyhow ... Oh, I know I'm very weak ...'

'You needn't apologize to me,' I smiled, to conceal a slight feeling of irritation: 'I'm not one of your analysts!'

I picked up the oars and began to row back towards the shore. As we reached the pier, Peter said:

'It seems funny to think of now – when I first met Otto, I thought we should live together for the rest of our lives.'

'Oh, my God!' The vision of a life with Otto opened before me, like a comic inferno. I laughed out loud. Peter laughed, too, wedging his locked hands between his knees. His face turned from pink to red, from red to purple. His veins bulged. We were still laughing when we got out of the boat.

In the garden the landlord was waiting for us. 'What a pity!' he exclaimed. 'The gentlemen are too late!' He pointed over the meadows, in the direction of the lake. We could see the smoke rising above the line of poplars, as the little train drew out of the station: 'Your friend was obliged to leave for Berlin, suddenly, on urgent business. I hoped the gentlemen might have been in time to see him off. What a pity!'

This time, both Peter and I ran upstairs. Peter's bedroom was in a terrible mess – all the drawers and cupboards were open. Propped up on the middle of the table was a note, in Otto's cramped, scrawling hand:

Dear Peter. Please forgive me I couldn't stand it any longer here so I am going home.

Love from Otto.

Don't be angry.

(Otto had written it, I noticed it, on a fly-leaf torn out of one of Peter's psychology books: *Beyond the Pleasure-Principle.*)

'Well ... !' Peter's mouth began to twitch. I glanced at him nervously, expecting a violent outburst, but he seemed fairly calm. After a moment, he walked over to the cupboards and began looking through the drawers. 'He hasn't taken much,' he announced, at the end of his search. 'Only a couple of my ties, three shirts – lucky my shoes don't fit him! – and, let's see ... about two hundred marks ...' Peter started to laugh, rather hysterically: 'Very moderate, on the whole!'

'Do you think he decided to leave quite suddenly?' I asked, for the sake of saying something.

'Probably he did. That would be just like him ... Now I come to think of it, I told him we were going out in that boat, this morning – and he asked me if we should be away for long...'

'I see ...'

I sat down on Peter's bed – thinking, oddly enough, that Otto has at last done something which I rather respect.

Peter's hysterical high spirits kept him going for the rest of the morning; at lunch he turned gloomy, and wouldn't say a word.

'Now I must go and pack,' he told me when we had finished.

'You're off, too?'

'Of course.'

'To Berlin?'

Peter smiled. 'No, Christopher. Don't be alarmed! Only to England...'

'Oh ...'

'There's a train which'll get me to Hamburg, late to-night. I shall probably go straight on ... I feel I've got to keep travelling until I'm clear of this bloody country ...'

There was nothing to say. I helped him pack, in silence. As Peter put his shaving-mirror into the bag, he asked: 'Do you remember how Otto broke this, standing on his head?'

'Yes, I remember.'

When we had finished, Peter went out on to the balcony of his room: 'There'll be plenty of whistling outside here, to-night', he said.

I smiled: 'I shall have to go down and console them.'

Peter laughed: 'Yes, you will!'

I went with him to the station. Luckily, the engine-driver was in a hurry. The train only waited a couple of minutes.

'What shall you do when you get to London?' I asked.

Peter's mouth curved down at the corners; he gave me a kind of inverted grin: 'Look round for another analyst, I suppose.'

'Well, mind you beat down his prices a bit!'

'I will.'

As the train moved out, he waved his hand: 'Well, good-bye, Christopher. Thank you for all your moral support!'

Peter never suggested that I should write to him, or visit him at home. I suppose he wants to forget this place, and everybody concerned with it. I can hardly blame him.

It was only this evening, turning over the pages of a book I have been reading, that I found another note from Otto, slipped between the leaves.

> Please dear Christoph don't you be angry with me too because you aren't an idiot like Peter. When you are back in Berlin I shall come and see you because I know where you live; I saw the address on one of your letters and we can have a nice talk,
>
> Your loving friend,
>
> Otto.

I thought, somehow, that he wouldn't be got rid of quite so easily.

Actually, I am leaving for Berlin in a day or two, now. I thought I should stay on till the end of August, and perhaps finish my novel, but, suddenly, the place seems so lonely. I miss Peter and Otto, and their daily quarrels, far more than I should have expected. And now even Otto's dancing-partners have stopped lingering sadly in the twilight, under my window.

The entrance to the Wassertorstrasse was a big stone archway, a bit of old Berlin, daubed with hammers and sickles and Nazi crosses and plastered with tattered bills which advertised auctions or crimes. It was a deep shabby cobbled street, littered with sprawling children in tears. Youths in woollen sweaters circled waveringly across it on racing bikes and whooped at girls passing with milk-jugs. The pavement was chalk-marked for the hopping game called Heaven and Earth. At the end of it, like a tall, dangerously sharp, red instrument, stood a church.

Frau Nowak herself opened the door to me. She looked far iller than when I had seen her last, with big blue rings under her eyes. She was wearing the same hat and mangy old black coat. At first, she didn't recognize me.

'Good afternoon, Frau Nowak.'

Her face changed slowly from poking suspicion to a brilliant, timid, almost girlish smile of welcome:

'Why, if it isn't Herr Christoph! Come in, Herr Christoph! Come in and sit down.'

'I'm afraid you were just going out, weren't you?'

'No, no, Herr Christoph – I've just come in; just this minute.' She was wiping her hands hastily on her coat before shaking mine: 'This is one of my charring days. I don't get finished till half-past two, and it makes the dinner so late.'

She stood aside for me to enter. I pushed open the door and, in doing so, jarred the handle of the frying-pan on the stove which stood just behind it. In the tiny kitchen there was barely room for the two of us together. A stifling smell of potatoes in cheap margarine filled the flat.

'Come and sit down, Herr Christoph,' she repeated, hastily doing the honours. 'I'm afraid it's terribly untidy. You must excuse that. I have to go out so early and my Grete's such a lazy great lump, though she's turned twelve. There's no getting her to do anything, if you don't stand over her all the time.'

The living-room had a sloping ceiling stained with old patches of damp. It contained a big table, six chairs, a sideboard and two large double-beds. The place was so full of furniture that you had to squeeze your way into it sideways.

'Grete!' cried Frau Nowak. 'Where are you? Come here this minute!'

'She's gone out,' came Otto's voice from the inner room.

'Otto! Come and see who's here!'

'Can't be bothered. I'm busy mending the gramophone.'

'Busy, indeed! You! You good-for-nothing! That's a nice way to speak to your mother! Come out of that room, do you hear me?'

She had flown into a rage instantly, automatically, with astonishing violence. Her face became all nose: thin, bitter and inflamed. Her whole body trembled.

'It doesn't really matter, Frau Nowak,' I said. 'Let him come out when he wants to. He'll get all the bigger surprise.'

'A nice son I've got! Speaking to me like that.'

She had pulled off her hat and was unpacking greasy parcels from a string bag: 'Dear me,' she fussed. 'I wonder where that child's got to? Always down in the street, she is. If I've told her once, I've told her a hundred times. Children have no consideration.'

'How has your lung been keeping, Frau Nowak?'

She sighed: 'Sometimes it seems to me it's worse than ever. I get such a burning, just here. And when I finish work it's as if I was too tired to eat. I come over so bilious . . . I don't think the doctor's satisfied either. He talks about sending me to a sanatorium later in the winter. I was there before, you know. But there's always so many waiting to go . . . Then, the flat's so damp at this time of year. You see those marks on the ceiling? There's days we have to put a foot-bath under them to catch the drips. Of course, they've no right to let these attics as dwellings at all, really. The Inspector's condemned them time and time again. But what are you to do? One must live somewhere. We applied for a transfer over a year ago and they keep promising they'll see about it. But there's a lot of others are worse off still, I dare say ... My husband was reading out of the newspaper the other day about the English and their Pound. It keeps on falling, they say. I don't understand such things, myself. I hope you haven't lost any money, Herr Christoph?'

'As a matter of fact, Frau Nowak, that's partly why I came down to see you to-day. I've decided to go into a cheaper room and I was wondering if there was anywhere round here you could recommend me?'

'Oh dear, Herr Christoph, I *am* sorry!'

She was quite genuinely shocked: 'But you can't live in this part of the town – a gentleman like you! Oh, no. I'm afraid it wouldn't suit you at all.'

'I'm not so particular as you think, perhaps. I just want a quiet, clean room for about twenty marks a month. It doesn't matter how small it is. I'm out most of the day.'

She shook her head doubtfully: 'Well, Herr Christoph, I shall have to see if I can't think of something ...'

'Isn't dinner ready yet, mother?' asked Otto, appearing in shirt-sleeves at the doorway of the inner room: 'I'm nearly starving!'

'How do you expect it to be ready when I have to spend the whole morning slaving for you, you great lump of laziness!' cried Frau Nowak, shrilly, at the top of her voice. Then, transposing without the least pause into her ingratiating social tone, she added: 'Don't you see who's here?'

'Why ... it's Christoph!' Otto, as usual, had begun acting at once. His face was slowly illuminated by a sunrise of extreme joy. His cheeks dimpled with smiles. He sprang forward, throwing one arm around my neck, wringing my hand: 'Christoph, you old soul, where have you been hiding all this time?' His voice became languishing, reproachful: 'We've missed you so much! Why have you never come to see us?'

'Herr Christoph is a very busy gentleman,' put in Frau Nowak reprovingly: 'He's got no time to waste running after a do-nothing like you.'

Otto grinned, winked at me: then he turned reproachfully upon Frau Nowak:

'Mother, what are you thinking of? Are you going to let Christoph sit there without so much as a cup of coffee? He must be thirsty, after climbing all these stairs!'

'What you mean is, Otto, that *you're* thirsty, don't you? No, thank you, Frau Nowak, I won't have anything – really. And I won't keep you from your cooking any longer ... Look here, Otto, will you come out with me now and help me find a room? I've just been telling your mother that I'm coming to live in this neighbourhood ... You shall have your cup of coffee with me outside.'

'What, Christoph – you're going to live here, in Hallesches Tor!' Otto began dancing with excitement: 'Oh mother, won't that be grand! Oh, I am so pleased!'

'You may just as well go out and have a look round with Herr Christoph, now,' said Frau Nowak. 'Dinner won't be ready for at least an hour, yet. You're only in my way here. Not *you*, Herr Christoph, of course. You'll come back and have something to eat with us, won't you?'

'Well, Frau Nowak, it's very kind of you indeed, but I'm afraid I can't to-day. I shall have to be getting back home.'

'Just give me a crust of bread before I go, mother,' begged Otto piteously. 'I'm so empty that my head's spinning round like a top.'

'All right,' said Frau Nowak, cutting a slice of bread and half throwing it at him in her vexation, 'but don't blame me if there's nothing in the house this evening when you want to make one of your sandwiches ... Good-bye, Herr Christoph. It was very kind of you to come and see us. If you really decide to live near here, I hope you'll look in often ... though I doubt if you'll find anything to your liking. It won't be what you've been accustomed to ...'

As Otto was about to follow me out of the flat she called him back. I heard them arguing; then the door shut. I descended slowly the five flights of stairs to the courtyard. The bottom of the court was clammy and dark, although the sun was shining on a cloud in the sky overhead. Broken buckets, wheels off prams and bits of bicycle tyre lay scattered about like things which have fallen down a well.

It was a minute or two before Otto came clattering down
the stairs to join me:

'Mother didn't like to ask you,' he told me, breathless. 'She
was afraid you'd be annoyed ... But I said that I was sure you'd
far rather be with us, where you can do just what you like and
you know everything's clean, than in a strange house full of
bugs ... Do say yes, Christoph, please! It'll be such fun! You
and I can sleep in the back room. You can have Lothar's bed –
he won't mind. He can share the double-bed with Grete ...
And in the mornings you can stay in bed as long as ever you
like. If you want, I'll bring your breakfast ... You will come,
won't you?'

And so it was settled.

My first evening as a lodger at the Nowaks was something of
a ceremony. I arrived with my two suit-cases soon after five
o'clock, to find Frau Nowak already cooking the evening meal.
Otto whispered to me that we were to have lung hash, as a
special treat.

'I'm afraid you won't think very much of our food,' said Frau
Nowak, 'after what you've been used to. But we'll do our best.'
She was all smiles, bubbling over with excitement, I smiled and
smiled, feeling awkward and in the way. At length, I clambered over the living-room furniture and sat down on my bed.
There was no space to unpack in, and nowhere, apparently, to
put my clothes. At the living-room table, Grete was playing
with her cigarette-cards and transfers. She was a lumpish child
of twelve years old, pretty in a sugary way, but round-
shouldered and too fat. My presence made her very self-
conscious. She wriggled, smirked and kept calling out, in an
affected, sing-song, 'grown-up' voice:

'Mummy! Come and look at the pretty flowers!'

'I've got no time for your pretty flowers,' exclaimed Frau
Nowak at length, in great exasperation: 'Here am I, with a
daughter the size of an elephant, having to slave all by myself,
cooking the supper!'

'Quite right, mother!' cried Otto, gleefully joining in. He

turned upon Grete, righteously indignant: 'Why don't you
help her, I should like to know? You're fat enough. You sit
around all day doing nothing. Get off that chair this instant, do
you hear! And put those filthy cards away, or I'll burn them!'

He grabbed at the cards with one hand and gave Grete a slap
across the face with the other. Grete, who obviously wasn't
hurt, at once set up a loud, theatrical wail: 'Oh, Otto, you've
hurt me!' She covered her face with her hands and peeped at
me between the fingers.

'*Will* you leave that child alone!' cried Frau Nowak shrilly
from the kitchen. 'I should like to know who *you* are, to talk
about laziness! And you, Grete, just you stop that howling – or
I'll tell Otto to hit you properly, so that you'll have something
to cry for. You two between you, you drive me distracted.'

'But, mother!' Otto ran into the kitchen, took her round the
waist and began kissing her: 'Poor little Mummy, little Mutti,
little Muttchen,' he crooned, in tones of the most mawkish
solicitude. 'You have to work so hard and Otto's so horrid to
you. But he doesn't mean to be, you know – he's just stupid ...
Shall I fetch the coal up for you to-morrow, Mummy? Would
you like that?'

'Let go of me, you great humbug!' cried Frau Nowak, laughing and struggling. 'I don't want any of your soft soap! Much
you care for your poor old mother! Leave me to get on with my
work in peace.'

'Otto's not a bad boy,' she continued to me, when he had let
go of her at last, 'but he's such a scatterbrain. Quite the opposite of my Lothar – there's a model son for you! He's not too
proud to do any job, whatever it is, and when he's scraped a few
groschen together, instead of spending them on himself he
comes straight to me and says: "Here you are, mother. Just
buy yourself a pair of warm house-shoes for the winter." Frau
Nowak held out her hand to me with the gesture of giving
money. Like Otto, she had the trick of acting every scene she
described.

'Oh, Lothar, this, Lothar that,' Otto interrupted crossly:
'It's always Lothar. But tell me this, mother, which of us was it
that gave you a twenty-mark note the other day? Lothar

couldn't earn twenty marks in a month of Sundays. Well, if that's how you talk, you needn't expect to get any more; not if you come to me on your knees.'

'You wicked boy,' she was up in arms again in an instant, 'have you no more shame than to speak of such things in front of Herr Christoph! Why, if he knew where that twenty marks came from – and plenty more besides – he'd disdain to stay in the same house with you another minute; and quite right, too! And the cheek of you – saying you *gave* me that money! You know very well that if your father hadn't seen the envelope . . .'

'That's right!' shouted Otto, screwing up his face at her like a monkey and beginning to dance with excitement: 'That's just what I wanted! Admit to Christoph that you stole it! You're a thief! You're a thief!'

'Otto, how dare you!' Quick as fury, Frau Nowak's hand grabbed up the lid of a saucepan. I jumped back a pace to be out of range, tripped over a chair and sat down hard. Grete uttered an affected little shriek of joy and alarm. The door opened. It was Herr Nowak, come back from his work.

He was a powerful, dumpy little man, with pointed moustache, cropped hair and bushy eyebrows. He took in the scene with a long grunt which was half a belch. He did not appear to understand what had been happening; or perhaps he merely did not care. Frau Nowak said nothing to enlighten him. She hung the saucepan-lid quietly on a hook. Grete jumped up from her chair and ran to him with outstretched arms: 'Pappi! Pappi!'

Herr Nowak smiled down at her, showing two or three nicotine-stained stumps of teeth. Bending, he picked her up, carefully and expertly, with a certain admiring curiosity, like a large valuable vase. By profession he was a furniture-remover. Then he held out his hand – taking his time about it, gracious, not fussily eager to please:

'Servus, Herr!"

'Aren't you glad that Herr Christoph's come to live with us, Pappi?' chanted Grete, perched on her father's shoulder, in her sugary sing-song tones. At this Herr Nowak, as if suddenly acquiring new energy, began shaking my hand again, much more warmly, and thumping me on the back:

'Glad? Yes, of course I'm glad!' He nodded his head in vigorous approval. 'Englisch Man? Anglais, eh? Ha, ha. That's right! Oh, yes, I talk French, you see. Forgotten most of it now. Learnt in the war. I was *Feldwebel* – on the West Front. Talked to lots of prisoners. Good lads. All the same as us . . .'

'You're drunk again, father!' exclaimed Frau Nowak in disgust. 'Whatever will Herr Christoph think of you!'

'Christoph doesn't mind; do you, Christoph?' Herr Nowak patted my shoulder.

'Christoph, indeed! He's *Herr* Christoph to you! Can't you tell a gentleman when you see one?'

'I'd much rather you called me Christoph,' I said.

'That's right! Christoph's right! We're all the same flesh and blood . . . *Argent*, money – all the same! Ha, ha!'

Otto took my other arm: 'Christoph's quite one of the family, already!'

Presently we sat down to an immense meal of lung hash, black bread, malt coffee and boiled potatoes. In the first recklessness of having so much money to spend (I had given her ten marks in advance for the week's board) Frau Nowak had prepared enough for a dozen people. She kept shovelling them on to my plate from a big saucepan, until I thought I should suffocate:

'Have some more, Herr Christoph. You're eating nothing.'

'I've never eaten so much in my whole life, Frau Nowak.'

'Christoph doesn't like our food,' said Herr Nowak. 'Never mind, Christoph, you'll get used to it. Otto was just the same when he came back from the seaside. He'd got used to all sorts of fine ways, with his Englishman . . .'

'Hold your tongue, father!' said Frau Nowak warningly. 'Can't you leave the boy alone? He's old enough to be able to decide for himself what's right and wrong – more shame to him!'

We were still eating when Lothar came in. He threw his cap on the bed, shook hands with me politely but silently, with a little bow, and took his place at the table. My presence did not appear to surprise or interest him in the least: his glance barely met mine. He was, I knew, only twenty; but he might well have been years older. He was a man already. Otto seemed almost childish beside him. He had a lean, bony, peasant's face, soured by racial memory of barren fields.

'Lothar's going to night-school,' Frau Nowak told me with pride. 'He had a job in a garage, you know; and now he wants to study engineering. They won't take you in anywhere nowadays unless you've got a diploma of some sort. He must show you his drawings, Herr Christoph, when you've got time to look at them. The teacher said they were very good indeed.'

'I should like to see them.'

Lothar didn't respond. I sympathized with him and felt rather foolish. But Frau Nowak was determined to show him off:

'What nights are your classes, Lothar?'

'Mondays and Thursdays.' He went on eating, deliberately, obstinately, without looking at his mother. Then perhaps to show that he bore me no ill-will, he added: 'From eight to ten-thirty.' As soon as he had finished, he got up without a word, shook hands with me, making the same small bow, took his cap and went out.

Frau Nowak looked after him and sighed: 'He's going round to his Nazis, I suppose. I often wish he'd never taken up with them at all. They put all kinds of silly ideas into his head. It makes him so restless. Since he joined them he's been a different boy altogether ... Not that I understand these politics myself. What I always say is – why can't we have the Kaiser back? Those were the good times, say what you like.'

'Ach, to hell with your old Kaiser,' said Otto. 'What we want is a communist revolution.'

'A communist revolution!' Frau Nowak snorted. 'The idea! The communists are all good-for-nothing lazybones like you, who've never done an honest day's work in their lives.'

'Christoph's a communist,' said Otto. 'Aren't you, Christoph?'

'Not a proper one, I'm afraid.'

Frau Nowak smiled: 'What nonsense will you be telling us

next! How could Herr Christoph be a communist? He's a gentleman.'

'What I say is—.' Herr Nowak put down his knife and fork and wiped his moustache carefully on the back of his hand: 'we're all equal as God made us. You're as good as me; I'm as good as you. A Frenchman's as good as an Englishman; an Englishman's as good as a German. You understand what I mean?'

I nodded.

'Take the war, now—.' Herr Nowak pushed back his chair from the table: 'One day I was in a wood. All alone, you understand. Just walking through the wood by myself, as I might be walking down the street . . . And suddenly – there before me, stood a Frenchman. Just as if he'd sprung out of the earth. He was no further away from me than you are now.' Herr Nowak sprang to his feet as he spoke. Snatching up the bread-knife from the table he held it before him, in a posture of defence, like a bayonet. He glared at me from beneath his bushy eyebrows, re-living the scene: 'There we stand. We look at each other. That Frenchman was as pale as death. Suddenly he cries: "Don't shoot me!" Just like that.' Herr Nowak clasped his hands in a piteous gesture of entreaty. The bread-knife was in the way now: he put it down on the table. ' "Don't shoot me! I have five children." (He spoke French, of course: but I could understand him. I could speak French perfectly in those days; but I've forgotten some of it now.) Well, I look at him and he looks at me. Then I say: "Ami." (That means Friend.) And then we shake hands.' Herr Nowak took my hand in both of his and pressed it with great emotion. 'And then we begin to walk away from each other – backwards; I didn't want him to shoot me in the back.' Still glaring in front of him Herr Nowak began cautiously retreating backwards, step by step, until he collided violently with the sideboard. A framed photograph fell off it. The glass smashed.

'Pappi! Pappi!' cried Grete in delight. 'Just look what you've done!'

'Perhaps that'll teach you to stop your fooling, you old clown!' exclaimed Frau Nowak angrily. Grete began loudly and affectedly laughing, until Otto slapped her face and she set up her stagey whine. Meanwhile, Herr Nowak had restored his wife's good temper by kissing her and pinching her cheek.

'Get away from me, you great lout!' she protested laughingly; coyly pleased that I was present: 'let me alone, you stink of beer!'

At that time, I had a great many lessons to give. I was out most of the day. My pupils were scattered about the fashionable suburbs of the west – rich, well-preserved women of Frau Nowak's age, but looking ten years younger; they liked to make a hobby of a little English conversation on dull afternoons when their husbands were away at the office. Sitting on silk cushions in front of open fireplaces, we discussed *Point Counter Point* and *Lady Chatterley's Lover*. A manservant brought in tea with buttered toast. Sometimes, when they got tired of literature, I amused them by descriptions of the Nowak household. I was careful, however, not to say that I lived there: it would have been bad for my business to admit that I was really poor. The ladies paid me three marks an hour; a little reluctantly, having done their best to beat me down to two marks fifty. Most of them also tried, deliberately or subconsciously, to cheat me into staying longer than my time. I always had to keep my eye on the clock.

Fewer people wanted lessons in the morning; and so it happened that I usually got up much later than the rest of the Nowak family. Frau Nowak had her charring, Herr Nowak went off to his job at the furniture-removers, Lothar, who was out of work, was helping a friend with a paper-round, Grete went to school. Only Otto kept me company; except on the mornings when, with endless nagging, he was driven out to the labour-bureau by his mother, to get his card stamped.

After fetching our breakfast, a cup of coffee and a slice of bread and dripping, Otto would strip off his pyjamas and do exercises, shadow-box or stand on his head. He flexed his muscles for my admiration. Squatting on my bed, he told me stories:

'Did I ever tell you, Christoph, how I saw the Hand?'

'No, I don't think so.'

'Well, listen ... Once, when I was very small, I was lying in bed at night. It was very dark and very late. And suddenly I woke up and saw a great big black hand stretching over the bed. I was so frightened I couldn't even scream. I just drew my legs up under my chin and stared at it. Then, after a minute or two, it disappeared and I yelled out. Mother came running in and I said: "Mother, I've seen the Hand." But she only laughed. She wouldn't believe it.'

Otto's innocent face, with its two dimples, like a bun, had become very solemn. He held me with his absurdly small bright eyes, concentrating all his narrative powers:

'And then, Christoph, several years later, I had a job as apprentice to an upholsterer. Well, one day – it was in the middle of the morning, in broad daylight – I was sitting working on my stool. And suddenly it seemed to go all dark in the room and I looked up and there was the Hand, as near to me as you are now, just closing over me. I felt my arms and legs turn cold and I couldn't breathe and I couldn't cry out. The master saw how pale I was and he said: "Why, Otto, what's the matter with you? Aren't you well?" And as he spoke to me it seemed as if the Hand drew right away from me again, getting smaller and smaller, until it was just a little black speck. And when I looked up again the room was quite light, just as it always was, and where I'd seen the black speck there was a big fly crawling across the ceiling. But I was so ill the whole day that the master had to send me home.'

Otto's face had gone quite pale during this recital and, for a moment, a really frightening expression of fear had passed over his features. He was tragic now; his little eyes bright with tears:

'One day I shall see the Hand again. And then I shall die.'

'Nonsense,' I said laughing. 'We'll protect you.'

Otto shook his head very sadly:

'Let's hope so, Christoph. But I'm afraid not. The Hand will get me in the end.'

'How long did you stay with the upholsterer?' I asked.

'Oh, not long. Only a few weeks. The master was so unkind

to me. He always gave me the hardest jobs to do – and I was such a little chap then. One day I got there five minutes late. He made a terrible row; called me a *verfluchter Hund*. And do you think I put up with that?' Otto leant forward, thrust his face, contracted into a dry monkey-like leer of malice, towards me. *'Nee, nee! Bei mir nicht!'* His little eyes focused upon me for a moment with an extraordinary intensity of simian hatred; his puckered-up features became startlingly ugly. Then they relaxed. I was no longer the upholsterer. He laughed gaily and innocently, throwing back his hair, showing his teeth: 'I pretended I was going to hit him. I frightened him, all right!' He imitated the gesture of a scared middle-aged man avoiding a blow. He laughed.

'And then you had to leave?' I asked.

Otto nodded. His face slowly changed. He was turning melancholy again.

'What did your father and mother say to that?'

'Oh, they've always been against me. Ever since I was small. If there were two crusts of bread, mother would always give the bigger one to Lothar. Whenever I complained they used to say: "Go and work. You're old enough. Get your own food. Why should we support you?"' Otto's eyes moistened with the most sincere self-pity: 'Nobody understands me here. Nobody's good to me. They all hate me really. They wish I was dead.'

'How can you talk such rubbish, Otto! Your mother certainly doesn't hate you.'

'Poor mother!' agreed Otto. He had changed his tone at once, seeming utterly unaware of what he had just said: 'It's terrible. I can't bear to think of her working like that, every day. You know, Christoph, she's very, very ill. Often, at night, she coughs for hours and hours. And sometimes she spits out blood. I lie awake wondering if she's going to die.'

I nodded. In spite of myself I began to smile. Not that I disbelieved what he had said about Frau Nowak. But Otto himself, squatting there on the bed, was so animally alive, his naked brown body so sleek with health, that his talk of death seemed ludicrous, like the description of a funeral by a painted clown. He must have understood this, for he grinned back, not in the least shocked at my apparent callousness. Straightening his legs he bent forward without effort and grasped his feet with his hands: 'Can you do that Christoph?'

A sudden notion pleased him: 'Christoph, if I show you something, will you swear not to tell a single soul?'

'All right.'

He got up and rummaged under his bed. One of the floorboards was loose in the corner by the window: lifting it, he fished out a tin box which had once contained biscuits. The tin was full of letters and photographs. Otto spread them out on the bed:

'Mother would burn these if she found then ... Look, Christoph, how do you like her? Her name's Hilde. I met her at the place where I go dancing. ... And this is Marie. Hasn't she got beautiful eyes? She's wild about me – all the other boys are jealous. But she's not really my type.' Otto shook his head seriously: 'You know, it's a funny thing, but as soon as I know that a girl's keen on me, I lose interest in her. I wanted to break with her altogether; but she came round here and made such a to-do in front of mother. So I have to see her sometimes to keep her quiet ... And here's Trude – honestly, Christoph, would you believe she was twenty-seven? It's a fact! Hasn't she a marvellous figure? She lives in the West End, in a flat of her own! She's been divorced twice. I can go there whenever I like. Here's a photo her brother took of her. He wanted to take some of us two together, but I wouldn't let him. I was afraid he'd sell them, afterwards – you can be arrested for it, you know ...' Otto smirked, handed me a packet of letters: 'Here, read these; they'll make you laugh. This one's from a Dutchman. He's got the biggest car I ever saw in my life. I was with him in the spring. He writes to me sometimes. Father got wind of it, and now he watches out to see if there's any money in the envelopes – the dirty dog! But I know a trick worth two of that! I've told all my friends to address their letters to the bakery on the corner. The baker's son is a pal of mine ...'

'Do you ever hear from Peter?' I asked.

Otto regarded me very solemnly for a moment: 'Christoph?'

'Yes?'

'Will you do me a favour?'

'What is it?' I asked cautiously: Otto always chose the least expected moments to ask for a small loan.

'Please . . .' he was gently reproachful, 'please, never mention Peter's name to me again . . .'

'Oh, all right,' I said, very much taken aback: 'If you'd rather not.'

'You see, Christoph . . . Peter hurt me very much. I thought he was my friend. And then, suddenly, he left me – all alone . . .'

Down in the murky pit of the courtyard where the fog, in this clammy autumn weather, never lifted, the street singers and musicians succeeded each other in a performance which was nearly continuous. There were parties of boys with mandolins, an old man who played the concertina and a father who sang with his little girls. Easily the favourite tune was: *Aus der Jugendzeit*. I often heard it a dozen times in one morning. The father of the girls was paralysed and could only make desperate throttled noises like a donkey; but the daughters sang with the energy of fiends: '*Sie kommt, sie kommt nicht mehr!*' they screamed in unison, like demons of the air, rejoicing in the frustration of mankind. Occasionally a groschen, screwed in a corner of newspaper, was tossed down from a window high above. It hit the pavement and ricocheted like a bullet, but the little girls never flinched.

Now and then the visiting nurse called to see Frau Nowak, shook her head over the sleeping arrangements and went away again. The inspector of housing, a pale young man with an open collar (which he obviously wore on principle), came also and took copious notes. The attic, he told Frau Nowak, absolutely insanitary and uninhabitable. He had a slightly reproachful air as he said this, as though we ourselves were partly to blame. Frau Nowak bitterly resented these visits. They were, she thought, simply attempts to spy on her. She was haunted by the fear that the nurse or the inspector would look in at a moment when the flat was untidy. So deep were her suspicions that she even told lies – pretending that the leak in the roof wasn't serious – to get them out of the house as quickly as possible.

Another regular visitor was the Jewish tailor and outfitter, who sold clothes of all kinds on the instalment plan. He was small and gentle and very persuasive. All day long he made his rounds of the tenements in the district, collecting fifty pfennigs here, a mark there, scratching up his precarious livelihood, like a hen, from this apparently barren soil. He never pressed hard for money; preferring to urge his debtors to take more of his goods and embark upon a fresh series of payments. Two years ago Frau Nowak had bought a suit and an overcoat for Otto for three hundred marks. The suit and the overcoat had been worn out long ago, but the money was not nearly repaid. Shortly after my arrival Frau Nowak invested in clothes for Grete to the value of seventy-five marks. The tailor made no objection at all.

The whole neighbourhood owed him money. Yet he was not unpopular: he enjoyed the status of a public character, whom people curse without real malice. 'Perhaps Lothar's right,' Frau Nowak would sometimes say: 'When Hitler comes, he'll show these Jews a thing or two. They won't be so cheeky then.' But when I suggested that Hitler, if he got his own way, would remove the tailor altogether, then Frau Nowak would immediately change her tone: 'Oh, I shouldn't like that to happen. After all, he makes very good clothes. Besides, a Jew will always let you have time if you're in difficulties. You wouldn't catch a Christian giving credit like he does ... You ask the people round here, Herr Christoph: they'd never turn out the Jews.'

Towards evening Otto, who had spent the day in gloomy lounging – either lolling about the flat or chatting with his friends downstairs at the courtyard entrance – would begin to brighten up. When I got back from work I generally found him changing already from his sweater and knickerbockers into his best suit, with its shoulders padded out to points, small tight double-breasted waistcoat and bell-bottomed trousers. He had quite a large selection of ties and it took him half an hour at least to choose one of them and to knot it to his satisfaction. He stood smirking in front of the cracked triangle of looking-glass in the kitchen, his pink plum-face dimpled with conceit, getting in Frau Nowak's way and disregarding all her protests. As soon as supper was over he was going out dancing.

I generally went out in the evenings, too. However tired I was, I couldn't go to sleep immediately after my evening meal: Grete and her parents were often in bed by nine o'clock. So I went to the cinema or sat in a café and read the newspapers and yawned. There was nothing else to do.

At the end of our street there was a cellar *lokal* called the Alexander Casino. Otto showed it to me one evening, when we happened to leave the house together. You went down four steps from the street level, opened the door, pushed aside the heavy leather curtain which kept out the draught and found yourself in a long, low, dingy room. It was lit by red Chinese lanterns and festooned with dusty paper streamers. Round the walls stood wicker tables and big shabby settees which looked like the seats of English third-class railway-carriages. At the far end were trellis-work alcoves, arboured over with imitation cherry-blossom twined on wires. The whole place smelt damply of beer.

I had been here before: a year ago, in the days when Fritz Wendel used to take me on Saturday evening excursions round 'the dives' of the city. It was all just as we had left it; only less sinister, less picturesque, symbolic no longer of a tremendous truth about the meaning of existence – because, this time, I wasn't in the least drunk. The same proprietor, an ex-boxer, rested his immense stomach on the bar, the same hangdog waiter shuffled forward in his soiled white coat: two girls, the very same, perhaps, were dancing together to the wailing of the loud-speaker. A group of youths in sweaters and leather jackets were playing Sheep's Head; the spectators leaning over to see the cards. A boy with tattooed arms sat by the stove, deep in a crime shocker. His shirt was open at the neck, with the sleeves rolled up to his armpits; he wore shorts and socks, as if about to take part in a race. Over in the far alcove, a man and a boy were sitting together. The boy had a round childish face and heavy reddened eyelids which looked swollen as if from lack of sleep. He was relating something to the elderly, shaven-headed, respectable-looking man, who sat rather unwillingly listening and smoking a short cigar. The boy told his story carefully and with great patience. At intervals, to emphasize a point, he laid his hand on the elderly man's knee and looked up into his face, watching its every movement shrewdly and intently, like a doctor with a nervous patient.

Later on, I got to know this boy quite well. He was called Pieps. He was a great traveller. He ran away from home at the age of fourteen because his father, a woodcutter in the Thuringian Forest, used to beat him. Pieps set out to walk to Hamburg. At Hamburg he stowed away on a ship bound for Antwerp and from Antwerp he walked back into Germany and along the Rhine. He had been in Austria, too, and Czechoslovakia. He was full of songs and stories and jokes: he had an extraordinarily cheerful and happy nature, sharing what he had with his friends and never worrying where his next meal was coming from. He was a clever pickpocket and worked chiefly in an amusement-hall in the Friedrichstrasse, not far from the Passage, which was full of detectives and getting too dangerous nowadays. In this amusement-hall there were punch-balls and peepshows and try-your-grip machines. Most of the boys from the Alexander Casino spent their afternoons there, while their girls were out working the Friedrichstrasse and the Linden for possible pickups.

Pieps lived together with his two friends, Gerhardt and Kurt, in a cellar on the canal-bank, near the station of the overhead railway. The cellar belonged to Gerhardt's aunt, an elderly Friedrichstrasse whore, whose legs and arms were tattooed with snakes, birds and flowers. Gerhardt was a tall boy with a vague, silly unhappy smile. He did not pick pockets, but stole from the big department-stores. He had never yet been caught, perhaps because of the lunatic brazenness of his thefts. Stupidly grinning, he would stuff things into his pockets right under the noses of the shop-assistants. He gave everything he stole to his aunt, who cursed him for his laziness and kept him very short of money. One day, when we were together, he took from his pocket a brightly coloured lady's leather belt: 'Look, Christoph, isn't it pretty?'

'Where did you get it from?'

'From Landauers',' Gerhardt told me. 'Why . . . what are you smiling at?'

'You see, the Landauers are friends of mine. It seems funny – that's all.'

At once, Gerhardt's face was the picture of dismay: 'You won't tell them, Christoph, will you?'

'No,' I promised. 'I won't.'

Kurt came to the Alexander Casino less often than the others. I could understand him better than I could understand Pieps of Gerhardt, because he was consciously unhappy. He had a reckless, fatal streak in his character, a capacity for pure sudden flashes of rage against the hopelessness of his life. The Germans call it *Wut*. He would sit silent in his corner, drinking rapidly, drumming with his fists on the table, imperious and sullen. Then, suddenly, he would jump to his feet, exclaim: '*Ach, Scheiss!*' and go striding out. In this mood, he picked quarrels deliberately with the other boys, fighting them three or four at a time, until he was flung out into the street, half stunned and covered with blood. On these occasions even Pieps and Gerhardt joined against him as against a public danger: they hit him as hard as anyone else and dragged him home between them afterwards without the least malice for the black eyes he often managed to give them. His behaviour did not appear to surprise them in the least. They were all good friends again next day.

By the time I arrived back Herr and Frau Nowak had probably been asleep for two or three hours. Otto generally arrived later still. Yet Herr Nowak, who resented so much else in his son's behaviour, never seemed to mind getting up and opening the door to him, whatever the time of night. For some strange reason, nothing would induce the Nowaks to let either of us have a latchkey. They couldn't sleep unless the door was bolted as well as locked.

In these tenements each lavatory served for four flats. Ours was on the floor below. If, before retiring, I wished to relieve nature, there was a second journey to be made through the living-room in the dark to the kitchen, skirting the table, avoiding the chairs, trying not to collide with the head of the Nowaks' bed or jolt the bed in which Lothar and Grete were sleeping. However cautiously I moved, Frau Nowak would wake up: she seemed to be able to see me in the dark, and embarrassed me with polite directions: 'No, Herr Christoph – not there, if you please. In the bucket on the left, by the stove.'

Lying in bed, in the darkness, in my tiny corner of the enormous human warren of the tenements, I could hear, with uncanny precision, every sound which came up from the courtyard below. The shape of the court must have acted as a gramophone-horn. There was someone going downstairs: our neighbour, Herr Müller, probably: he had a night-shift on the railway. I listened to his steps getting fainter, flight by flight; then they crossed the court, clear and sticky on the wet stone. Straining my ears, I heard, or fancied I heard, the grating of the key in the lock of the big street door. A moment later, the door closed with a deep, hollow boom. And now, from the next room, Frau Nowak had an outburst of coughing. In the silence which followed it, Lothar's bed creaked as he turned over muttering something indistinct and threatening in his sleep. Somewhere on the other side of the court a baby began to scream, a window was slammed to, something very heavy, deep in the innermost recesses of the building, thudded dully against a wall. It was alien and mysterious and uncanny, like sleeping out in the jungle alone.

Sunday was a long day at the Nowaks. There was nowhere to go in this wretched weather. We were all of us at home. Grete and Herr Nowak were watching a trap for sparrows which Herr Nowak had made and fixed up in the window. They sat there, hour by hour, intent upon it. The string which worked the trap was in Grete's hand. Occasionally, they giggled at each other and looked at me. I was sitting on the opposite side of the table, frowning at a piece of paper on which I had writ-

ten: 'But, Edward, can't you *see*?' I was trying to get on with
my novel. It was about a family who lived in a large country
house on unearned incomes and were very unhappy. They
spent their time explaining to each other why they couldn't
enjoy their lives; and some of the reasons – though I say it
myself – were most ingenious. Unfortunately I found myself
taking less and less interest in my unhappy family: the atmosphere of the Nowak household was not very inspiring. Otto,
in the inner room with the door open, was amusing himself
by balancing ornaments on the turntable of an old gramophone, which was now minus sound-box and tone-arm, to see
how long it would be before they flew off and smashed. Lothar
was filing keys and mending locks for the neighbours, his pale
sullen face bent over his work in obstinate concentration. Frau
Nowak, who was cooking, began a sermon about the Good and
the Worthless Brother: 'Look at Lothar. Even when he's out
of a job he keeps himself occupied. But all you're good for is
to smash things. You're no son of mine.'

Otto lolled sneering on his bed, occasionally spitting out
an obscene word or making a farting noise with his lips.
Certain tones of his voice were maddening: they made one
want to hurt him – and he knew it. Frau Nowak's shrill scolding rose to a scream:

'I've a good mind to turn you out of the house! What have
you ever done for us? When there's any work going you're too
tired to do it; but you're not too tired to go gallivanting about
half the night – you wicked unnatural good-for-nothing . . .'

Otto sprang to his feet, and began dancing about the room
with cries of animal triumph. Frau Nowak picked up a piece of
soap and flung it at him. He dodged, and it smashed the
window. After this Frau Nowak sat down and began to cry.
Otto ran to her at once and began to soothe her with noisy
kisses. Neither Lothar nor Herr Nowak took much notice of
the row. Herr Nowak seemed even rather to have enjoyed it:
he winked at me slyly. Later, the hole in the window was
stopped with a piece of cardboard. It remained unmended;
adding one more to the many draughts in the attic.

During supper, we were all jolly. Herr Nowak got up from

the table to give imitations of the different ways in which Jews and Catholics pray. He fell down on his knees and bumped his head several times vigorously on the ground, gabbling nonsense which was supposed to represent Hebrew and Latin prayers: 'Koolyvotchka, koolyvotchka, koolyvotchka. Amen.' Then he told stories of executions, to the horror and delight of Grete and Frau Nowak: 'William the First – the old William – never signed a death-warrant; and do you know why? Because once, quite soon after he'd come to the throne, there was a celebrated murder-case and for a long time the judges couldn't agree whether the prisoner was guilty or innocent, but at last they condemned him to be executed. They put him on the scaffold and the executioner took his axe – so; and swung it – like this; and brought it down: *Kernack!* (They're all trained men, of course: You or I couldn't cut a man's head off with one stroke, if they gave us a thousand marks.) And the head fell into the basket – flop!' Herr Nowak rolled up his eyes, let his tongue hang out from the corner of his mouth and gave a really most vivid and disgusting imitation of the decapitated head: 'And then the head spoke, all by itself, and said: "I am innocent!" (Of course, it was only the nerves; but it spoke, just as plainly as I'm speaking now.) "I am innocent!" it said ... And a few months later, another man confessed on his death-bed that he'd been the real murderer. So, after that, William never signed a death-warrant again!'

In the Wassertorstrasse one week was much like another. Our leaky stuffy little attic smelt of cooking and bad drains. When the living-room stove was alight, we could hardly breathe; when it wasn't we froze. The weather had turned very cold. Frau Nowak tramped the streets, when she wasn't at work, from the clinic to the board of health offices and back again: for hours she waited on benches in draughty corridors or puzzled over complicated application-forms. The doctors couldn't agree about her case. One was in favour of sending her to a sanatorium at once. Another thought she was too far gone to be worth sending at all – and told her so. Another assured her that there was nothing serious the matter: she merely

needed a fortnight in the Alps. Frau Nowak listened to all
three of them with the greatest respect and never failed to impress upon me, in describing these interviews, that each was
the kindest and cleverest professor to be found in the whole of
Europe.

She returned home, coughing and shivering, with sodden
shoes, exhausted and semi-hysterical. No sooner was she inside
the flat than she began scolding at Grete or at Otto, quite
automatically, like a clockwork doll unwinding its spring:

'You mark my words – you'll end in prison! I wish I'd
packed you off to a reformatory when you were fourteen. It
might have done you some good . . . And to think that, in my
whole family, we've never had anybody before who wasn't
respectable and decent!'

"*You* respectable!' Otto sneered: 'When you were a girl you
went around with every pair of trousers you could find.'

'I forbid you to speak to me like that! Do you hear? I forbid
you! Oh, I wish I'd died before I bore you, you wicked, unnatural child!'

Otto skipped around her, dodging her blows, wild with glee
at the row he had started. In his excitement he pulled hideous
grimaces.

'He's mad!' exclaimed Frau Nowak: 'Just look at him now,
Herr Christoph. I ask you, isn't he just a raving madman?
I must take him to the hospital to be examined.'

This idea appealed to Otto's romantic imagination. Often,
when we were alone together, he would tell me with tears in his
eyes:

'I shan't be here much longer, Christoph. My nerves are
breaking down. Very soon they'll come and take me away.
They'll put me in a strait-waistcoat and feed me through a
rubber tube. And when you come to visit me, I shan't know
who you are.'

Frau Nowak and Otto were not the only ones with 'nerves.'
Slowly but surely the Nowaks were breaking down my powers
of resistance. Every day I found the smell from the kitchen
sink a little nastier: every day Otto's voice when quarrelling
seemed harsher and his mother's a little shriller. Grete's whine

made me set my teeth. When Otto slammed a door I winced irritably. At nights I couldn't get to sleep unless I was half drunk. Also, I was secretly worrying about an unpleasant and mysterious rash: it might be due to Frau Nowak's cooking, or worse.

I now spent most of my evenings at the Alexander Casino. At a table in the corner by the stove I wrote letters, talked to Pieps and Gerhardt or simply amused myself by watching the other guests. The place was usually very quiet. We all sat round or lounged at the bar, waiting for something to happen. No sooner came the sound of the outer door than a dozen pairs of eyes were turned to see what new visitor would emerge from behind the leather curtain. Generally, it was only a biscuit-seller with his basket, or a Salvation Army girl with her collecting-box and tracts. If the biscuit-seller had been doing good business or was drunk he would throw dice with us for packets of sugar-wafers. As for the Salvation Army girl, she rattled her way drably round the room, got nothing and departed, without making us feel in the least uncomfortable. Indeed, she had become so much a part of the evening's routine that Gerhardt and Pieps did not even make jokes about her when she was gone. Then an old man would shuffle in, whisper something to the barman and retire with him into the room behind the bar. He was a cocaine-addict. A moment later he reappeared, raised his hat to all of us with a vague courteous gesture, and shuffled out. The old man had a nervous tic and kept shaking his head all the time, as if saying to Life: No. No. No.

Sometimes the police came, looking for wanted criminals or escaped reformatory boys. Their visits were usually expected and prepared for. At any rate you could always, as Pieps explained to me, make a last-minute exit through the lavatory window into the courtyard at the back of the house: 'But you must be careful, Christoph,' he added: 'Take a good big jump. Or you'll fall down the coal-shoot and into the cellar. I did, once. And Hamburg Werner, who was coming after me, laughed so much that the bulls caught him.'

On Saturday and Sunday evenings the Alexander Casino was full. Visitors from the West End arrived, like ambassadors from another country. There were a good number of foreigners – Dutchmen mostly, and Englishmen. The Englishmen talked in loud, high, excited voices, they discussed communism and Van Gogh and the best restaurants. Some of them seemed a little scared: perhaps they expected to be knifed in this den of thieves. Pieps and Gerhardt sat at their tables and mimicked their accents, cadging drinks and cigarettes. A stout man in horn spectacles asked: 'Were you at that delicious party Bill gave for the negro singers?' And a young man with a monocle murmured: 'All the poetry in the world is in that face.' I knew what he was feeling at that moment: I could sympathize with, even envy him. But it was saddening to know that, two weeks hence, he would boast about his exploits here to a select party of clubmen or dons – warmed discreet smilers around a table furnished with historic silver and legendary port. It made me feel older.

At last the doctors made up their minds: Frau Nowak was to be sent to the sanatorium after all: and quite soon – shortly before Christmas. As soon as she heard this she ordered a new dress from the tailor. She was as excited and pleased as if she had been invited to a party: 'The matrons are always very particular, you know, Herr Christoph. They see to it that we keep ourselves neat and tidy. If we don't we get punished – and quite right, too ... I'm sure I shall enjoy being there,' Frau Nowak sighed, 'if only I can stop myself worrying about the family. What they'll do when I'm gone, goodness only knows. They're as helpless as a lot of sheep ...' In the evenings she spent hours stitching warm flannel underclothes, smiling to herself, like a woman who is expecting a child.

On the afternoon of my departure Otto was very depressed.
'Now you're going, Christoph, I don't know what'll happen to me. Perhaps, six months from now, I shan't be alive at all.'
'You got on all right before I came, didn't you?'
'Yes ... but now mother's going, too. I don't suppose father'll give me anything to eat.'

'What rubbish!'

'Take me with you, Christoph. Let me be your servant. I could be very useful, you know. I could cook for you and mend your clothes and open the door for your pupils ...' Otto's eyes brightened as he admired himself in this new role. 'I'd wear a little white jacket – or perhaps blue would be better, with silver buttons ...'

'I'm afraid you're a luxury I can't afford.'

'Oh, but, Christoph, I shouldn't want any wages, of course.' Otto paused, feeling that this offer had been a bit too generous. 'That is,' he added cautiously, 'only just a mark or two to go dancing, now and then.'

'I'm very sorry.'

We were interrupted by the return of Frau Nowak. She had come home early to cook me a farewell meal. Her string-bag was full of things she had bought; she had tired herself out carrying it. She shut the kitchen-door behind her with a sigh and began to bustle about at once, her nerves on edge, ready for a row.

'Why, Otto, you've let the stove go out! After I specially told you to keep an eye on it! Oh, dear, can't I rely on anybody in this house to help me with a single thing?'

'Sorry, mother,' said Otto. 'I forgot.'

'Of course you forgot! Do you ever remember anything? You *forgot*!' Frau Nowak screamed at him, her features puckered into a sharp little stabbing point of fury: 'I've worked myself into my grave for you, and that's my thanks. When I'm gone I hope your father'll turn you out into the streets. We'll see how you like that! You great, lazy, hulking lump! Get out of my sight, do you hear! Get out of my sight!'

'All right. Christoph, you hear what she says?' Otto turned to me, his face convulsed with rage; at that moment the resemblance between them was quite startling; they were like creatures demoniacally possessed. 'I'll make her sorry for it as long as she lives!'

He turned and plunged into the inner bedroom, slamming the rickety door behind him. Frau Nowak turned at once to the stove and began shovelling out the cinders. She was trem-

bling all over and coughing violently. I helped her, putting fire-
wood and pieces of coal into her hands; she took them from
me blindly, without a glance or a word. Feeling, as usual, that I
was only in the way. I went into the living-room and stood
stupidly by the window, wishing that I could simply disappear.
I had had enough. On the window-sill lay a stump of pencil. I
picked it up and drew a small circle on the wood, thinking: I
have left my mark. Then I remembered how I had done exactly
the same thing, years ago, before leaving a boarding-house in
North Wales. In the inner room all was quiet. I decided to confront Otto's sulks. I had still got my suit-cases to pack.

When I opened the door Otto was sitting on his bed. He was
staring as if hypnotized at a gash in his left wrist, from which
the blood was trickling down over his open palm and spilling in
big drops on the floor. In his right hand, between finger and
thumb, he held a safety-razor blade. He didn't resist when I
snatched it from him. The wound itself was nothing much; I
bandaged it with his handkerchief. Otto seemed to turn faint
for a moment and lolled against my shoulder.

'How on earth did you manage to do it?'

'I wanted to show her,' said Otto. He was very pale. He had
evidently given himself a nasty scare: 'You shouldn't have
stopped me, Christoph.'

'You little idiot,' I said angrily, for he had frightened me,
too: 'One of these days you'll really hurt yourself – by mistake.'

Otto gave me a long, reproachful look. Slowly his eyes filled
with tears.

'What does it matter, Christoph? I'm no good ... What'll become of me, do you suppose, when I'm older?'

'You'll get work.'

'Work ...' The very thought made Otto burst into tears.
Sobbing violently, he smeared the back of his hand across
his nose.

I pulled out the handkerchief from my pocket. 'Here. Take
this.'

'Thanks, Christoph ...' He wiped his eyes mournfully and
blew his nose. Then something about the handkerchief itself

caught his attention. he began to examine it, listlessly at first, then with extreme interest.

'Why, Christoph,' he exclaimed indignantly, 'this is one of mine!'

One afternoon, a few days after Christmas, I visited the Wassertorstrasse again. The lamps were alight already, as I turned in under the archway and entered the long, damp street, patched here and there with dirty snow. Weak yellow gleams shone out from the cellar shops. At a hand-cart under a gas-flare, a cripple was selling vegetables and fruit. A crowd of youths, with raw, sullen faces, stood watching two boys fighting at a doorway: a girl's voice screamed excitedly as one of them tripped and fell. Crossing the muddy courtyard, inhaling the moist, familiar rottenness of the tenement buildings, I thought: Did I really ever live here? Already, with my comfortable bed-sitting room in the West End and my excellent new job, I had become a stranger to the slums.

The lights on the Nowaks' staircase were out of order: it was pitch-dark. I groped my way upstairs without much difficulty and banged on their door. I made as much noise as I could because, to judge from the shouting and singing and shrieks of laughter within, a party was in progress.

'Who's there?' bawled Herr Nowak's voice.

'Christoph.'

'Aha! Christoph! Anglais! Englisch Man! Come in! Come in!'

The door was flung open. Herr Nowak swayed unsteadily on the threshold, with arms open to embrace me. Behind him stood Grete, shaking like a jelly, with tears of laughter pouring down her cheeks. There was nobody else to be seen.

'Good old Christoph!' cried Herr Nowak, thumping me on the back. 'I said to Grete: I know he'll come. Christoph won't desert us!' With a large burlesque gesture of welcome he pushed me violently into the living-room. The whole place was fearfully untidy. Clothing of various kinds lay in a confused heap on one of the beds; on the other were scattered cups, saucers, shoes, knives and forks. On the sideboard was a frying-

pan full of dried fat. The room was lighted by three candles
stuck into empty beer-bottles.

'All light's been cut off,' explained Herr Nowak, with a negli-
gent sweep of his arm: 'The bill isn't paid ... Must pay it
sometime, of course. Never mind – it's nicer like this, isn't it?
Come on, Grete, let's light up the Christmas tree.'

The Christmas tree was the smallest I had ever seen. It was
so tiny and feeble that it could only carry one candle, at the
very top. A single thin strand of tinsel was draped around it.
Herr Nowak dropped several lighted matches on the floor before he could get the candle to burn. If I hadn't stamped them
out the table-cloth might easily have caught fire.

'Where are Lothar and Otto?' I asked.

'Don't know. Somewhere about ... They don't show themselves much, nowadays – it doesn't suit them, here ... Never
mind, we're quite happy by ourselves, aren't we Grete?' Herr
Nowak executed a few elephantine dance-steps and began to
sing:

'O *Tannenbaum! O Tannenbaum!* ... Come on, Christoph,
all together now! *Wie treu sind Deine Blätter!*'

After this was over I produced my presents: cigars for Herr
Nowak, for Grete chocolates and a clockwork mouse. Herr
Nowak then brought out a bottle of beer from under the bed.
After a long search for his spectacles, which were finally discovered hanging on the water-tap in the kitchen, he read me a
letter which Frau Nowak had written from the sanatorium.
He repeated every sentence three or four times, got lost in
the middle, swore, blew his nose, and picked his ears. I could
hardly understand a word. Then he and Grete began playing
with the clockwork mouse, letting it run about the table,
shrieking and roaring whenever it neared the edge. The mouse
was such a success that my departure was managed briefly,
without any fuss. 'Good-bye, Christoph. Come again soon,' said
Herr Nowak and turned back to the table at once. He and Grete
were bending over it with the eagerness of gamblers as I
made my way out of the attic.

Not long after this I had a call from Otto himself. He had

come to ask me if I would go with him the next Sunday to see Frau Nowak. The sanatorium had its monthly visiting-day: there would be a special bus running from Hallesches Tor.

'You needn't pay for me, you know,' Otto added grandly. He was fairly shining with self-satisfaction.

'That's very handsome of you, Otto ... A new suit?'

'Do you like it?'

'It must have cost a good bit.'

'Two hundred and fifty marks.'

'My word! Has your ship come home?'

'Otto smirked: 'I'm seeing a lot of Trude now. Her uncle's left her some money. Perhaps, in the spring, we'll get married.'

'Congratulations ... I suppose you're still living at home?'

'Oh, I look in there occasionally,' Otto drew down the corners of his mouth in a grimace of languid distaste, 'but father's always drunk.'

'Disgusting, isn't it?' I mimicked his tone. We both laughed.

'My goodness, Christoph, is it as late as that? I must be getting along ... Till Sunday. Be good.'

We arrived at the sanatorium about midday.

There was a bumpy cart-track winding for several kilometres through snowy pine-woods and then, suddenly, a Gothic brick gateway like the entrance to a churchyard, with big red buildings rising behind. The bus stopped. Otto and I were the last passengers to get out. We stood stretching ourselves and blinking at the bright snow: out here in the country everything was dazzling white. We were all very stiff, for the bus was only a covered van, with packing-cases and school-benches for seats. The seats had not shifted much during the journey, for we had been packed together as tightly as books on a shelf.

And now the patients came running out to meet us – awkward padded figures muffled in shawls and blankets, stumbling and slithering on the trampled ice of the path. They were in such a hurry that their blundering charge ended in a slide. They shot skidding into the arms of their friends and relations, who staggered under the violence of the collision. One couple, amid shrieks of laughter, had tumbled over.

'Otto!'

'Mother!'

'So you've really come! How well you're looking!'

'Of course we've come, mother! What did you expect?'
Frau Nowak disengaged herself from Otto to shake hands with
me. 'How do you do, Herr Christoph?'

She looked years younger. Her plump, oval, innocent face,
lively and a trifle crafty, with its small peasant eyes, was like the
face of a young girl. Her cheeks were brightly dabbed with
colour. She smiled as though she could never stop.

'Ah, Herr Christoph, how nice of you to come! How nice of
you to bring Otto to visit me!'

She uttered a brief, queer, hysterical little laugh. We mounted
some steps into the house. The smell of the warm, clean, anti-
septic building entered my nostrils like a breath of fear.

'They've put me in one of the smaller wards,' Frau Nowak
told us. 'There's only four of us altogether. We get up to all
sorts of games.' Proudly throwing open the door, she made
the introductions: 'This is Muttchen – she keeps us in order!
And this is Erna. And this is Erika – our baby!'

Erika was a weedy blonde girl of eighteen, who giggled:
'So here's the famous Otto! We've been looking forward to
seeing him for weeks!'

Otto smiled subtly, discreetly, very much at his ease. His
brand new brown suit was vulgar beyond words; so were his
lilac spats and his pointed yellow shoes. On his finger was an
enormous signet-ring with a square, chocolate-coloured stone.
Otto was extremely conscious of it and kept posing his hand in
graceful attitudes, glancing down furtively to admire the effect.
Frau Nowak simply couldn't leave him alone. She must keep
hugging him and pinching his cheeks.

'Doesn't he look well!' she exclaimed. 'Doesn't he look
splendid! Why, Otto, you're so big and strong, I believe you
could pick me up with one hand!'

Old Muttchen had a cold, they said. She wore a bandage
round her throat, tight under the high collar of her old-
fashioned black dress. She seemed a nice old lady, but somehow
slightly obscene, like an old dog with sores. She sat on the edge

of her bed with the photographs of her children and grand-children on the table beside her, like prizes she had won. She looked slyly pleased, as though she were glad to be so ill. Frau Nowak told us that Muttchen had been three times in this sanatorium already. Each time she had been discharged as cured, but within nine months or a year she would have a re-lapse and have to be sent back again.

'Some of the cleverest professors in Germany have come here to examine her,' Frau Nowak added, with pride, 'but you always fool them, don't you, Muttchen dear?'

The old lady nodded, smiling, like a clever child which is being praised by its elders.

'And Erna is here for the second time,' Frau Nowak continued. 'The doctors said she'd be all right; but she didn't get enough to eat. So now she's come back to us, haven't you, Erna?'

'Yes, I've come back,' Erna agreed.

She was a skinny, bobbed-haired woman of about thirty-five, who must once have been very feminine, appealing, wistful, and soft. Now, in her extreme emaciation, she seemed possessed by a kind of desperate resolution, a certain defiance. She had immense, dark, hungry eyes. The wedding-ring was loose on her bony finger. When she talked and became excited her hands flitted tirelessly about in sequences of aimless gestures, like two shrivelled moths.

'My husband beat me and then ran away. The night he went he gave me such a thrashing that I had the marks afterwards for months. He was such a great strong man. He nearly killed me.' She spoke calmly, deliberately, yet with a certain suppressed excitement, never taking her eyes from my face. Her hungry glance bored into my brain, reading eagerly what I was thinking. 'I dream about him now, sometimes,' she added, as if faintly amused.

Otto and I sat down at the table while Frau Nowak fussed around us with coffee and cakes which one of the sisters had brought. Everything which happened to me to-day was curiously without impact: my senses were muffled, insulated, functioning as if in a vivid dream. In this calm, white room, with its great windows looking out over the silent snowy pine-woods – the Christmas-tree on the table, the paper festoons above the beds, the nailed-up photographs, the plate of heart-shaped chocolate biscuits – these four women lived and moved. My eyes could explore every corner of their world: the tem-perature-charts, the fire extinguisher, the leather screen by the door. Dressed daily in their best clothes, their clean hands no longer pricked by the needle or roughened from scrubbing, they lay out on the terrace, listening to the wireless, forbidden to talk. Women being shut up together in this room had bred an atmosphere which was faintly nauseating, like soiled linen locked in a cupboard without air. They were playful with each other and shrill, like overgrown schoolgirls. Frau Nowak and Erika indulged in sudden furtive bouts of ragging. They plucked at each other's clothes, scuffled silently, exploded into shrilly strained laughter. They were showing off in front of us.

'You don't know how we've looked forward to to-day,' Erna told me. 'To see a real live man!'

Frau Nowak giggled.

'Erika was such an innocent girl until she came here ... You didn't know anything, did you, Erika?'

Erika sniggered.

'I've learnt enough since then ...'

'Yes, I should think you have! Would you believe it, Herr Christoph – her aunt sent her this little mannikin for Christ-mas, and now she takes it to bed with her every night, because she says she must have a man in her bed!'

Erika laughed boldly. 'Well, it's better than nothing, isn't it?'

She winked at Otto, who rolled his eyes, pretending to be shocked.

After lunch Frau Nowak had to put in an hour's rest. So Erna and Erika took possession of us for a walk in the grounds.

'We'll show them the cemetery first,' Erna said.

The cemetery was for pet animals belonging to the sana-torium staff which had died. There were about a dozen little crosses and tombstones, pencilled with mock-heroic inscrip-tions in verse. Dead birds were buried there and white mice and rabbits, and a bat which had been found frozen after a storm.

'It makes you feel sad to think of them lying there, doesn't it?' said Erna. She scooped away the snow from one of the graves. There were tears in her eyes.

But, as we walked away down the path, both she and Erika were very gay. We laughed and threw snowballs at each other. Otto picked up Erika and pretended he was going to throw her into a snowdrift. A little further on we passed close to a summer-house, standing back from the path on a mound among the trees. A man and a woman were just coming out of it.

'That's Frau Klemke,' Erna told me. 'She's got her husband here to-day. Just think, that old hut's the only place in the whole grounds where two people can be alone together ...'

'It must be pretty cold in this weather.'

'Of course it is! To-morrow her temperature will be up again and she'll have to stay in bed for a fortnight ... But who cares! If I were in her place I'd do the same myself.' Erna squeezed my arm: 'We've got to live while we're young, haven't we?'

'Of course we have!'

Erna looked up quickly into my face; her big dark eyes fastened on to mine like hooks; I could imagine I felt them pulling me down.

'I'm not really a consumptive, you know, Christoph ... You didn't think I was, did you, just because I'm here?'

'No, Erna, of course I didn't.'

'Lots of the girls here aren't. They just need looking after for a bit, like me ... The doctor says that if I take care of myself I shall be as strong as ever I was ... And what do you think the first thing is I shall do when they let me out of here?'

'What?'

'First I shall get my divorce, and then I shall find a husband.' Erna laughed, with a kind of bitter triumph. 'That won't take me long – I can promise you!'

After tea we sat upstairs in the ward. Frau Nowak had

borrowed a gramophone so that we could dance. I danced with
Erna. Erika danced with Otto. She was tomboyish and
clumsy, laughing loudly whenever she slipped or trod on his
toes. Otto, sleekly smiling, steered her backwards and forwards
with skill, his shoulders hunched in the fashionable chimpan-
zee stoop of Hallesches Tor. Old Muttchen sat looking on from
her bed. When I held Erna in my arms I felt her shivering all
over. It was almost dark now, but nobody suggested turning on
the light. After a while we stopped dancing and sat round in
a circle on the beds. Frau Nowak had begun to talk about her
childhood days, when she had lived with her parents on a farm
in East Prussia. 'We had a saw-mill of our own,' she told us,
'and thirty horses. My father's horses were the best in the district; he won prizes with them, many a time, at the show ...'
the ward was quite dark now. The windows were big pale rect-
angles in the darkness. Erna, sitting beside me on the bed, felt
down for my hand and squeezed it; then she reached behind me
and drew my arm round her body. She was trembling violently.
'Christoph ...' she whispered in my ear.

'... and in the summer time,' Frau Nowak was saying, 'we
used to go dancing in the big barn down by the river ...'

My mouth pressed against Erna's hot, dry lips. I had no
particular sensation of contact: all this was part of the long,
rather sinister symbolic dream which I seemed to have been
dreaming throughout the day. 'I'm so happy, this evening ...'
Erna whispered.

'The postmaster's son used to play the fiddle,' said Frau
Nowak. 'He played beautifully ... it made you want to cry ...'

From the bed on which Erika and Otto were sitting came
sounds of scuffling and a loud snigger: 'Otto, you naughty boy
... I'm surprised at you! I shall tell your mother!'

Five minutes later a sister came to tell us that the bus was
ready to start.

'My word, Christoph,' Otto whispered to me, as we were putting on our overcoats, 'I could have done anything I liked with
that girl! I felt her all over ... Did you have a good time with
yours? A bit skinny, wasn't she – but I bet she's hot stuff!'

Then we were clambering into the bus with the other passengers. The patients crowded round to say good-bye. Wrapped and hooded in their blankets, they might have been the members of an aboriginal forest tribe.

Frau Nowak had begun crying, though she tried hard to smile.

'Tell father I'll be back soon ...'

'Of course you will, mother! You'll soon be well now. You'll soon be home.'

'It's only a short time ...' sobbed Frau Nowak; the tears running down over her hideous frog-like smile. And suddenly she started coughing – her body seemed to break in half like a hinged doll. Clasping her hands over her breast, she uttered short yelping coughs like a desperate injured animal. The blanket slipped back from her head and shoulders: a wisp of hair, working loose from the knot, was getting into her eyes – she shook her head blindly to avoid it. Two sisters gently tried to lead her away, but at once she began to struggle furiously. She wouldn't go with them.

'Go in, mother,' begged Otto. He was almost in tears himself. 'Please go in! You'll catch your death of cold!'

'Write to me sometimes, won't you, Christoph?' Erna was clutching my hand as though she were drowning. Her eyes looked up at me with a terrifying intensity of unashamed despair. 'It doesn't matter if it's only a postcard ... just sign your name.'

'Of course I will ...'

They all thronged round us for a moment in the little circle of light from the panting bus, their lit faces ghastly like ghosts against the black stems of the pines. This was the climax of my dream: the instant of nightmare in which it would end. I had an absurb pang of fear that they were going to attack us – a gang of terrifyingly soft muffled shapes – clawing us from our seats, dragging us hungrily down, in dead silence. But the moment passed. They drew back – harmless, after all, as mere ghosts – into the darkness, while our bus, with a great churning of its wheels, lurched forward towards the city, through the deep unseen snow.

One night in October 1930, about a month after the Elections, there was a big row on the Leipzigerstrasse. Gangs of Nazi roughs turned out to demonstrate against the Jews. They manhandled some dark-haired, large-nosed pedestrians, and smashed the windows of all the Jewish shops. The incident was not, in itself, very remarkable; there were no deaths, very little shooting, not more than a couple of dozen arrests. I remember it only because it was my first introduction to Berlin politics.

Frl. Mayr, of course, was delighted: 'Serve them right!' she exclaimed. 'This town is sick with Jews. Turn over any stone, and a couple of them will crawl out. They're poisoning the very water we drink! They're strangling us, they're robbing us, they're sucking our life-blood. Look at all the big department stores: Wertheim, K.D.W., Landauers'. Who owns them? Filthy thieving Jews!'

'The Landauers are personal friends of mine,' I retorted icily, and left the room before Frl. Mayr had time to think of a suitable reply.

This wasn't strictly true. As a matter of fact, I had never met any member of the Landauer family in my life. But, before leaving England, I had been given a letter of introduction to them by a mutual friend. I mistrust letters of introduction, and should probably never have used this one, if it hadn't been for Frl. Mayr's remark. Now, perversely, I decided to write to Frau Landauer at once.

Natalia Landauer, as I saw her, for the first time, three days later, was a schoolgirl of eighteen. She had dark fluffy hair; far too much of it – it made her face, with its sparkling eyes, appear too long and too narrow. She reminded me of a young fox. She shook hands straight from the shoulder in the modern student manner. 'In here, please.' Her tone was peremptory and brisk.

The sitting-room was large and cheerful, pre-War in taste, a little over-furnished. Natalia had begun talking at once, with terrific animation, in eager stumbling English, showing me gramophone records, pictures, books. I wasn't allowed to look at anything for more than a moment:

'You like Mozart? Yes? Oh, I also! Vairy much! ... These picture is in the Kronprinz Palast. You have not seen it? I shall show you one day, yes? ... You are fond of Heine? Say quite truthfully, please.' She looked up from the bookcase, smiling, but with a certain schoolmarm severity: 'Read. It's beautiful, I find.'

I hadn't been in the house for more than a quarter of an hour before Natalia had put aside four books for me to take with me when I left – *Tonio Krüger*, Jacobsen's stories, a volume of Stefan George, Goethe's letters. 'You are to tell me your truthful opinion,' she warned me.

Suddenly a maid parted the sliding glass doors at the end of the room, and we found ourselves in the presence of Frau Landauer, a large, pale woman with a mole on her left cheek and her hair brushed back smooth into a knot, seated placidly at the dining-room table, filling glasses from a samovar with tea. There were plates of ham and cold cut wurst and a bowl of those thin wet slippery sausages which squirt you with hot water when their skins are punctured by a fork; as well as cheese, radishes, pumpernickel and bottled beer. 'You will drink beer,' Natalia ordered, returning one of the glasses of tea to her mother.

Looking round me, I noticed that the few available wall-spaces between pictures and cupboards were decorated with eccentric life-sized figures, maidens with flying hair or oblique-eyed gazelles, cut out of painted paper and fastened down with drawing-pins. They made a comically ineffectual protest against the bourgeois solidity of the mahogany furniture. I knew, without being told, that Natalia must have designed them. Yes, she'd made them and fixed them up there for a party; now she wanted to take them down, but her mother

wouldn't let her. They had a little argument about this –
evidently part of the domestic routine. 'Oh, but they're
tairrible, I find!' cried Natalia, in English. 'I think they're
very pretty,' replied Frau Landauer placidly, in German,
without raising her eyes from the plate, her mouth full of
pumpernickel and radish.

As soon as we had finished supper, Natalia made it clear
that I was to say a formal good-night to Frau Landauer. We
then returned to the sitting-room. She began to cross-examine
me. Where was my room? How much was I paying for it?
When I told her, she said immediately that I'd chosen quite the
wrong district (Wilmersdorf was far better), and that I'd been
swindled. I could have got exactly the same thing, with running water and central heating thrown in, for the same price.
'You should have asked me,' she added, apparently quite for-
getting that we'd met that evening for the first time: 'I
should have found it for you myself.'

'Your friend tells us you are a writer?' Natalia challenged
suddenly.

'Not a real writer,' I protested.

'But you have written a book? Yes?'

Yes, I had a written a book.

Natalia was triumphant: 'You have written a book and
you say you are not a writer. You are mad, I think.'

Then I had to tell her the whole history of *All The
Conspirators*, why it had that title, what it was about, when
it was published, and so forth.

'You will bring me a copy, please.'

'I haven't got one,' I told her, with satisfaction, 'and it's out
of print.'

This rather dashed Natalia for the moment, then she sniffed
eagerly at a new scent: 'And this what you will write in
Berlin? Tell me, please.'

To satisfy her, I began to tell the story of a story I had
written years before, for a college magazine at Cambridge. I
improved it as much as possible extempore, as I went along.
Telling this story again quite excited me – so much so that I
began to feel that the idea in it hadn't been so bad after all,

and that I might really be able to rewrite it. At the end of every sentence, Natalia pressed her lips tight together and nodded her head so violently that the hair flopped up and down over her face.

'Yes, yes,' she kept saying. 'Yes, yes.'

It was only after some minutes that I realized she wasn't taking in anything I said. She evidently couldn't understand my English, for I was talking much faster now, and not choosing my words. In spite of her tremendous devotional effort of concentration, I could see that she was noticing the way I parted my hair, and that my tie was worn shiny at the knot. She even flashed a furtive glance at my shoes. It would have been rude to stop short and most unkind to spoil Natalia's pleasure in the mere fact that I was talking so intimately to her about something which really interested me, although we were practically strangers.

When I had finished, she asked at once: 'And it will be ready — how soon?' For she had taken possession of the story, together with all my other affairs. I answered that I didn't know. I was lazy.

'You are lazy?' Natalia opened her eyes mockingly. 'So? Then I am sorry. I can't help you.'

Presently, I said that I must go. She came with me to the door: 'And you will bring me this story soon,' she persisted.

'Yes.'

'How soon?'

'Next week,' I feebly promised.

It was a fortnight before I called on the Landauers again. After dinner, when Frau Landauer had left the room, Natalia informed me that we were to go together to the cinema. 'We are the guests of my mother.' As we stood up to go, she suddenly grabbed two apples and an orange from the sideboard and stuffed them into my pockets. She had evidently made up her mind that I was suffering from undernourishment. I protested weakly.

'When you say another word, I am angry,' she warned me.

'And you have brought it?' she asked, as we were leaving the house.

Knowing perfectly well that she meant the story, I made my voice as innocent as I could: 'Brought what?'

'You know. What you promised.'

'I don't remember promising anything.'

'Don't *remember*?' Natalie laughed scornfully. 'Then I'm sorry. I can't help you.'

By the time we got to the cinema, she had forgiven me, however. The big film was a Pat and Patachon. Natalia remarked severely: 'You do not like this kind of film, I think? It isn't something clever enough for you?'

I denied that I only liked 'clever' films, but she was sceptical: 'Good. We shall see.'

All through the film, she kept glancing at me to see if I was laughing. At first, I laughed exaggeratedly. Then, getting tired of this, I stopped laughing altogether. Natalia got more and more impatient with me. Towards the end of the film, she even began to nudge me at moments when I should laugh. No sooner were the lights turned up, than she pounced:

'You see? I was right. You did not like it, no?'

'I liked it very much indeed.'

'Oh yes, I believe! And now say truthfully.'

'I have told you. I liked it.'

'But you did not laugh. You are sitting always with your face so . . .' Natalia tried to imitate me, 'and not once laughing.'

'I never laugh when I am amused,' I said.

'Oh yes, perhaps! That shall be one of your English customs, not to laugh?'

'No Englishman ever laughs when he's amused.'

'You wish I believe that? Then I will tell you your Englishmen are mad.'

'That remark is not very original.'

'And must always my remarks be so original, my dear sir?'

'When you are with me, yes.'

'Imbecile!'

We sat for a little in a café near the Zoo Station and ate ices. The ices were lumpy and tasted slightly of potato. Suddenly, Natalia began to talk about her parents:

'I do not understand what this modern books mean when they say: the mother and father always must have quarrel with the children. You know, it would be impossible that I can have quarrel with my parents. Impossible.'

Natalia looked hard at me to see whether I believed this. I nodded.

'Absolute impossible,' she repeated solemnly. 'Because I know that my father and my mother love me. And so they are thinking always not of themselves but of what is for me the best. My mother, you know, she is not strong. She is having sometimes the most tairrible headaches. And then, of course, I cannot leave her alone. Vairy often, I would like to go out to a cinema or theatre or concert, and my mother, she say nothing, but I look at her and see that she is not well, and so I say No, I have change my mind, I will not go. But never it happens that she say one word about the pain she is suffered. Never.'

(When next I called on the Landauers, I spent two marks fifty on roses for Natalia's mother. It was worth it. Never once did Frau Landauer have a headache on an evening when I proposed going out with Natalia.)

'My father will always that I have the best of everything,' Natalia continued. 'My father will always that I say: My parents are rich, I do not need to think for money.' Natalia sighed: 'But I am different than this. I await always that the worst will come. I know how things are in Germany to-day, and suddenly it can be that my father lose all. You know, that is happened once already? Before the war, my father has had a big factory in Posen. The War comes, and my father has to go. To-morrow, it can be here the same. But my father, he is such a man that to him it is equal. He can start with one pfennig and work and work until he gets all back.'

'And that is why,' Natalia went on, 'I wish to leave school and begin to learn something useful, that I can win my bread. I cannot know how long my parents have money. My father will that I make my Abitur and go to the university. But now I will speak with him and ask if I cannot go to Paris and study art. If I can draw and paint I can perhaps make my life; and also I will learn cookery. Do you know that I cannot cook, not the simplest thing?'

'Neither can I.'

'For a man, that is not so important, I find. But a girl must be prepared for all.'

'If I want,' added Natalia earnestly, 'I shall go away with the man I love and I shall live with him; even if we cannot become married it will not matter. Then I must be able to do all for myself, you understand? It is not enough to say: I have made my Abitur, I have my degree at the university. He will answer: "Please, where is my dinner?" '

There was a pause.

'You are not shocked at what I say just now,' asked Natalia suddenly. 'That I would live with a man without that we were married?'

'No, of course not.'

'Do not misunderstand me, please. I do not admirate the women who is going always from one man to another – that is all so,' Natalia made a gesture of distaste, 'so degenerated, I find.'

'You don't think that women should be allowed to change their minds?'

'I do not know. I do not understand such questions . . . But it is degenerated.'

I saw her home. Natalia had a trick of leading you right up on to the doorstep, and then, with extraordinary rapidity, shaking hands, whisking into the house and slamming the door in your face.

'You ring me up? Next week? Yes?' I can hear her voice now. And then the door slammed and she was gone without waiting for an answer.

Natalia avoided all contacts, direct and indirect. Just as she wouldn't stand chatting with me on her own doorstep, she preferred always, I noticed, to have a table between us if we sat down. She hated me to help her into her coat: 'I am not yet sixty years, my dear sir!' If we stood up to leave a

café or a restaurant and she saw my eye moving towards the
peg from which her coat hung, she would pounce instantly
upon it and carry it off with her into a corner, like an animal
guarding its food.

One evening, we went into a café and ordered two cups of
chocolate. When the chocolate came, we found that the wait-
ress had forgotten to bring Natalia a spoon. I'd already sipped
my cup and had stirred it with my spoon after sipping it. It
seemed quite natural to offer my spoon to Natalia, and I was
surprised and a little impatient when she refused it with
an expression of slight distaste. She declined even this indirect contact with my mouth.

Natalia got tickets for a concert of Mozart concertos. The
evening was not a success. The severe Corinthian hall was
chilly, and my eyes were uncomfortably dazzled by the classic
brilliance of the electric lights. The shiny wooden chairs were
austerely hard. The audience plainly regarded the concert as
a religious ceremony. Their taut, devotional enthusiasm oppressed me like a headache; I couldn't, for a moment, lose
consciousness of all those blind half-frowning, listening heads.
And despite Mozart, I couldn't help feeling: What an
extraordinary way this is of spending an evening!

On the way home, I was tired and sulky, and this resulted
in a little tiff with Natalia. She began it by talking about
Hippi Bernstein. It was Natalia who had got me my job with
the Bernsteins: she and Hippi went to the same school. A
couple of days before, I had given Hippi her first English
lesson.

'And how do you like her?' Natalia asked.

'Very much. Don't you?'

'Yes, I also ... But she's got two bad faults. I think you
will not have notice them yet?'

As I didn't rise to this, she added solemnly: 'You know, I
wish you would tell me truthfully what are *my* faults?'

In another mood, I should have found this amusing, and
even rather touching. As it was, I only thought: 'She's fishing,' and snapped:

'I don't know what you mean by "faults." I don't judge

people on a half-term-report basis. You'd better ask one of your teachers.'

This shut Natalia up for the moment. But, presently, she started again. Had I read any of the books she'd lent me?

I hadn't, but said: Yes, I'd read Jacobsen's *Frau Marie Grubbe*.

And what did you think of it?

'It's very good,' I said, peevish because guilty.

Natalia looked at me sharply: 'I'm afraid you are vairy insincere. You do not give your real meaning.'

I was suddenly, childishly cross:

'Of course I don't. Why should I? Arguments bore me. I don't intend to say anything which you're likely to disagree with.'

'But if that is so,' she was really dismayed, 'then it is no use for us to speak of anything seriously.'

'Of course it isn't.'

'Then shall we not talk at all?' asked poor Natalia.

'The best of all,' I said, 'would be for us to make noises like farmyard animals. I like hearing the sound of your voice but I don't care a bit what you're saying. So it'd be far better if we just said *Bow-wow* and *Baa* and *Meaow*.'

Natalia flushed. She was bewildered and deeply hurt. Presently, after a long silence, she said: 'Yes. I see.'

As we approached her house, I tried to patch things up and turn the whole business into a joke, but she didn't respond. I went home feeling very much ashamed of myself.

Some days after this, however, Natalia rang up of her own accord and asked me to lunch. She opened the door herself – she had evidently been waiting to do so – and greeted me by exclaiming: 'Bow-wow! Baa! Meaow!'

For a moment, I really thought she must have gone mad. Then I remembered our quarrel. But Natalia, having made her joke, was quite ready to be friends again.

We went into the sitting-room, and she began putting aspirin tablets into the bowls of flowers – to revive them, she said. I asked what she'd been doing during the last few days.

'All this week,' said Natalia, 'I am not going in the school. I have been unwell. Three days ago, I stand by the piano, and suddenly I fall down – so. How do you say – *ohnmächtig*?'

'You mean you fainted?'

Natalia nodded vigorously: 'Yes, that's right. I am *ohnmächtig*.'

'But in that case you ought to be in bed now.' I felt suddenly very masculine and protective: 'How are you feeling?'

Natalia laughed gaily, and, certainly, I had never seen her looking better:

'Oh it is not so important!'

'There is one thing I must tell you,' she added. 'It shall be a nice surprise for you, I think – to-day is coming my father, and my cousin Bernhard.'

'How very nice.'

'Yes! Is it not? My father makes us great joy when he comes, for now he is often on travel. He has much business everywhere, in Paris, in Vienna, in Prague. Always he must be going in the train. You shall like him, I think.'

'I'm certain I shall.'

And sure enough, when the glass doors parted, there was Herr Landauer, waiting to receive me. Beside him stood Bernhard Landauer, Natalia's cousin, a tall pale young man in a dark suit, only a few years older than myself. 'I am very pleased to make your acquaintance,' Bernhard said, as we shook hands. He spoke English without the faintest trace of a foreign accent.

Herr Landauer was a small lively man, with dark leathery wrinkled skin, like an old well-polished boot. He had shiny brown boot-button eyes and low-comedian's eyebrows – so thick and black that they looked as if they had been touched up with burnt cork. It was evident that he adored his family. He opened the door for Frau Landauer in a way which suggested that she was a very beautiful young girl. His benevolent, de-lighted smile embraced the whole party – Natalia sparkling with joy at her father's return, Frau Landauer faintly flushed, Bernhard's smooth and pale and politely enigmatic: even I myself was included. Indeed, Herr Landauer addressed almost the whole of his conversation to me, carefully avoiding any reference to family affairs which might have reminded me that I was a stranger at his table.

'Thirty-five years ago I was in England,' he told me, speaking with a strong accent. 'I came to your capital to write a thesis for my doctorate, on the condition of Jewish workers in the East End of London. I saw a great deal that your English officials did not desire me to see. I was quite a young fellow then: younger, I suspect, than you are to-day. I had some exceedingly interesting conversations with dock-hands and prostituted women and the keepers of your so-called Public Houses. Very interesting ...' Herr Landauer smiled reminiscently: 'And this insignificant little thesis of mine caused a great deal of discussion. It has been translated into no less than five languages.'

'Five languages!' repeated Natalia, in German, to me. 'You see, my father is a writer, too!'

'Ah, that was thirty-five years ago! Long before you were born, my dear.' Herr Landauer shook his head deprecatingly, his boot-button eyes twinkling with benevolence: 'Now I have not the time for such studies.' He turned to me again: 'I have just been reading a book in the French language about your great English poet, Lord Byron. A most interesting book. Now I should be very glad to have your opinion, as a writer, on this most important question – was Lord Byron guilty of the crime of incest? What do you think, Mr Isherwood?'

I felt myself beginning to blush. For some odd reason, it was the presence of Frau Landauer, placidly chewing her lunch, not of Natalia, which chiefly embarrassed me at this moment. Bernhard kept his eyes on his plate, subtly smiling. 'Well,' I began, 'it's rather difficult ...'

'This is a very interesting problem,' interrupted Herr Landauer, looking benevolently round upon us all and masticating with the greatest satisfaction: 'Shall we allow that the man of genius is an exceptional person who may do exceptional things? Or shall we say: No – you may write a beautiful poem or paint a beautiful picture, but in your daily life you must behave like an ordinary person, and you must obey these laws which we have made for ordinary persons? We will not allow you to be *extra*-ordinary.' Herr Landauer fixed each of us in turn, triumphantly, his mouth full of food. Suddenly his eyes focused beamingly upon me: 'Your dramatist Oscar Wilde ... this is another case. I put this case to you, Mr Isherwood. I should like very much to hear your opinion. Was your English Law justified in punishing Oscar Wilde, or was it not justified? Please tell me what you think?'

Herr Landauer regarded me delightedly, a forkful of meat poised half-way up to his mouth. In the background, I was aware of Bernhard, discreetly smiling.

'Well ...' I began, feeling my ears burning red. This time, however, Frau Landauer unexpectedly saved me, by making a remark to Natalia in German, about the vegetables. There was a little discussion, during which Herr Landauer seemed to forget all about his question. He went on eating contentedly. But now Natalia must needs chip in:

'Please tell my father the name of your book. I could not remember it. It's such a funny name.'

I tried to direct a private frown of disapproval at her which the others would not notice. '*All the Conspirators*,' I said, coldly.

'*All the Conspirators* ... oh, yes, of course!'

'Ah, you write criminal romances, Mr Isherwood?' Herr Landauer beamed approvingly.

'I'm afraid this book has nothing to do with criminals,' I said, politely. Herr Landauer looked puzzled and disappointed: 'Not to do with criminals?'

'You will explain to him, please,' Natalia ordered.

I drew a long breath: 'The title was meant to be symbolic ... It's taken from Shakespeare's *Julius Caesar* ...'

Herr Landauer brightened at once: 'Ah, Shakespeare! Splendid! This is most interesting ...'

'In German,' I smiled slightly at my own cunning: I was luring him down a side-track, 'you have wonderful translations of Shakespeare, I believe?'

'Indeed, yes! These translations are among the finest works

in our language. Thanks to them, your Shakespeare has become, as it were, almost a German poet ...'

'But you do not tell,' Natalia persisted, with what seemed really devilish malice, 'what your book is about?'

I set my teeth: 'It's about two young men. One of them is an artist and the other a student of medicine.'

'Are these the only two persons in your book, then?' Natalia asked.

'Of course not ... But I'm surprised at your bad memory. I told you the whole story only a short time ago.'

'Imbecile! It is not for myself I ask. Naturally, I remember all what you have told me. But my father has not yet heard. So you will please tell ... And what is then?'

'The artist has a mother and a sister. They are all very unhappy.'

'But why are they unhappy? My father and my mother and I, we are not unhappy.'

I wished the earth would swallow her: 'Not all people are alike,' I said carefully, avoiding Herr Landauer's eye.

'Good,' said Natalia. 'They are unhappy ... And what then?'

'The artist runs away from home and his sister gets married to a very unpleasant young man.'

Natalia evidently saw that I wouldn't stand much more of this. She delivered one final pin-prick: 'And how many copies did you sell?'

'Five.'

'Five! But that is very few, isn't it?'

'Very few indeed.'

At the end of lunch, it seemed tacitly understood that Bernhard and his uncle and aunt were to discuss family affairs together. 'Do you like,' Natalia asked me, 'that we shall walk together a little?'

Herr Landauer took a ceremonial farewell of me: 'At all times, Mr Isherwood, you are welcome under my roof.' We both bowed profoundly. 'Perhaps,' said Bernhard, giving me his card, 'you would come one evening and enliven my solitude for a little?' I thanked him and said that I should be delighted.

'And what do you think of my father?' Natalia asked, as soon as we were out of the house.

'I think he's the nicest father I've ever met.'

'You do truthfully?' Natalia was delighted.

'Yes truthfully.'

'And now confess to me, my father shocked you when he was speaking of Lord Byron – no? You were quite red as a lobster in your cheeks.'

I laughed: 'Your father makes me feel old-fashioned. His conversation's so modern.'

Natalia laughed triumphantly: 'You see, I was right! You were shocked. Oh, I am so glad! You see, I say to my father: A vairy intelligent young man is coming here to see us – and so he wish to show you that he also can be modern and speak of all subjects. You thought my father would be a stupid old man? Tell the truth, please.'

'No,' I protested. 'I never thought that!'

'Well, he is not stupid, you see ... He is vairy clever. Only he does not have so much time for reading, because he must work always. Sometimes he must work eighteen and nineteen hours in the day; it is tairrible ... And he is the best father in the whole world!'

'Your cousin Bernhard is your father's partner, isn't he?'

Natalia nodded: 'It is he who manages the store, here in Berlin. He is also vairy clever.'

'I suppose you see a good deal of him?'

'No ... It is not often that he come to our house ... He is a strange man, you know? I think he like to be vairy much alone. I am surprised when he ask you to make him a visit ... You must be careful.'

'Careful? Why on earth should I be careful?'

'He is vairy sarcastical, you see. I think perhaps he laugh at you.'

'Well, that wouldn't be very terrible, would it? Plenty of people laugh at me ... You do, yourself, sometimes.'

'Oh, I! That is different.' Natalia shook her head solemnly: 'When I laugh, it is to make fun, you know? But when Bernhard laugh at you, it is not nice ...'

Bernhard had a flat in a quiet street not far from the Tiergarten. When I rang at the outer entrance, a gnome-like caretaker peeped up at me through a tiny basement window, asked whom I wished to visit, and finally, after regarding me for a few moments with profound mistrust, pressed a button releasing the lock of the outer door. This door was so heavy that I had to push it open with both hands; it closed behind me with a hollow boom, like the firing of a cannon. Then came a pair of doors opening into the courtyard, then the door of the Gartenhaus, then five flights of stairs, then the door of the flat. Four doors to protect Bernhard from the outer world.

This evening, he was wearing a beautifully embroidered kimono over his town clothes. He was not quite as I remembered him from our first meeting: I hadn't seen him, then, as being in the least oriental – the kimono, I suppose, brought this out. His overcivilized, prim, finely drawn, beaky profile gave him something of the air of a bird in a piece of Chinese embroidery. He was soft, negative, I thought, yet curiously potent, and with the static potency of a carved ivory figure in a shrine. I noticed again his beautiful English, and the deprecatory gestures of his hands, as he showed me a twelfth-century sandstone head of Buddha from Khmer which stood at the foot of his bed – 'keeping watch over my slumbers.' On the low white bookcase were little Greek and Siamese and Indo-Chinese statuettes and stone heads, most of which Bernhard had brought home with him from his travels. Amongst volumes of Kunst-Geschichte, photographic reproductions and monographs on sculpture and antiquities, I saw Vachell's *The Hill* and Lenin's *What is to be done?* The flat might well have been in the depths of the country: you couldn't hear the faintest outside sound. A staid housekeeper in an apron served supper. I had soup, fish, a chop and savoury; Bernhard drank milk, ate only tomatoes and rusks.

We talked of London, which Bernhard had never visited, and of Paris, where he had studied for a time in a sculptor's atelier. In his youth, he had wanted to be a sculptor, 'but,' Bernhard sighed, smiled gently, 'Providence has ordained otherwise.'

I wanted to talk to him about the Landauer business, but didn't – fearing it might not be tactful. Bernhard himself referred to it, however, in passing: 'You must pay us a visit, one day, if it would interest you – for I suppose that it is interesting, if only as a contemporary economic phenomenon.' He smiled, and his face crossed my mind that he was perhaps suffering from a fatal disease.

After supper, he seemed brighter, however. A few years before, he had been right round the world – gently inquisitive, mildly satiric, poking his delicate beak-like nose into everything: Jewish village communities in Palestine, Jewish settlements on the Black Sea, revolutionary committees in India, rebel armies in Mexico. Hesitating, delicately choosing his words, he described a conversation with a Chinese ferryman about demons, and a barely credible instance of the brutality of the police in New York.

Four or five times during the evening, the telephone bell rang, and, on each occasion, it seemed that Bernhard was being asked for help and advice. 'Come and see me tomorrow,' he said, in his tired, soothing voice. 'Yes ... I'm sure it can all be arranged ... And now, please don't worry any more. Go to bed and sleep. I prescribe two or three tablets of aspirin ...' He smiled softly, ironically. Evidently he was about to lend each of his applicants some money.

'And please tell me,' he asked, just before I left, 'if I am not being impertinent – what has made you come to live in Berlin?'

'To learn German,' I said. After Natalia's warning, I wasn't going to trust Bernhard with the history of my life.

'And you are happy here?'

'Very happy.'

'That is wonderful, I think ... Most wonderful ...' Bernhard laughed his gentle ironical laugh: 'A spirit possessed of such vitality that it can be happy, even in Berlin. You must teach me your secret. May I sit at your feet and learn wisdom?'

His smile contracted, vanished. Once again, the impassivity of mortal weariness fell like a shadow across his strangely youthful face. 'I hope,' he said, 'that you will ring me up whenever you have nothing better to do.'

· Soon after this, I went to call on Bernhard at the business. Landauers' was an enormous steel and glass building, not far from the Potsdamer Platz. It took me nearly a quarter of an hour to find my way through departments of underwear, outfitting, electrical appliances, sport and cutlery to the private world behind the scenes – the wholesale, travellers' and buying rooms, and Bernhard's own little suite of offices. A porter showed me into a small waiting-room, panelled in some highly polished streaky wood, with a rich blue carpet and one picture, an engraving of Berlin in the year 1803. After a few moments, Bernhard himself came in. This morning, he looked younger, sprucer, in a bow-tie and a light grey suit. 'I hope that you give your approval to this room,' he said. 'I think that, as I keep so many people waiting here, they ought at least to have a more or less sympathetic atmosphere to allay their impatience.'

'It's very nice,' I said, and added, to make conversation – for I was feeling a little embarrassed: 'What kind of wood is this?'

'Caucasian Nut.' Bernhard pronounced the words with his characteristic primness, very precisely. He grinned suddenly. He seemed, I thought, in much better spirits: 'Come and see the shop.'

In the hardware department, an overalled woman demonstrator was exhibiting the merits of a patent coffee-strainer. Bernhard stopped to ask her how the sales were going, and she offered us cups of coffee. While I sipped mine, he explained that I was a well-known coffee-merchant from London, and that my opinion would therefore be worth having. The woman half believed this, at first, but we both laughed so much that she became suspicious. Then Bernhard dropped his coffee-cup and broke it. He was quite distressed and apologized profusely. 'It doesn't matter,' the demonstrator reassured him – as though he were a minor employee who might get sacked for his clumsiness: 'I've got two more.'

Presently we came to the toys. Bernhard told me that he and his uncle wouldn't allow toy soldiers or guns to be sold at Landauers'. Lately, at a directors' meeting, there had been a heated argument about toy tanks, and Bernhard had succeeded in getting his own way. 'But this is really the thin end of the wedge,' he added, sadly, picking up a toy tractor with caterpillar wheels.

Then he showed me a room in which the children could play while their mothers were shopping. A uniformed nurse was helping two little boys to build a castle of bricks. 'You observe,' said Bernhard, 'that a little philanthropy is here combined with advertisement. Opposite this room, we display specially cheap and attractive hats. The mothers who bring their children here fall immediately into temptation ... I'm afraid you will think us sadly materialistic ...'

I asked why there was no book department.

'Because we dare not have one. My uncle knows that I should remain there all day.'

All over the store, there were brackets of coloured lamps, red, green, blue and yellow. I asked what they were for, and Bernhard explained that each of these lights was the signal for one of the heads of the firm: 'I am the blue light. That is, perhaps, to some degree, symbolic.' Before I had time to ask what he meant, the blue lamp we were looking at began to flicker. Bernhard went to the nearest telephone and was told that somebody wished to speak to him in his office. So we said good-bye. On the way out, I bought a pair of socks.

During the early part of that winter, I saw a good deal of Bernhard. I cannot say that I got to know him much better through these evenings spent together. He remained curiously remote from me – his face impassive with exhaustion under the shaded lamplight, his gentle voice moving on through sequences of mildly humorous anecdotes. He would describe, for instance, a lunch with some friends who were very strict

Jews. 'Ah,' Bernhard had said, conversationally, 'so we're having lunch out of doors to-day? How delightful! The weather's so warm for the time of year, isn't it? And your garden's looking lovely.' Then, suddenly, it had occurred to him that his hosts were regarding him rather sourly, and he remembered, with horror, that this was the feast of Tabernacles.

I laughed. I was amused. Bernhard told stories very well. But, all the time, I was aware of feeling a certain impatience. Why does he treat me like a child, I thought. He treats us all as children – his uncle and aunt, Natalia, myself. He tells us stories. He is sympathetic, charming. But his gestures, offering me a glass of wine or a cigarette, are clothed in arrogance, in the arrogant humility of the East. He is not going to tell me what he is really thinking or feeling, and he despises me because I do not know. He will never tell me anything about himself, or about the things which are most important to him. And because I am not as he is, because I am the opposite of this, and would gladly share my thoughts and sensations with forty million people if they cared to read them, I half admire Bernhard but also half dislike him.

We seldom talked about the political condition of Germany, but, one evening, Bernhard told me a story of the days of the civil war. He had been visited by a student friend who was taking part in the fighting. The student was very nervous and refused to sit down. Presently he confessed to Bernhard that he had been ordered to take a message through to one of the newspaper office-buildings which the police were besieging; to reach this office, it would be necessary to climb and crawl over roofs which were exposed to machine-gun fire. Naturally, he wasn't anxious to start. The student was wearing a remarkably thick overcoat, which Bernhard pressed him to take off, for the room was well heated and his face was literally streaming with sweat. At length, after much hesitation, the student did so, revealing, to Bernard's intense alarm, that the lining of the coat was fitted with inside pockets stuffed full of hand-grenades. 'And the worst of it was,' said Bernhard, 'that he'd made up his mind not to take any more risks, but to leave the overcoat with me. He wanted to put it into the bath and turn on the cold water tap. At last I persuaded him that it would be much better to take it out after dark and to drop it into the canal – and this he ultimately succeeded in doing ... He is now one of the most distinguished professors in a certain provincial university. I am sure that he has long since forgotten this somewhat embarrassing escapade ...'

'Were *you* ever a communist, Bernhard?' I asked.

At once – I saw it in his face – he was on the defensive. After a moment, he said slowly:

'No, Christopher. I'm afraid I was always constitutionally incapable of bringing myself to the required pitch of enthusiasm.'

I felt suddenly impatient with him; angry, even: '– ever to believe in anything?'

Bernhard smiled faintly at my violence. It may have amused him to rouse me like this.

'Perhaps ...' Then he added, as if to himself: 'No ... that is not quite true ...'

'What *do* you believe in, then?' I challenged.

Bernhard was silent for some moments, considering this – his beaky delicate profile impassive, his eyes half-closed. At last he said: 'Possibly I believe in discipline.'

'In discipline?'

'You don't understand that, Christopher? Let me try to explain ... I believe in discipline for myself, not necessarily for others. For others, I cannot judge. I know only that I myself must have certain standards which I obey and without which I am quite lost ... Does that sound very dreadful?'

'No,' I said – thinking: He is like Natalia.

'You must not condemn me too harshly, Christopher.' The mocking smile was spreading over Bernhard's face. 'Remember that I am a cross-breed. Perhaps, after all, there is one drop of pure Prussian blood in my polluted veins. Perhaps this little finger,' he held it up to the light, 'is the finger of a Prussian drill-sergeant ... You, Christopher, with your centuries of Anglo-Saxon freedom behind you, with your Magna Charta engraved upon your heart, cannot understand that we poor barbarians need the stiffness of a uniform to keep us standing upright.'

'Why do you always make fun of me, Bernhard?'

'Make fun of you, my dear Christopher! I shouldn't dare!'

Yet, perhaps, on this occasion, he told me a little more than he had intended.

I had long meditated the experiment of introducing Natalia to Sally Bowles. I think I knew beforehand what the result of their meeting would be. At any rate, I had the sense not to invite Fritz Wendel.

We were to meet at a smart café in the Kurfüstendamm. Natalia was the first to arrive, She was a quarter of an hour late – probably because she'd wanted to have the advantage of coming last. But she had reckoned without Sally: she hadn't the nerve to be late in the grand manner. Poor Natalia! She had tried to make herself look more grown up – with the result that she appeared merely rather dowdy. The long townified dress she'd put on didn't suit her at all. On the side of her head, she had planted a little hat – an unconscious parody of Sally's page-boy cap. But Natalia's hair was much too fuzzy for it: it rode the waves like a half-swamped boat on a rough sea.

'How do I look?' she immediately asked, sitting down opposite me, rather flurried.

'You look very nice.'

'Tell me, please, truthfully, what will she think of me?'

'She'll like you very much.'

'How can you say that?' Natalia was indignant. 'You do not know!'

'First you want my opinion, and then you say I don't know!'

'Imbecile! I do not ask for compliments!'

'I'm afraid I don't quite understand what you *do* ask for.'

'Oh no?' cried Natalia scornfully. 'You do not understand? Then I am sorry. I can't help you!'

At this moment, Sally arrived.

'Hilloo, darling,' she exclaimed, in her most cooing accents, 'I'm *terribly* sorry I'm late – can you forgive me?' She sat down daintily, enveloping us in wafts of perfume, and began, with languid miniature gestures, to take off her gloves: 'I've been making love to a dirty old Jew producer. I'm hoping he'll give me a contract – but no go, so far ...'

I kicked Sally hastily, under the table, and she stopped short, with an expression of absurd dismay – but now, of course, it was too late. Natalia froze before our eyes. All I'd said and hinted beforehand, in the hypothetic pre-excuse of Sally's conduct, was instantly made void. After a moment's glacial pause, Natalia asked me if I'd seen *Sous les Toits de Paris*. She spoke German. She wasn't going to give Sally a chance of laughing at her English.

Sally immediately chipped in, however, quite unabashed. *She'd* seen the film, and thought it was marvellous, and wasn't Prejean marvellous, and did we remember the scene where a train goes past in the background while they're starting to fight? Sally's German was so much more than usually awful that I wondered whether she wasn't deliberately exaggerating it in order, somehow, to make fun of Natalia.

During the rest of the interview I suffered mental pins and needles. Natalia hardly spoke at all. Sally prattled on in her murderous German, making what she imagined to be light general conversation, chiefly about the English film industry. But as every anecdote involved explaining that somebody was someone else's mistress, that this one drank and that one took drugs, this didn't make the atmosphere any more agreeable. I found myself getting increasingly annoyed with both of them – with Sally for her endless silly pornographic talk; with Natalia for being such a prude. At length, after what seemed an eternity but was, in fact, barely twenty minutes, Natalia said that she must be going.

'My God, so must I!' cried Sally, in English. 'Chris, darling, you'll take me as far as the Eden, won't you?'

In my cowardly way, I glanced at Natalia, trying to convey my helplessness. This, I knew only too well, was going to be regarded as a test of my loyalty – and, already, I had failed it. Natalia's expression showed no mercy. Her face was set. She was very angry, indeed.

'When shall I see you?' I ventured to ask.

'I don't know,' said Natalia – and she marched off down the Kurfüstendamm as if she never wished to set eyes on either of us again.

Although we had only a few hundred yards to go, Sally insisted that we must take a taxi. It would never do, she explained, to arrive at the Eden on foot.

'That girl didn't like me much, did she?' she remarked, as we were driving off.

'No, Sally. Not much.'

'I'm sure I don't know why ... I went out of my way to be nice to her.'

'If that's what you call being nice ...!' I laughed, in spite of my vexation.

'Well, what ought I to have done?'

'It's more of a question of what you ought *not* to have done ... Haven't you *any* small-talk except adultery?'

'People have got to take me as I am,' retorted Sally, grandly.

'Finger-nails and all?' I'd noticed Natalia's eyes returning to them again and again, in fascinated horror.

Sally laughed: 'Today, I specially didn't paint my toe-nails.'

'Oh, rot, Sally! Do you really?'

'Yes, of course I do.'

'But what on earth's the point? I mean, nobody—' I corrected myself, 'very few people can see them ...'

Sally gave me her most fatuous grin: 'I know, darling ... But it makes me feel so marvellously sensual ...'

From this meeting, I date the decline of my relations with Natalia. Not that there was ever any open quarrel between us, or definite break. Indeed, we met again only a few days later; but at once I was aware of a change in the temperature of our friendship. We talked, as usual, of art, music, books – carefully avoiding the personal note. We had been walking about the Tiergarten for the best part of an hour, when Natalia abruptly asked:

'You like Miss Bowles vairy much?' Her eyes, fixed on the leaf-strewn path, were smiling maliciously.

'Of course I do ... We're going to be married, soon.'

'Imbecile!'

We marched on for several minutes in silence.

'You know,' said Natalia suddenly, with the air of one who makes a surprising discovery: 'I do not like your Miss Bowles?'

'I know you don't.'

My tone vexed her – as I intended that it should: 'What I think, it is not of importance?'

'Not in the least.' I grinned teasingly.

'Only your Miss Bowles, she is of importance?'

'She is of great importance.'

Natalia reddened and bit her lip. She was getting angry: 'Some day, you will see that I am right.'

'I've no doubt I shall.'

We walked all the way back to Natalia's home without exchanging a single word. On the doorstep, however, she asked, as usual: 'Perhaps you will ring me up, one day ...' then paused, delivered her parting shot: 'if your Miss Bowles permits?'

I laughed: 'Whether she permits or not, I shall ring you up very soon.' Almost before I had finished speaking, Natalia had shut the door in my face.

Nevertheless, I didn't keep my word. It was a month before I finally dialled Natalia's number. I had half intended to do so, many times, but, always, my disinclination had been stronger than my desire to see her again. And when, at length, we did meet, the temperature had dropped several degrees lower still; we seemed mere acquaintances. Natalia was convinced, I suppose, that Sally had become my mistress, and I didn't see why I should correct her mistake – doing so would only have involved a long heart-to-heart talk for which I simply wasn't in the mood. And, at the end of all the explanations, Natalia would probably have found herself quite as much shocked as she was at present, and a good deal more jealous. I didn't flatter myself that Natalia had ever wanted me as a lover, but she had certainly begun to behave towards me, as a kind of bossy elder sister, and it was just this role – absurdly enough – which Sally had stolen from her. No, it was a pity, but on the whole, I decided, things were better as they were. So I played up to Natalia's indirect questions and insinuations, and even let drop a few hints of domestic bliss: 'When Sally and I were having breakfast together, this morning . . .' or 'How do you like this tie? Sally chose it . . .' Poor Natalia received them in glum silence; and, as so often before. I felt guilty and un-kind. There were two more meetings, equally unsuccessful. Then, towards the end of February, I rang up her home, and was told that she'd gone abroad.

Bernhard, too, I hadn't seen for some time. Indeed, I was quite surprised to hear his voice on the telephone one morn-ing. He wanted to know if I would go with him that evening 'into the country' and spend the night. This sounded very mysterious, and Bernhard only laughed when I tried to get out of him where we were going and why.

He called for me about eight o'clock, in a big closed car with a chauffeur. The car, Bernhard explained, belonged to the busi-ness. Both he and his uncle used it. It was typical, I thought, of the patriarchal simplicity in which the Landauers lived that Natalia's parents had no private car of their own, and that Bernhard even seemed inclined to apologize to me for the existence of this one. It was a complicated simplicity, the negation of a negation. Its roots were entangled deep in the awful guilt of possession. Oh dear, I sighed to myself, shall I ever get to the bottom of these people, shall I ever understand them? The mere act of thinking about the Landauers' psychic make-up overcame me, as always, with a sense of absolute, defeated exhaustion.

'You are tired?' Bernhard asked, solicitous, at my elbow.

'Oh no . . .' I roused myself. 'Not a bit.'

'You will not mind if we call first at the house of a friend of mine? There is somebody else coming with us, you see . . . I hope you don't object?'

'No, of course not,' I said politely.

'He is very quiet. An old friend of the family.' Bernhard, for some reason, seemed amused. He chuckled faintly to himself.

The car stopped outside a villa in the Fasanenstrasse. Bernhard rang the bell and was let in: a few moments later, he reappeared, carrying in his arms a Skye terrier. I laughed.

'You were exceedingly polite,' said Bernhard, smiling. 'All the same, I think I detected a certain uneasiness on your part ... Am I right?'

'Perhaps ...'

'I wonder whom you were expecting? Some terribly boring old gentleman, perhaps?' Bernhard patted the terrier. 'But I fear, Christopher, that you are far too well bred ever to confess that to me now.'

The car slowed down and stopped before the toll-gate of the Avus motor-road.

'Where are we going?' I asked. 'I wish you'd tell me!'

Bernhard smiled his soft expansive Oriental smile: 'I'm very mysterious, am I not?'

'Very.'

'Surely it must be a wonderful experience for you to be driving away into the night, not knowing whither you are bound? If I tell you that we are going to Paris, or to Madrid, or to Moscow, then there will no longer be any mystery and you will have lost half your pleasure ... Do you know, Christopher, I quite envy you because you do not know where we are going?'

'That's one way of looking at it, certainly ... But, at any rate, I know already we aren't going to Moscow. We're driving in the opposite direction.'

Bernhard laughed: 'You are so very English sometimes, Christopher. Do you realize that, I wonder?'

'You bring out the English side of me, I think,' I answered, and immediately felt a little uncomfortable, as though this remark were somehow insulting. Bernhard seemed aware of my thought.

'Am I to understand that as a compliment, or as a reproof?'

'As a compliment, of course.'

The car whirled along the black Avus, into the immense darkness of the winter countryside. Giant reflector signs glittered for a moment like burnt-out matches. Already Berlin was a reddish glow in the sky behind us, dwindling rapidly beyond a converging forest of pines. The searchlight on the Funkturm swung its little ray through the night. The straight black road roared headlong to meet us, as if to its destruction. In the upholstered darkness of the car, Bernhard was patting the restless dog upon his knees.

'Very well, I will tell you ... We are going to a place on the shores of the Wannsee which used to belong to my father. What you call in England a country cottage.'

'A cottage? Very nice ...?'

My tone amused Bernhard. I could hear from his voice that he was smiling:

'I hope you won't find it too uncomfortable?'

'I'm sure I shall love it.'

'It may seem a little primitive, at first ...' Bernhard laughed quietly to himself: 'Nevertheless, it is amusing ...'

'It must be ...'

I suppose I had been vaguely expecting an hotel, lights, music, very good food. I reflected bitterly that only a rich, decadently over-civilized town-dweller would describe camping out for the night in a poky, damp country cottage in the middle of the winter as 'amusing.' And how typical that he should drive me to that cottage in a luxurious car! Where would the chauffeur sleep? Probably in the best hotel in Potsdam ... As we passed the lamps of the toll-house at the far end of the Avus, I saw that Bernhard was still smiling to himself.

The car swung to the right, downhill, along a road through silhouetted trees. There was a feeling of nearness to the big lake lying invisible behind the woodland on our left. I had hardly realized that the road had ended in a gateway and a private drive: we pulled up at the door of a large villa.

'Where's this?' I asked Bernhard, supposing confusedly that he must have something else to call for – another terrier, perhaps. Bernhard laughed gaily:

'We have arrived at our destination, my dear Christopher! Out you get!'

A manservant in a striped jacket opened the door. The dog jumped out, and Bernhard and I followed. Resting his hand upon my shoulder, he steered me across the hall and up the stairs. I was aware of a rich carpet and framed engravings. He opened the door of a luxurious pink and white bedroom, with a luscious quilted silk eiderdown on the bed. Beyond was a bathroom, gleaming with polished silver, and hung with fleecy white towels.

Bernhard grinned:

'Poor Christopher! I fear you are disappointed in our cottage? It is too large for you, too ostentatious? You were looking forward to the pleasure of sleeping on the floor – amidst the black-beetles?'

The atmosphere of this joke surrounded us through dinner. As the manservant brought in each new course on its silver dish, Bernhard would catch my eye and smile a deprecatory smile. The dining-room was tame baroque, elegant and rather colourless. I asked him when the villa had been built.

'My father built this house in 1904. He wanted to make it as much as possible like an English home – for my mother's sake ...'

After dinner we walked down the windy garden, in the darkness. A strong wind was blowing up through the trees, from over the water. I followed Bernhard, stumbling against the body of the terrier which kept running between my legs, down flights of stone steps to a landing-stage. The dark lake was full of waves, and beyond, in the direction of Potsdam, a sprinkle of bobbing lights were comet-tailed in the black water. On the parapet, a dismantled gas-bracket rattled in the wind, and, below us, the waves splashed uncannily soft and wet, against unseen stone.

'When I was a boy, I used to come down these steps in the winter evenings and stand for hours here ...' Bernhard had begun to speak. His voice was pitched so low that I could hardly hear it; his face was turned away from me, in the darkness, looking out over the lake. When a stronger puff of wind blew, his words came more distinctly – as though the wind itself were talking: 'That was during the War-time. My elder brother had been killed, right at the beginning of the War . . . Later, certain business rivals of my father began to make propaganda against him, because his wife was an English woman, so that nobody would come to visit us, and it was rumoured that we were spies. At last, even the local trades-people did not wish to call at the house . . . It was all rather rid-iculous, and at the same time rather terrible, that human beings could be possessed by so much malice . . .'

I shivered a little, peering out over the water. It was cold. Bernhard's soft, careful voice continued in my ear:

'I used to stand here on those winter evenings and pretend to myself that I was the last human being left alive in the world . . . I was a queer sort of boy, I suppose . . . I never got on well with other boys, although I wished very much to be popular and to have friends. Perhaps that was my mistake – I was too eager to be friendly. The boys saw this and it made them cruel to me. Objectively, I can understand that . . . pos-sibly I might even have been capable of cruelty myself, had the circumstances been otherwise. It is difficult to say . . . But, being what I was, school was a kind of Chinese torture . . . So you can understand that I liked to come down here at night to the lake, and be alone. And then there was the War . . . At this time, I believed that the War would go on for ten, or fif-teen, or even twenty years. I knew that I myself should soon be called up. Curiously enough, I don't remember that I felt at all afraid. I accepted it. It seemed quite natural that we should all have to die. I suppose that this was the general wartime mentality. But I think that, in my case, there was also some-thing characteristically Semitic in my attitude . . . It is very difficult to speak quite impartially of these things. Some-times one is unwilling to make certain admissions to oneself, because they are displeasing to one's self-esteem . . .'

We turned slowly and began to climb the slope of the garden from the lake. Now and then, I heard the panting of the terrier, out hunting in the dark. Bernhard's voice went on, hesitating, choosing its words:

'After my brother had been killed, my mother scarcely ever left this house and its grounds. I think she tried to forget that such a land as Germany existed. She began to study Hebrew and to concentrate her whole mind upon ancient Jewish history and literature. I suppose that this is really symptomatic of a modern phase of Jewish development – this turning away from European culture and European traditions. I am aware of it, sometimes, in myself ... I remember my mother going about the house like a person walking in sleep. She grudged every moment which she did not spend at her studies, and this was rather terrible because, all the while, she was dying of cancer ... As soon as she knew what was the matter with her, she refused to see a doctor. She feared an operation ... At last, when the pain became very bad, she killed herself ...'

We had reached the house. Bernhard opened a glass door, and we passed through a little conservatory into a big drawing-room full of jumping shadows from the fire burning in an open English fireplace. Bernhard switched on a number of lamps, making the room quite dazzlingly bright.

'Need we have such illumination?' I asked. 'I think the fire-light is much nicer.'

'Do you?' Bernhard smiled subtly. 'So do I . . . But I thought, somehow, that you would prefer the lamps.'

'Why on earth should I?' I mistrusted his tone at once.

'I don't know. It's merely part of my conception of your character. How very foolish I am!'

Bernhard's voice was mocking. I made no reply. He got up and turned out all but one small lamp on a table at my side. There was a long silence.

'Would you care to listen to the wireless?'

This time his tone made me smile: 'You don't have to entertain me, you know! I'm perfectly happy just sitting here by the fire.'

'If you are happy, then I am glad ... It was foolish of me – I had formed the opposite impression.'

'What do you mean?'

'I was afraid, perhaps, that you were feeling bored.'

'Of course not! What nonsense!'

'You are very polite, Christopher. You are always very polite. But I can read quite clearly what you are thinking ...' I had never heard Bernhard's voice sound like this, before; it was really hostile: 'You are wondering why I brought you to this house. Above all, you are wondering why I told you what I told you just now.'

'I'm glad you told me ...'

'No Christopher. That is not true. You are a little shocked. One does not speak of such things, you think. It disgusts your English public-school training, a little – this Jewish emotionalism. You like to flatter yourself that you are a man of the world and that no form of weakness disgusts you, but your training is too strong for you. People ought not to talk to each other like this, you feel. It is not good form.'

'Bernhard, you're being fantastic!'

'Am I? Perhaps ... But I do not think so. Never mind ... Since you wish to know, I will try to explain to you why I brought you here ... I wished to make an experiment.'

'An experiment? Upon me, you mean?'

'No. An experiment upon myself. That is to say ... For ten years, I have never spoken intimately, as I have spoken to you to-night, to any human soul ... I wonder if you can put yourself in my place, imagine what that means? And this evening ... Perhaps, after all, it is impossible to explain ... Let me put it another way. I bring you down here, to this house, which has no associations for you. You have no reason to feel oppressed by the past. Then I tell you my story ... It is possible that, in this way, one can lay ghosts ... I can express myself very badly. Does it sound very absurd as I say it?'

'No not in the least ... But why did you choose me for your experiment?'

'Your voice was very hard as you said that, Christopher. You are thinking that you despise me.'

'No, Bernhard. I'm thinking that you must despise *me* ... I often wonder why you have anything to do with me at all. I feel sometimes that you actually dislike me, and that you say and do things to show it – and yet, in a way, I suppose you don't, or you wouldn't keep asking me to come and see you

... All the same, I'm getting rather tired of what you call your experiments. To-night wasn't the first of them by any means. The experiments fail, and then you're angry with me. I must say, I think that's very unjust ... But what I can't stand is that you show your resentment by adopting this mock-humble attitude ... Actually, you're the least humble person I've ever met.'

Bernhard was silent. He had lit a cigarette, and now expelled the smoke slowly through his nostrils. At last he said:

'I wonder if you are right ... I think not altogether. But partly ... Yes, there is some quality in you which attracts me and which I very much envy, and yet this very quality of yours also arouses my antagonism ... Perhaps that is merely because I am also partly English, and you represent to me an aspect of my own character ... No, that is not true, either ... It is not so simple as I would wish ... I'm afraid,' Bernhard passed his hand over his forehead and eyes, 'that I am a quite unnecessarily complicated piece of mechanism.'

There was a moment's silence. Then he added:

'But this is all stupid egotistical talk. You must forgive me. I have no right to speak to you in this way.'

He rose softly to his feet, went softly across the room, and switched on the wireless. In rising, he had rested his hand for an instant on my shoulder. Followed by the first strains of the music, he came back to his chair before the fire, smiling. His smile was soft, and yet curiously hostile. It had the hostility of something ancient. I thought of one of the Oriental statuettes in his flat.

'This evening,' he smiled softly, 'they are relaying the last act of *Die Meistersänger*.'

'Very interesting,' I said.

Half an hour later, Bernhard took me up to my bedroom door, his hand upon my shoulder, still smiling. Next morning, at breakfast, he looked tired, but was gay and amusing. He did not in any way refer to our conversation of the evening before.

We drove back to Berlin, and he dropped me on the corner of the Nollendorfplatz.

'Ring me up soon,' I said.

'Of course. Early next week.'

'And thank you very much.'

'Thank you for coming, my dear Christopher.'

I didn't see him again for nearly six months.

One Sunday, early in August, a referendum was held to decide the fate of the Brüning government. I was back at Frl. Schroeder's, lying in bed through the beautiful hot weather, cursing my toe: I had cut it on a piece of tin, bathing for the last time at Rügen, and now it had suddenly festered and was full of poison. I was quite delighted when Bernhard unexpectedly rang me up.

'You remember a certain little country cottage on the shores of the Wansee? You do? I was wondering if you would care to spend a few hours there, this afternoon ... Yes, your landlady has told me already about your misfortune. I am so sorry ... I can send the car for you. I think it will be good to escape for a little from this city? You can do whatever you like there – just lie quiet and rest. Nobody will interfere with your liberty.'

Soon after lunch, the car duly arrived to pick me up. It was a glorious afternoon, and, during the drive, I blessed Bernhard for his kindness. But when we arrived at the villa, I got a nasty shock: the lawn was crowded with people.

I was really annoyed. It was a dirty trick, I thought. Here was I, in my oldest clothes, with a bandaged foot and a stick, lured into the middle of a slap-up garden-party! And here was Bernhard in flannel trousers and a boyish jumper. It was astonishing how young he looked. Bounding to meet me, he vaulted over the low railing:

'Christopher! Here you are at last! Make yourself comfortable!'

In spite of my protests, he forcibly removed my coat and hat. As ill-luck would have it, I was wearing braces. Most of the other guests were in smart Riviera flannels. Smiling sourly, adopting instinctively the armour of sulky eccentricity which protects me on such occasions, I advanced hobbling into their midst. Several couples were dancing to a portable gramophone; two young men were pillow-fighting with cushions, cheered on by their respective women; most of the party were lying chatting on rugs on the grass. It was all so very informal, and the footmen and the chauffeurs stood discreetly aside, watching their antics, like the nursemaids of titled children.

What were they doing here? Why had Bernhard asked them? Was this another and more elaborate attempt to exorcize his ghosts? No, I decided; it was more probably only a duty-party, given once a year, to all the relatives, friends and dependants of the family. And mine was just another name to be ticked off, far down the list. Well, it was silly to be ungracious. I was here. I would enjoy myself.

Then, to my great surprise, I saw Natalia. She was dressed in some light yellow material, with small puffed sleeves, and carried a big straw hat in her hand. She looked so pretty that I should hardly have recognized her. She advanced gaily to welcome me:

'Ah, Christopher! You know, I am so pleased!'

'Where have you been, all the time?'

'In Paris ... You did not know? Truthfully? I await always a letter from you – and there is nothing!'

'But Natalia, you never sent me your address.'

'Oh, I *did*!'

'Well, in that case, I never got the letter ... I've been away, too, you know.'

'So? You have been away? Then I'm sorry ... I can't help you!'

We both laughed. Natalia's laugh had changed, like everything else about her. It was no longer the laugh of the severe schoolgirl who had ordered me to read Jacobsen and Goethe. And there was a dreamy, delighted smile upon her face – as though, I thought, she were listening, all the time, to lively, pleasant music. Despite her obvious pleasure at seeing me again, she seemed hardly to be attending to our conversation.

'And what are you doing in Paris? Are you studying art, as you wanted to?'

'But of course!'

'Do you like it?'

'Wonderful!' Natalia nodded vigorously. Her eyes were sparkling. But the word seemed intended to describe something else.

'Is your mother with you?'

'Yes. Yes ...'

'Have you got a flat together?'

'Yes ...' Again she nodded. 'A flat ... Oh, it's wonderful!'

'And you go back there, soon?'

'Why, yes ... Of course! To-morrow!' She seemed quite surprised that I should ask the question – surprised that the whole world didn't know ... How well I knew that feeling! I was certain, now: Natalia was in love.

We talked for several minutes more – Natalia always smiling, always dreamily listening, but not to me. Then, all at once, she was in a hurry. She was late, she said. She'd got to pack. She must go at once. She squeezed my hand, and I watched her run gaily across the lawn to a waiting car. She had forgotten, even, to ask me to write, or to give me her address. As I waved goodbye to her, my poisoned toe gave a sharp twinge of envy.

Later, the younger members of the party bathed, splashing about in the dirty lake-water at the foot of the stone stairs. Bernhard bathed, too. He had a white, strangely innocent body, like a baby's, with a baby's round, slightly protruding stomach. He laughed and splashed and shouted louder than anybody. When he caught my eye, he made more noise than ever – was it, I imagined, with a certain defiance? Was he thinking, as I was of what he had told me, standing in this very place, six months ago? 'Come in, too, Christopher!' he shouted. 'It'll do your foot good!' When, at last, they had all come out of the water and were drying themselves, he and a few other young men chased each other, laughing, among the garden trees.

Yet, in spite of all Bernhard's frisking, the party didn't

really 'go.' It split up into groups and cliques; and, even when the fun was at its height, at least a quarter of the guests were talking politics in low, serious voices. Indeed, some of them had so obviously come to Bernhard's house merely to meet each other and to discuss their own private affairs that they scarcely troubled to pretend to take part in the sociabilities. They might as well have been sitting in their own offices, or at home.

When it got dark, a girl began to sing. She sang in Russian, and, as always, it sounded sad. The footmen brought out glasses and a huge bowl of claret-cup. It was getting chilly on the lawn. There were millions of stars. Out on the great calm brimming lake, the last ghost-like sails were tacking hither and thither with the faint uncertain night breeze. The gramophone played. I lay back on the cushions, listening to a Jewish surgeon who argued that France cannot understand Germany because the French have experienced nothing comparable to the neurotic post-War life of the German people. A girl laughed suddenly, shrilly, from the middle of a group of young men. Over there, in the city, the votes were being counted. I thought of Natalia: She has escaped – none too soon, perhaps. However often the decision may be delayed, all these people are ultimately doomed. This evening is the dress-rehearsal of a disaster. It is like the last night of an epoch.

At half-past ten, the party began to break up. We all stood about in the hall or around the front door while someone telephoned through to Berlin to get the news. A few moments' hushed waiting, and the dark listening face at the telephone relaxed into a smile. The Government was safe, he told us. Several of the guests cheered, semi-ironical but relieved. I turned to find Bernhard at my elbow: 'Once again, Capitalism is saved.' He was subtly smiling.

He had arranged that I should be taken home in the dicky of a Berlin-bound car. As we came down the Tauentzienstrasse, they were selling papers with the news of the shooting on the Bülowplatz. I thought of our party lying out there on the lawn by the lake, drinking our claret-cup while the gramophone played; and of that police-officer, revolver in hand, stumbling mortally wounded up the cinema steps to fall dead at the feet of a cardboard figure advertising a comic film.

Another pause – eight months, this time. And here I was, ringing the bell of Bernhard's flat. Yes, he was in.

'This is a great honour, Christopher. And, unfortunately, a very rare one.'

'Yes, I'm sorry. I've so often meant to come and see you ... I don't know why I haven't ...'

'You've been in Berlin all this time? You know, I rang up twice at Frl. Schroeder's, and a strange voice answered and said that you'd gone away, to England.'

'I told Frl. Schroeder that. I didn't want her to know that I was still here.'

'Oh, indeed? You had a quarrel?'

'On the contrary. I told her that I was going to England, because, otherwise, she'd have insisted on supporting me. I got a bit hard up ... Everything's perfectly all right again, now,' I added hastily, seeing a look of concern on Bernhard's face.

'Quite certain? I am very glad ... But what have you been doing with yourself, all this time?'

'Living with a family of five in a two-room attic in Halleshes Tor.'

Bernhard smiled: 'By Jove, Christopher – what a romantic life you lead!'

'I'm glad you call that kind of thing romantic. I don't!' We both laughed.

'At any rate,' Bernhard said, 'it seems to have agreed with you. You're looking the picture of health.'

I couldn't return the compliment. I thought I had never seen Bernhard looking so ill. His face was pale and drawn; the weariness did not lift from it even when he smiled. There were deep sallow half-moons under his eyes. His hair seemed thinner. He might have added ten years to his age.

'And how have you been getting on?' I asked.

'My existence, in comparison with yours, is sadly humdrum, I fear ... Nevertheless, there are certain tragi-comic diversions.'

'What sort of diversions?'

'This for example—' Bernhard went over to his writing-desk, picked up a sheet of paper and handed it to me: 'It arrived by post this morning.'

I read the typed words:

Bernhard Landauer, beware. We are going to settle the score with you and your uncle and all other filthy Jews. We give you twenty-four hours to leave Germany. If not, you are dead men.

Bernhard laughed: 'Bloodthirsty, isn't it?'

'It's incredible ... Who do you suppose sent it?'

'An employee who has been dismissed, perhaps. Or a practical joker. Or a madman. Or a hot-headed Nazi school-boy.'

'What shall you do?'

'Nothing.'

'Surely you'll tell the police?'

'My dear Christopher, the police would very soon get tired of hearing such nonsense. We receive three or four such letters every week.'

'All the same, this one may quite well be in earnest ... The Nazis may write like schoolboys, but they're capable of any-thing. That's just why they're so dangerous. People laugh at them, right up to the last moment ...'

Bernhard smiled his tired smile: 'I appreciate very much this anxiety of yours on my behalf. Nevertheless, I am quite unworthy of it ... My existence is not of such vital im-portance to myself or to others that the forces of the Law should be called upon to protect me ... As for my uncle he is at present in Warsaw ...'

I saw that he wished to change the subject:

'Have you any news of Natalia and Frau Landauer?'

'Oh yes, indeed! Natalia is married. Didn't you know? To a young French doctor ... I hear that they are very happy.'

'I'm so glad!'

'Yes ... It's pleasant to think of one's friends being happy, isn't it?' Bernhard crossed to the waste paper basket and dropped the letter into it: 'Especially in another country ...' He smiled, gently and sadly.

'And what so you think will happen in Germany, now?' I asked. 'Is there going to be a Nazi putsch or a communist revolution?'

Bernhard laughed: 'You have lost none of your enthusiasm, I see! I only wish that this question seemed as momentous to me as it does to you ...'

'It'll seem momentous enough, one of these fine mornings' – the retort rose to my lips: I am glad now that I didn't utter it. Instead, I asked: 'Why do you wish that?'

'Because it would be a sign of something healthier in my own character ... It is right, nowadays, that one should be interested in such things; I recognize that. It is sane. It is healthy ... And because all this seemed to me a little unreal, a little – please don't be offended, Christopher – trivial, I know that I am getting out of touch with existence. That is bad, of course ... One must preserve a sense of proportion ... Do you know, there are times when I sit here alone in the evenings, amongst these books and stone figures, and there comes to me such a strange sensation of unreality, as if this were my whole life? Yes, actually, sometimes I have felt a doubt as to whether our firm – that great building packed from floor to roof with all our accumulation of property – really exists at all, except in my imagination ... And then I have had an unpleasant feeling, such as one has in a dream, that I myself do not exist. It is very morbid, very unbalanced, no doubt ... I will make a confession to you, Christopher ., . One evening, I was so much troubled by this hallucination of the non-existence of Landauers' that I picked up my telephone and had a long conversation with one of the night-watchmen, making some stupid excuse for having troubled him. Just to reassure myself, you understand? Don't you think I must be becoming insane?'

'I don't think anything of the kind ... It could have happened to anyone who has overworked.'

'You recommend a holiday? A month in Italy, just as the spring is beginning? Yes ... I remember the days when a month of Italian sunshine would have solved all my troubles. But now, alas, that drug has lost its power. Here is a paradox for you! Landauers' is no longer real to me, yet I am more than ever its slave! You see the penalty of a life of sordid materialism. Take my nose away from the grindstone, and I become positively unhappy ... Ah, Christopher, be warned by my fate'

He smiled, spoke lightly, half banteringly. I didn't like to pursue the subject further.

'You know,' I said, 'I really *am* going to England, now. I'm leaving in three or four days.'

'I am sorry to hear it. How long do you expect to stay there?'

'Probably the whole summer.'

'You are tired of Berlin, at last?'

'Oh no ... I feel more as if Berlin had got tired of me.'

'Then you will come back?'

'Yes I expect so.'

'I believe that you will always come back to Berlin, Christopher. You seem to belong here.'

'Perhaps I do, in a way.'

It is strange how people seem to belong to places — especially to places where they were not born ... When I first went to China, it seemed to me that I was at home there, for the first time in my life ... Perhaps, when I die, my spirit will be wafted to Peking.'

'It'd be better if you let a train waft your body there, as soon as possible!'

Bernhard laughed: 'Very well ... I will follow your advice! But on two conditions — first, that you come with me; second, that we leave Berlin this evening.'

'You mean it?'

'Certainly I do.'

'What a pity ! I should like to have come ... Unfortunately, I've only a hundred and fifty marks in the world.'

'Naturally, you would be my guest.'

'Oh, Bernhard, how marvellous! We'd stop a few days in Warsaw, to get the visas. Then on to Moscow, and take the trans-Siberian ...'

'So you'll come?'

'Of course!'

'This evening?'

I pretended to consider: 'I'm afraid I can't this evening ... I'd have to get my washing back from the laundry, first ... What about tomorrow?'

'Tomorrow is too late.'

'What a pity!'

'Yes, isn't it?'

We both laughed. Bernhard seemed to be specially tickled by his joke. There was even something a little exaggerated in his laughter, as though the situation had some further dimension of humour to which I hadn't penetrated. We were still laughing when I said good-bye.

Perhaps I am slow at jokes. At any rate, it took me nearly eighteen months to see the point of this one – to recognize it as Bernhard's last, most daring and most cynical experiment upon us both. For now I am certain – absolutely convinced – that his offer was perfectly serious.

When I returned to Berlin, in the autumn of 1932, I duly rang Bernhard up, only to be told that he was away on business, in Hamburg. I blame myself now – one always does blame oneself afterwards – for not having been more persistent. But there was so much for me to do, so many pupils, so many other people to see; the weeks turned into months; Christmas came – I sent Bernhard a card but got no answer: he was away again, most likely; and then the New Year began.

Hitler came, and the Reichstag fire, and the mock-elections. I wondered what was happening to Bernhard. Three times I rang him up – from call-boxes, lest I should get Frl. Schroeder into trouble: there was never any reply. Then, one evening early in April, I went round to his house. The caretaker put his head out of the tiny window, more suspicious than ever:

at first, he seemed even inclined to deny that he knew Bernhard at all. Then he snapped: 'Herr Landauer has gone away ... gone right away.'

'Do you mean he's moved from here?' I asked. 'Can you give me his address?'

'He's gone away,' the caretaker repeated, and slammed the window shut.

I left it at that – concluding, not unnaturally, that Bernhard was somewhere safe abroad.

On the morning of the Jewish boycott, I walked round to take a look at Landauers'. Things seemed very much as usual, superficially. Two or three uniformed S.A. boys were posted at each end of the big entrances. Whenever a shopper approached, one of them would say: 'Remember this is a Jewish business!' The boys were quite polite, grinning, making jokes among themselves. Little knots of passers-by collected to watch the performance – interested, amused or merely apathetic; still uncertain whether or not to approve. There was nothing of the atmosphere one read of later in the smaller provincial towns, where purchasers were forcibly disgraced with a rubber ink-stamp on the forehead and cheek. Quite a lot of people went into the building. I went in myself, bought the first thing I saw – it happened to be a nutmeg-grater – and strolled out again, twirling my small parcel. One of the boys at the door winked and said something to his companion. I remembered having seen him once or twice at the Alexander Casino, in the days when I was living with the Nowaks.

In May, I left Berlin for the last time. My first stop was at Prague – and it was there, sitting one evening alone, in a cellar restaurant, that I heard, indirectly, my last news of the Landauer family.

Two men were at the next table, talking German. One of them was certainly an Austrian; the other I couldn't place – he was fat and sleek, about forty-five, and might well have

owned a small business in any European capital, from
Belgrade to Stockholm. Both of them were undoubtedly pros-
perous, technically Aryan, and politically neuter. The fat man
startled me into attention by saying:

'You know Landauers'— Landauers' of Berlin?'

The Austrian nodded: 'Sure, I do ... Did a lot of business
with them, one time ... Nice place they've got there. Must
have cost a bit ...'

'Seen the papers, this morning?'

'No. Didn't have time ... Moving into our new flat, you
know. The wife's coming back.'

'She's coming back? You don't say! Been in Vienna, hasn't
she?'

'That's right.'

'Had a good time?'

'Trust her! It cost enough, anyway.'

'Vienna's pretty dear, these days.'

'It is that.'

'Food's dear.'

'It's dear everywhere.'

'I guess you're right.' The fat man began to pick his teeth:
'What was I saying?'

'You were saying about Landauers'.'

'So I was ... You didn't read the papers, this morning?'

'No, I didn't read them.'

'There was a bit in about Bernhard Landauer.'

'Bernhard?' said the Austrian. 'Let's see – he's the son, isn't
he?'

'I wouldn't know ...' The fat man dislodged a tiny fragment
of meat with the point of his toothpick. Holding it up to the
light, he regarded it thoughtfully.

'I think he's the son,' said the Austrian. 'Or maybe the
nephew ... No, I think he's the son.'

'Whoever he is,' the fat man flicked the scrap of meat on to
his plate with a gesture of distaste: 'He's dead.'

'You don't say!'

'Heart failure.' The fat man frowned, and raised his hand
to cover a belch. He was wearing three gold rings: 'That's

what the newspapers said.'

'Heart failure!' The Austrian shifted uneasily in his chair:
'You don't say!'

'There's a lot of heart failure,' said the fat man, 'in Germany
these days.'

The Austrian nodded: 'You can't believe all you hear.
That's a fact.'

'If you ask me,' said the fat man, 'anyone's heart's liable to
fail, if it gets a bullet inside it.'

The Austrian looked very uncomfortable: 'Those Nazis ...'
he began.

'They mean business.' The fat man seemed rather to enjoy
making his friend's flesh creep. 'You mark my words: they're
going to clear the Jews right out of Germany. Right out.'

The Austrian shook his head: 'I don't like it.'

'Concentration camps,' said the fat man lighting a cigar.
They get them in there, make them sign things ... Then
their hearts fail.'

'I don't like it,' said the Austrian. 'It's bad for trade.'

'Yes,' the fat man agreed. 'It's bad for trade.'

'Makes everything so uncertain.'

'That's right. Never know who you're doing business with.'
The fat man laughed. In his own way he was rather macabre:
'It might be a corpse.'

The Austrian shivered a little: 'What about the old man,
old Landauer? Did they get him, too?'

'No, he's all right. Too smart for them. He's in Paris.'

'You don't say!'

'I reckon the Nazis'll take over the business. They're doing
that, now.'

'Then old Landauer'll be ruined, I guess?'

'Not him!' The fat man flicked the ash from his cigar, con-
temptuously. 'He'll have a bit put by, somewhere. You'll see.
He'll start something else. They're smart, those Jews ...'

'That's right,' the Austrian agreed. 'You can't keep a Jew
down.'

The thought seemed to cheer him, a little. He brightened:
'That reminds me! I knew there was something I wanted to

tell you ... Did you ever hear the story about the Jew and the Goy girl with the wooden leg?'

'No.' The fat man puffed at his cigar. His digestion was working well, now. He was in the right after-dinner mood: 'Go ahead ...'

A BERLIN DIARY
(Winter 1932–3)

To-night, for the first time this winter, it is very cold. The dead cold grips the town in utter silence, like the silence of intense midday summer heat. In the cold the town seems actually to contract, to dwindle to a small black dot, scarcely larger than hundreds of other dots, isolated and hard to find, on the enormous European map. Outside, in the night, beyond the last new-built blocks of concrete flats, where the streets end in frozen allotment gardens, are the Prussian plains. You can feel them all round you, to-night, creeping in upon the city, like an immense waste of unhomely ocean – sprinkled with leafless copses and ice-lakes and tiny villages which are remembered only as the outlandish names of battlefields in half-forgotten wars. Berlin is a skeleton which aches in the cold: it is my own skeleton aching. I feel in my bones the sharp ache of the frost in the girders of the overhead railway, in the ironwork of balconies, in bridges, tramlines, lamp-standards, latrines. The iron throbs and shrinks, the stone and the bricks ache dully, the plaster is numb.

Berlin is a city with two centres – the cluster of expensive hotels, bars, cinemas, shops round the Memorial Church, a sparkling nucleus of light, like a sham diamond, in the shabby twilight of the town; and the self-conscious civic centre of buildings round the Unter den Linden, carefully arranged. In grand international styles, copies of copies, they assert our dignity as a capital city – a parliament, a couple of museums, a State bank, a cathedral, an opera, a dozen embassies, a triumphal arch; nothing has been forgotten. And they are all so pompous, so very correct – all except the cathedral, which betrays, in its architecture, a flash of that hysteria which flickers always behind every grave, grey Prussian façade. Extinguished by its absurd dome, it is, at first sight, so startlingly funny that one searches for a name suitably preposterous – the Church of the Immaculate Consumption.

But the real heart of Berlin is a small damp black wood – the Tiergarten. At this time of the year, the cold begins to drive the peasant boys out of their tiny unprotected villages into the city, to look for food, and work. But the city, which glowed so brightly and invitingly in the night sky above the plains, is cold and cruel and dead. Its warmth is an illusion, a mirage of the winter desert. It will not receive these boys. It has nothing to give. The cold drives them out of its streets, into the wood which is its cruel heart. And there they cower on benches, to starve and freeze, and dream of their far-away cottage stoves.

Frl. Schroeder hates the cold. Huddled in her fur-lined velvet jacket, she sits in the corner with her stockinged feet on the stove. Sometimes she smokes a cigarette, sometimes she sips a glass of tea, but mostly she just sits, staring dully at the stove tiles in a kind of hibernation-doze She is lonely, nowadays. Frl. Mayr is away in Holland, on a cabaret-tour. So Frl. Schroeder has nobody to talk to, except Bobby and myself.

Bobby, anyhow, is in deep disgrace. Not only is he out of work and three months behind with the rent, but Frl. Schroeder has reason to suspect him of stealing money from her bag. 'You know, Herr Issyvoo,' she tells me, 'I shouldn't wonder at all if he didn't pinch those fifty marks from Frl. Kost ... He's quite capable of it, the pig! To think I could ever have been so mistaken in him! Will you believe it, Herr Issyvoo, I treated him as if he were my own son – and this is the thanks I get! He says he'll pay me every pfennig if he gets this job as barman at the Lady Windermere ... if, *if* ...' Frl. Schroeder sniffs with intense scorn: 'I dare say! If my grandmother had wheels, she'd be an omnibus!'

Bobby has been turned out of his old room and banished to the 'Swedish Pavilion.' It must be terribly draughty, up there.

Sometimes poor Bobby looks quite blue with cold. He has changed very much during the last year – his hair is thinner, his clothes are shabbier, his cheekiness has become defiant and rather pathetic. People like Bobby *are* their jobs – take the job away and they partially cease to exist. Sometimes, he sneaks into the living-room, unshaven, his hands in his pockets, and lounges about uneasily defiant, whistling to himself – the dance tunes he whistles are no longer quite new. Frl. Schroeder throws him a word, now and then, like a grudging scrap of bread, but she won't look at him or make room for him by the stove. Perhaps she has never really forgiven him for his affair with Frl. Kost. The tickling and bottom-slapping days are over.

Yesterday we had a visit from Frl. Kost herself. I was out at the time: when I got back I found Frl. Schroeder quite excited. 'Only think, Herr Issyvoo – I wouldn't have known her! She's quite the lady now! Her Japanese friend has bought her a fur coat – real fur, I shouldn't like to think what he must have paid for it! And her shoes – genuine snakeskin! Well, well, I bet she earned them! That's the one kind of business that still goes well, nowadays . . . I think I shall have to take to the line myself!' But however much Frl. Schroeder might effect sarcasm at Frl. Kost's expense, I could see that she'd been greatly and not unfavourably impressed. And it wasn't so much the fur coat or the shoes which had impressed her: Frl. Kost had achieved something higher – the hall-mark of respectability in Frl. Schroeder's world – she had had an operation in a private nursing home. 'Oh, not what you think, Herr Issyvoo! It was something to do with her throat. Her friend paid for that, too, of course . . . Only imagine – the doctors cut something out of the back of her nose; and now she can fill her mouth with water and squirt it out through her nostrils, just like a syringe! I wouldn't believe it at first – but she did it to show me! My word of honour, Herr Issyvoo, she could squirt it right across the kitchen! There's no denying, she's very much improved, since the time when she used to live here . . . I shouldn't be surprised if she married a bank director one of these days. Oh, yes, you mark my words, that girl will go far . . .'

Herr Krampf, a young engineer, one of my pupils, describes his childhood during the days of the War and the Inflation. During the last years of the War, the straps disappeared from the windows of railway carriages: people had cut them off in order to sell the leather. You even saw men and women going about in clothes made from the carriage upholstery. A party of Krampf's school friends broke into a factory one night and stole all the leather driving belts. Everybody stole. Everybody sold what they had to sell – themselves included. A boy of fourteen, from Krampf's class, peddled cocaine between school hours, in the streets.

Farmers and butchers were omnipotent. Their slightest whim had to be gratified, if you wanted vegetables or meat. The Krampf family knew of a butcher in a little village outside Berlin who always had meat to sell. But the butcher had a peculiar sexual perversion. His greatest erotic pleasure was to pinch and slap the cheeks of a sensitive, well-bred girl or woman. The possibility of thus humiliating a lady like Frau Krampf excited him enormously: unless he was allowed to realize his fantasy, he refused, absolutely, to do business. So, every Sunday, Krampf's mother would travel out to the village with her children, and patiently offer her cheeks to be slapped and pinched, in exchange for some cutlets or a steak.

At the far end of the Potsdamerstrasse, there is a fairground, with merry-go-rounds, swings and peep-shows. One of the chief attractions of the fair-ground is a tent where boxing and wrestling matches are held. You pay your money and go in, the wrestlers fight three or four rounds, and the referee then announces that, if you want to see any more, you must pay an extra ten pfennigs. One of the wrestlers is a bald man with a very large stomach: he wears a pair of canvas trousers rolled up at the bottoms, as though he were going paddling. His opponent wears black tights, and leather kneelets which look as if they had come off an old cab-horse. The wrestlers throw each other about as much as possible, turning somersaults in the air to amuse the audience. The fat man who plays the part of loser pretends to get very angry when he is beaten, and threatens to fight the referee.

One of the boxers is a negro. He invariably wins. The boxers hit each other with the open glove, making a tremendous amount of noise. The other boxer, a tall, well-built young man, about twenty years younger and obviously much stronger than the negro, is 'knocked out' with absurd ease. He writhes in great agony on the floor, nearly manages to struggle to his feet at the count of ten, then collapses again, groaning. After this fight, the referee collects ten more pfennigs and calls for a challenger from the audience. Before any bona fide challenger can apply, another young man, who has been quite openly chatting and joking with the wrestlers, jumps hastily into the ring and strips off his clothes, revealing himself already dressed in shorts and boxer's boots. The referee announces a purse of five marks; and, this time, the negro is 'knocked out.'

The audience took the fights dead seriously, shouting encouragement to the fighters, and even quarrelling and betting amongst themselves on the results. Yet nearly all of them had been in the tent as long as I had, and stayed on after I had left. The political moral is certainly depressing: these people could be made to believe in anybody or anything.

Walking this evening along the Kleiststrasse, I saw a little crowd gathered round a private car. In the car were two girls. On the pavement stood two young Jews, engaged in a violent argument with a large blond man who was obviously rather drunk. The Jews, it seemed, had been driving slowly along the street, on the look-out for a pick-up, and had offered these girls a ride. The two girls had accepted and got into the car. At this moment, however, the blond man intervened. He was a Nazi, he told us, and as such felt it his mission to defend the honour of all German women against the obscene anti-Nordic menace. The two Jews didn't seem in the least intimidated; they told the Nazi energetically to mind his own business. Meanwhile, the girls, taking advantage of the row, slipped out of the car and ran off down the street. The Nazi then tried to drag one of the Jews with him to find a policeman, and the Jew whose arm he had seized gave him an uppercut which laid him sprawling on his back. Before the Nazi could get to his feet, both young men had jumped into their car and driven away. The crowd dispersed slowly, arguing. Very few of them sided

openly with the Nazi: several supported the Jews; but the
majority confined themselves to shaking their heads dubiously
and murmuring: *'Allerhand!'*

When, three hours later, I passed the same spot, the Nazi
was still patrolling up and down, looking hungrily for more
German womanhood to rescue.

We have just got a letter from Frl. Mayr; Frl. Schroeder
called me in to listen to it. Frl. Mayr doesn't like Holland. She
has been obliged to sing in a lot of second-rate cafés in third-
rate towns, and her bedroom is badly heated. The Dutch, she
writes, have no culture; she has only met one truly refined and
superior gentleman, a widower. The widower tells her that she
is a really womanly woman – he has no use for young chits
of girls. He has shown his admiration for her art by presenting
her with a complete new set of underclothes.

Frl. Mayr has also had trouble with her colleagues. At one
town, a rival actress, jealous of Frl. Mayr's vocal powers, tried
to stab her in the eye with a hat-pin. I can't help admiring
that actress's courage. When Frl. Mayr had finished with her,
she was so badly injured that she couldn't appear on the stage
again for a week.

Last night, Fritz Wendel proposed a tour of 'the dives.' It
was to be in the nature of a farewell visit, for the Police have
begun to take a great interest in these places. They are frequently raided, and the names of their clients are written down.
There is even talk of a general Berlin clean-up.

I rather upset him by insisting on visiting the Salomé, which
I had never seen. Fritz, as a connoisseur of night-life, was most
contemptuous. It wasn't even genuine, he told me, The man-
agement run it entirely for the benefit of provincial sight-
seers.

The Salomé turned out to be very expensive and even more
depressing than I had imagined. A few stage lesbians and
some young men with plucked eyebrows lounged at the bar,
uttering occasional raucous guffaws or treble hoots – supposed, apparently, to represent the laughter of the damned.
The whole premises are painted gold and inferno-red – crim-

son plush inches thick, and vast gilded mirrors. It was pretty full. The audience consisted chiefly, of respectable middle-aged tradesmen and their families, exclaiming in good-humoured amazement: 'Do they really?' and 'Well, I never!' We went out half-way through the cabaret performance, after a young man in a spangled crinoline and jewelled breast-caps had painfully but successfully executed three splits.

At the entrance we met a party of American youths, very drunk, wondering whether to go in. Their leader was a small stocky young man in pince-nez, with an annoyingly prominent jaw.

'Say,' he asked Fritz, 'what's on here?'

'Men dressed as women,' Fritz grinned.

The little American simply couldn't believe it. 'Men dressed as *women*? As *women* hey? Do you mean they're *queer*?'

'Eventually we're all queer,' drawled Fritz solemnly, in lugubrious tones. The young man looked us over slowly. He had been running and was still out of breath. The others grouped themselves awkwardly behind him, ready for anything – though their callow, open-mouthed faces in the greenish lamp-light looked a bit scared.

'You *queer*, too, hey?' demanded the little American, turning suddenly on me.

'Yes,' I said, 'very queer indeed.'

He stood before me a moment, panting, thrusting out his jaw, uncertain it seemed, whether he ought not to hit me in the face. Then he turned, uttered some kind of wild college battle-cry, and, followed by the others, rushed headlong into the building.

'Ever been to that communist dive near the Zoo?' Fritz asked me, as we were walking away from the Salomé. 'Eventually we should cast an eye in there ... In six months, maybe, we'll all be wearing red shirts ...'

I agreed. I was curious to know what Fritz's idea of a 'communist dive' would be like.

It was, in fact, a small whitewashed cellar. You sat on long wooden benches at big bare tables; a dozen people together –

like a school dining-hall. On the walls were scribbled expressionist drawings involving actual newspaper clippings, real playing-cards, nailed-on beer-mats, match-boxes, cigarette cartons, and heads cut out of photographs. The café was full of students, dressed mostly with aggressive political untidiness – the men in sailor's sweaters and stained baggy trousers, the girls in ill-fitting jumpers, skirts held visibly together with safety-pins and carelessly knotted gaudy gipsy scarves. The proprietress was smoking a cigar. The boy who acted as a waiter lounged about with a cigarette between his lips and slapped customers on the back when taking their orders.

It was all thoroughly sham and gay and jolly: you couldn't help feeling at home, immediately. Fritz, as usual, recognized plenty of friends. He introduced me to three of them – a man called Martin, an art student named Werner, and Inge, his girl. Inge was broad and lively – she wore a little hat with feather in it which gave her a kind of farcical resemblance to Henry the Eighth. While Werner and Inge chattered, Martin sat silent: he was thin and dark and hatchet-faced, with the sardonically superior smile of the conscious conspirator. Later in the evening, when Fritz and Werner and Inge had moved down the table to join another party, Martin began to talk about the coming civil war. When the war breaks out, Martin explained, the communists, who have very few machine-guns, will get command of the roof tops. They will then keep the Police at bay with hand-grenades. It will only be necessary to hold out for three days, because the Soviet fleet will make an immediate dash for Swinemünde and begin to land troops. 'I spend most of my time now making bombs,' Martin added. I nodded and grinned, very much embarrassed – uncertain whether he was making fun of me, or deliberately committing some appalling indiscretion. He certainly wasn't drunk, and he didn't strike me as merely insane.

Presently, a strikingly handsome boy of sixteen or seventeen came into the café. His name was Rudi. He was dressed in a Russian blouse, leather shorts and despatch-rider's boots, and he strode up to our table with all the heroic mannerisms of a messenger who returns successful from a desperate mission. He had, however, no message of any kind to deliver. After his whirlwind entry, and a succession of curt, martial hand shakes, he sat down quite quietly beside us and ordered a glass of tea.

This evening, I visited the 'communist' café again. It is really a fascinating little world of intrigue and counter-intrigue. Its Napoleon is the sinister bomb-making Martin; Werner is its Danton; Rudi its Joan of Arc. Everybody suspects everybody else. Already Martin has warned me against Werner: he is 'politically unreliable' – last summer he stole the entire funds of a communist youth organization. And Werner has warned me against Martin: he is either a Nazi agent, or a police spy, or in the pay of the French Government. In addition to this, both Martin and Werner earnestly advised me to have nothing to do with Rudi – they absolutely refused to say why.

But there was no question of having nothing to do with Rudi. He planted himself down beside me and began talking at once – a hurricane of enthusiasm. His favourite word is 'Knorke': 'Oh, *ripping*!' He is a pathfinder. He wanted to know what the boy scouts were like in England. Had they got the spirit of adventure? 'All German boys are adventurous. Adventure is ripping. Our Scoutmaster is a ripping man. Last year he went to Lapland and lived in a hut, all through the summer, alone . . . Are you a communist?'

'No. Are you?'

Rudi was pained.

'Of course! We all are, here . . . I'll lend you some books, if you like . . . You ought to come and see our club-house. It's ripping . . . We sing the Red Flag, and all the forbidden songs . . . Will you teach me English? I want to learn all languages.'

I asked if there were any girls in his pathfinder group. Rudi was as shocked as if I'd said something really indecent.

'Women are no good,' he told me bitterly. 'They spoil everything. They haven't got the spirit of adventure. Men understand each other much better when they're alone together. Uncle Peter (that's our Scoutmaster) says women should stay at home and mend socks. That's all they're fit for!'

'Is Uncle Peter a communist, too?'

'Of course!' Rudi looked at me suspiciously. 'Why do you ask that?'

'Oh, no special reason,' I replied hastily. 'I think perhaps I was mixing him up with somebody else . . .'

This afternoon I travelled out to the reformatory to visit one of my pupils, Herr Brink, who is a master there. He is a small, broad-shouldered man, with the thin, dead-looking fair hair, mild eyes, and bulging, over-heavy forehead of the German vegetarian intellectual. He wears sandals and an open-necked shirt. I found him in the gymnasium, giving physical instruction to a class of mentally deficient children – for the reformatory houses mental deficients as well as juvenile delinquents. With a certain melancholy pride, he pointed out the various cases: one little boy was suffering from hereditary syphilis – he had a fearful squint; another, the child of elderly drunkards, couldn't stop laughing. They clambered about the wall-bars like monkeys, laughing and chattering, seemingly quite happy.

Then we went up to the workshop, where older boys in blue overalls – all convicted criminals – were making boots. Most of the boys looked up and grinned when Brink came in, only a few were sullen. But I couldn't look them in the eyes. I felt horribly guilty and ashamed: I seemed, at that moment, to have become the sole representative of their gaolers, of Capitalist Society. I wondered if any of them had actually been arrested in the Alexander Casino, and, if so, whether they recognized me.

We had lunch in the matron's room. Herr Brink apologized for giving me the same food as the boys themselves ate – potato soup with two sausages, and a dish of apples and stewed prunes. I protested – as no doubt, I was intended to protest – that it was very good. And yet the thought of the boys having to eat it, or any other kind of meat, in that building made each spoonful stick in my throat. Institution food has an indescribable, perhaps purely imaginary, taste. (One of the most vivid and sickening memories of my own school life, is the smell of ordinary white bread.)

'You don't have any bars or locked gates here,' I said. 'I thought all reformatories had them ... Don't your boys often run away?'

'Hardly ever,' said Brink, and the admission seemed to make him positively unhappy; he sank his head wearily in his hands. 'Where shall they run to? Here it is bad. At home it is worse. The majority of them know that.'

'But isn't there a kind of natural instinct for freedom?'

'Yes, you are right. But the boys soon lose it. The system helps them to lose it. I think perhaps that, in Germans, this instinct is never very strong.'

'You don't have much trouble here, then?'

'Oh, yes. Sometimes ... Three months ago, a terrible thing happened. One boy stole another boy's overcoat. He asked for permission to go into the town – that is allowed – and possibly he meant to sell it. But the owner of the overcoat followed him, and they had a fight. The boy to whom the overcoat belonged took up a big stone and flung it at the other boy; and this boy, feeling himself hurt, deliberately smeared dirt into the wound, hoping to make it worse and so escape punishment. The wound did get worse. In three days the boy died of blood-poisoning. And when the other boy heard of this he killed himself with a kitchen knife ...' Brink sighed deeply: 'Sometimes I almost despair,' he added. 'It seems as if there were a kind of badness, a disease, infecting the world to-day.'

'But what can you really do for these boys?' I asked.

'Very little. We teach them a trade. Later, we try to find them work – which is almost impossible. If they have work in the neighbourhood, they can still sleep here at nights ... The Principal believes that their lives can be changed through the teachings of the Christian religion. I'm afraid I cannot feel this. The problem is not so simple. I'm afraid that most of them if they cannot get work, will take to crime. After all, people cannot be ordered to starve.'

'Isn't there any alternative?'

Brink rose and led me to the window.

'You see those two buildings? One is the engineering-works, the other is the prison. For the boys of this district there used to be two alternatives . . . But now the works are bankrupt. Next week they will close down.'

This morning I went to see Rudi's club-house, which is also the office of a pathfinders' magazine. The editor and scout-master, Uncle Peter, is a haggard, youngish man, with a parch-ment-coloured face and deeply sunken eyes, dressed in corduroy jacket and shorts. He is evidently Rudi's idol. The only time Rudi will stop talking is when Uncle Peter has some-thing to say. They showed me dozens of photographs of boys, all taken with the camera tilted upwards, from beneath, so that they look like epic giants, in profile against enormous clouds. The magazine itself has articles on hunting, tracking, and pre-paring food – all written in super-enthusiastic style, with a curious underlying note of hysteria, as though the actions described were part of a religious or erotic ritual. There were half-a-dozen other boys in the room with us: all of them in a state of heroic semi-nudity, wearing the shortest of shorts and the thinnest of shirts or singlets, although the weather is so cold.

When I had finished looking at the photographs, Rudi took me into the club meeting-room. Long coloured banners hung down the walls, embroidered with initials and mysterious totem devices. At one end of the room was a low table covered with a crimson embroidered cloth – a kind of altar. On the table were candles in brass candlesticks.

'We light them on Thursdays,' Rudi explained, 'when we have our camp-fire palaver. Then we sit round in a ring on the floor, and sing songs and tell stories.'

Above the table with the candlesticks was a sort of icon – the framed drawing of a young pathfinder of unearthly beauty, gazing sternly into the far distance, a banner in his hand. The whole place made me feel profoundly uncomfortable. I excused myself and got away as soon as I could.

Overheard in a café: a young Nazi is sitting with his girl; they are discussing the future of the Party: The Nazi is drunk.

'Oh, I know we shall win, all right,' he exclaims impatiently, 'but that's not enough!' He thumps the table with his fist: 'Blood must flow!'

The girl strokes his arm reassuringly. She is trying to get him to come home. 'But, *of course*, it's going to flow, darling,' she coos soothingly, 'the Leader's promised that in our programme.'

To-day is 'Silver Sunday.' The streets are crowded with shoppers. All along the Tauentzienstrasse, men, women and boys are hawking postcards, flowers, song-books, hair-oil, bracelets. Christmas-trees are stacked for sale along the central path between the tramlines. Uniformed S.A. men rattle their collecting boxes. In the side-streets, lorry-loads of police are waiting; for any large crowd, nowadays, is capable of turning into a political riot. The Salvation Army have a big illuminated tree on the Wittenbergplatz, with a blue electric star. A group of students were standing round it, making sarcastic remarks. Among them I recognized Werner, from the 'Communist' café.

'This time next year,' said Werner, 'that star will have changed its colour!' He laughed violently – he was in an excited, slightly hysterical mood. Yesterday, he told me, he'd had a great adventure: 'You see, three other comrades and myself decided to make a demonstration at the Labour Exchange in Neukölln. I had to speak, and the others were to see I wasn't interrupted. We went round there at about half-past ten, when the bureau's most crowded. Of course, we'd planned it all beforehand – each of the comrades had to hold one of the doors, so that none of the clerks in the office could get out. There they were, cooped up like rabbits . . . Of course, we couldn't prevent their telephoning for the Police, we knew that. We reckoned we'd got six or seven minutes . . . Well, as soon as the doors were fixed, I jumped on to a table. I just yelled out whatever came into my head – I don't know what I said. They liked it, anyhow . . . In half a minute I had them so excited I got quite scared. I was afraid they'd break into the office and lynch somebody. There was a fine old shindy, I can tell you! But just when things were beginning to look properly lively, a comrade came up from below to tell us the Police were there already – just getting out of their car. So we had to make a dash for it ... I think they'd have got us, only the crowd was on our side, and wouldn't let them through until we were out by the other door, into the street ...' Werner finished breathlessly. 'I tell you, Christopher,' he added, 'the capitalist system can't possibly last much longer now. The workers are on the move!'

Early this evening I was in the Bülowstrasse. There had been a big Nazi meeting at the Sportpalast, and groups of men and boys were just coming away from it, in their brown or black uniforms. Walking along the pavement ahead of me were three S.A. men. They all carried Nazi banners on their shoulders, like rifles, rolled tight round the staves – the banner-staves had sharp metal points, shaped into arrow-heads.

All at once, the three S.A. men came face to face with a youth of seventeen or eighteen, dressed in civilian clothes, who was hurrying along in the opposite direction. I heard one of the Nazis shout: 'That's him!' and immediately all three of them flung themselves upon the young man. He uttered a scream, and tried to dodge, but they were too quick for him. In a moment they had jostled him into the shadow of a house entrance, and were standing over him, kicking him and stabbing at him with the sharp metal points of their banners. All this happened with such incredible speed that I could hardly believe my eyes – already, the three S.A. men had left their victim, and were barging their way through the crowd; they made for the stairs which led up to the station of the Overhead Railway.

Another passer-by and myself were the first to reach the doorway where the young man was lying. He lay huddled crookedly in the corner, like an abandoned sack. As they picked him up, I got a sickening glimpse of his face – his left eye was poked half out, and blood poured from the wound. He wasn't dead. Somebody volunteered to take him to the hospital in a taxi.

By this time, dozens of people were looking on. They seemed surprised, but not particularly shocked – this sort of thing happened too often, nowadays. 'Allerhand ...' they murmured. Twenty yards away, at the Potsdamerstrasse corner, stood a group of heavily armed policemen. With their chests out, and their hands on their revolver belts, they magnificently disregarded the whole affair.

Werner has become a hero. His photograph was in the *Rote Fahne* a few days ago, captioned: 'Another victim of the Police blood-bath.' Yesterday, which was New Year's day, I went to visit him in hospital.

Just after Christmas, it seems, there was a street-fight near the Stettiner Bahnhof. Werner was on the edge of the crowd, not knowing what the fight was about. On the off-chance that it might be something political, he began yelling: 'Red Front!' A policeman tried to arrest him. Werner kicked the policeman in the stomach. The policeman drew his revolver and shot Werner three times through the leg. When he had finished shooting, he called another policeman, and together they carried Werner into a taxi. On the way to the police-station, the policemen hit him on the head with their truncheons, until he fainted. When he has sufficiently recovered, he will, most probably, be prosecuted.

He told me all this with the greatest satisfaction, sitting up in bed surrounded by his admiring friends, including Rudi and Inge, in her Henry the Eighth hat. Around him, on the blanket, lay his press cuttings. Somebody had carefully underlined each mention of Werner's name with a red pencil.

Today, January 22nd, the Nazis held a demonstration on the Bülowplatz, in front of the Karl Liebknecht House. For the last week the communists have been trying to get the demonstration forbidden: they say it is simply intended as a provocation – as, of course, it was. I went along to watch it with Frank, the newspaper correspondent.

As Frank himself said afterwards, this wasn't really a Nazi demonstration at all, but a Police demonstration – there were at least two policemen to every Nazi present. Perhaps General Schleicher only allowed the march to take place in order to show who are the real masters of Berlin. Everybody says he's going to proclaim a military dictatorship.

But the real masters of Berlin are not the Police, or the Army, and certainly not the Nazis. The masters of Berlin are the workers – despite all the propaganda I've heard and read, all the demonstrations I've attended, I only realized this, for the first time to-day. Comparatively few of the hundreds of people in the streets round the Bülowplatz can have been organized communists, yet you had the feeling that every single one of them was united against this march. Somebody began to sing the 'International,' and, in a moment, everyone had joined in – even the women with their babies, watching from top-storey windows. The Nazis slunk past, marching as fast as they knew how, between their double rows of protectors. Most of them kept their eyes on the ground, or glared glassily ahead : a few attempted sickly, furtive grins. When the procession had passed, an elderly fat little S.A. man, who had somehow got left behind, came panting along at the double, desperately scared at finding himself alone, and trying vainly to catch up with the rest. The whole crowd roared with laughter.

During the demonstration nobody was allowed on the Bülowplatz itself. So the crowd surged uneasily about, and things began to look nasty. The police, brandishing their rifles, ordered us back; some of the less experienced ones, getting rattled, made as if to shoot. Then an armoured car appeared, and started to turn its machine-gun slowly in our direction. There was a stampede into house doorways and cafés; but no sooner had the car moved on, than everybody rushed out into the street again, shouting and singing. It was too much like a naughty schoolboy's game to be seriously alarming. Frank enjoyed himself enormously, grinning from ear to ear, and hopping about, in his flapping overcoat and huge owlish spectacles, like a mocking, ungainly bird.

Only a week since I wrote the above. Schleicher has resigned. The monocles did their stuff. Hitler has formed a cabinet with Hugenberg. Nobody thinks it can last till the spring.

The newspapers are becoming more and more like copies of a school magazine. There is nothing in them but new rules, new punishments, and lists of people who have been 'kept in.' This morning, Göring has invented three fresh varieties of high treason.

Every evening, I sit in the big half-empty artists' café by the Memorial Church, where the Jews and left-wing intellectuals bend their heads together over the marble tables, speaking in low, scared voices. Many of them know that they will certainly be arrested – if not to-day, then to-morrow or next week. So they are polite and mild with each other, and raise their hats and enquire after their colleagues' families. Notorious literary tiffs of several years' standing are forgotten.

Almost every evening, the S.A. men come into the café. Sometimes they are only collecting money; everybody is compelled to give something. Sometimes they have come to make an arrest. One evening a Jewish writer, who was present, ran into the telephone-box to ring up the Police. The Nazis dragged him out, and he was taken away. Nobody moved a finger. You could have heard a pin drop, till they were gone.

The foreign newspaper correspondents dine every night at the same little Italian restaurant, at a big round table, in the corner. Everybody else in the restaurant is watching them and trying to overhear what they are saying. If you have a piece of news to bring them – the details of an arrest, or the address of a victim whose relatives might be interviewed – then one of the journalists leaves the table and walks up and down with you outside, in the street.

A young communist I know was arrested by the S.A. men, taken to a Nazi barracks, and badly knocked about. After three or four days, he was released and went home. Next morning there was a knock at the door. The communist hobbled over to open it, his arm in a sling – and there stood a Nazi with a collecting-box. At the sight of him the communist completely lost his temper. 'Isn't it enough,' he yelled, 'that you beat me up? And you dare to come and ask me for money?'

But the Nazi only grinned. 'Now, now, comrade! No political squabbling! Remember, we're living in the Third Reich! We're all brothers! You must try and drive that silly political hatred from your heart!'

This evening I went into the Russian tea-shop in the Kleistrasse, and there was D. For a moment I really thought I must be dreaming. He greeted me quite as usual, beaming all over his face.

'Good God!' I whispered. 'What on earth are you doing here?'

D beamed. 'You thought I might have gone abroad?'

'Well, naturally . . .'

'But the situation nowadays is so interesting . . .'

I laughed. 'That's one way of looking at it, certainly . . . But isn't it awfully dangerous for you?'

D merely smiled. Then he turned to the girl he was sitting with and said, 'This is Mr Isherwood . . . You can speak quite openly to him. He hates the Nazis as much as we do. Oh, yes! Mr Isherwood is a confirmed anti-fascist!'

He laughed very heartily and slapped me on the back. Several people who were sitting near us overheard him. Their reactions were curious. Either they simply couldn't believe their ears, or they were so scared that they pretended to hear nothing, and went on sipping their tea in a state of deaf horror. I have seldom felt so uncomfortable in my whole life.

(D's technique appears to have had its points, all the same. He was never arrested. Two months later, he successfully crossed the frontier into Holland.)

This morning, as I was walking down the Bülowstrasse, the Nazis were raiding the house of a small liberal pacifist publisher. They had brought a lorry and were piling it with the publisher's books. The driver of the lorry mockingly read out the titles of the books to the crowd:

'*Nie Wieder Krieg!*' he shouted, holding up one of them by the corner of the cover, disgustedly, as though it were a nasty kind of reptile. Everybody roared with laughter.

' "No More War!" ' echoed a fat, well-dressed woman, with a scornful, savage laugh. 'What an idea!'

At present, one of my regular pupils is Herr N, a police chief under the Weimar régime. He comes to me every day. He wants to brush up his English, for he is leaving very soon to take up a job in the United States. The curious thing about these lessons is that they are all given while we are driving about the streets in Herr N's enormous closed car. Herr N himself never comes into our house: he sends up his chauffeur to fetch me, and the car moves off at once. Sometimes we stop for a few minutes at the edge of the Tiergarten, and stroll up and down the paths – the chauffeur always following us at a respectful distance.

Herr N talks to me chiefly about his family. He is worried about his son, who is very delicate, and whom he is obliged to leave behind, to undergo an operation. His wife is delicate, too. He hopes the journey won't tire her. He describes her symptoms, and the kind of medicine she is taking. He tells me stories about his son as a little boy. In a tactful, impersonal way we have become quite intimate. Herr N is always charmingly polite, and listens gravely and carefully to my explanations of grammatical points. Behind everything he says I am aware of an immense sadness.

We never discuss politics; but I know that Herr N must be an enemy of the Nazis, and, perhaps, even in hourly danger of arrest. One morning, when we were driving along the Unter den Linden, we passed a group of self-important S.A. men, chatting to each other and blocking the whole pavement. Passers-by were obliged to walk in the gutter. Herr N smiled faintly and sadly: 'One sees some queer sights in the streets nowadays.' That was his only comment.

Sometimes he will bend forward to the window and regard a building or a square with a mournful fixity, as if to impress its image upon his memory and to bid it good-bye.

To-morrow I am going to England. In a few weeks I shall return, but only to pick up my things, before leaving Berlin altogether.

Poor Frl. Schroeder is inconsolable: 'I shall never find another gentleman like you, Herr Issyvoo – always so punctual with the rent . . . I'm sure I don't know what makes you want to leave Berlin, all of a sudden, like this . . .'

It's no use trying to explain to her, or talking politics. Already she is adapting herself, as she will adapt herself to every new régime. This morning I even heard her talking reverently about 'Der Führer' to the porter's wife. If anybody were to remind her that, at the elections last November, she voted communist, she would probably deny it hotly, and in perfect good faith. She is merely acclimatizing herself, in accordance with a natural law, like an animal which changes its coat for the winter. Thousands of people like Frl. Schroeder are acclimatizing themselves. After all, whatever government is in power, they are doomed to live in this town.

Today the sun is brilliantly shining; it is quite mild and warm. I go out for my last morning walk, without an overcoat or hat. The sun shines, and Hitler is master of this city. The sun shines, and dozens of my friends – my pupils at the Workers' School, the men and women I met at the I.A.H. – are in prison, possibly dead. But it isn't of them that I am thinking – the clear-headed ones, the purposeful, the heroic; they recognized and accepted the risks. I am thinking of poor Rudi, in his absurd Russian blouse. Rudi's make-believe, story-book game has become earnest; the Nazis will play it with him. The Nazis won't laugh at him; they'll take him on trust for what he pretended to be. Perhaps at this very moment Rudi is being tortured to death.

I catch sight of my face in the mirror of a shop, and am horrified to see that I am smiling. You can't help smiling, in such beautiful weather. The trams are going up and down the Kleiststrasse, just as usual. They, and the people on the pavement, and the tea-cosy dome of the Nollendorfplatz station have an air of curious familiarity, of striking resemblance to something one remembers as normal and pleasant in the past – like a very good photograph.

No. Even now I can't altogether believe that any of this has really happened ...

The world's greatest novelists now available in Triad/Panther Books

Ernest Hemingway

The Old Man and The Sea	£1.50	☐
Fiesta	£1.95	☐
For Whom the Bell Tolls	£2.50	☐
A Farewell to Arms	£1.95	☐
The Snows of Kilimanjaro	£1.95	☐
The Essential Hemingway	£2.95	☐
To Have and Have Not	£1.95	☐
Green Hills of Africa	£2.50	☐
Men Without Women	£2.50	☐
A Moveable Feast	£1.95	☐
The Torrents of Spring	£2.50	☐
Across the River and Into the Trees	£1.95	☐
Winner Take Nothing	£1.95	☐
The Fifth Column	£1.95	☐
Death in the Afternoon (non-fiction)	£2.95	☐

Richard Hughes

A High Wind in Jamaica	£1.25	☐
In Hazard	£1.50	☐
Fox in the Attic	£1.50	☐
The Wooden Shepherdess	£1.50	☐

James Joyce

Dubliners	£1.95	☐
A Portrait of the Artist as a Young Man	£1.95	☐
Stephen Hero	£1.95	☐
The Essential James Joyce	£2.95	☐
Exiles (play)	£1.25	☐

To order direct from the publisher just tick the titles you want and fill in the order form.

All these books are available at your local bookshop or newsagent, or can be ordered direct from the publisher.

To order direct from the publisher just tick the titles you want and fill in the form below.

Name _____

Address _____

_____

Send to:
Panther Cash Sales
PO Box 11, Falmouth, Cornwall TR10 9EN.

Please enclose remittance to the value of the cover price plus:

UK 45p for the first book, 20p for the second book plus 14p per copy for each additional book ordered to a maximum charge of £1.63.

BFPO and Eire 45p for the first book, 20p for the second book plus 14p per copy for the next 7 books, thereafter 8p per book.

Overseas 75p for the first book and 21p for each additional book.

Panther Books reserve the right to show new retail prices on covers, which may differ from those previously advertised in the text or elsewhere.